Stone Voice Rising

C. Lee Tocci

HARCOURT
Houghton Mifflin Harcourt
Boston New York 2009

All rights reserved. Requests for permission to make copies of any part of the
work should be submitted online at www.harcourt.com/contact or mailed to the
following address: Permissions Department, Houghton Mifflin Harcourt
Publishing Company, 6277 Sea Harbor Drive, Orlando, Florida 32887-6777.

Harcourt is an imprint of Houghton Mifflin Harcourt Publishing Company.

www.hmhbooks.com

Text set in Adobe Jenson
Book design by Sheila Smallwood

Library of Congress Cataloging-in-Publication Data
Tocci, C. Lee.
Stone Voice rising / C. Lee Tocci.
p. cm.
Summary: In a world of whispering stones and corporate evil, Lilibit
and six other orphaned children with mysterious powers battle
a shape-shifting enemy and his helicopter army to reach Kiva,
a sacred place where Lilibit's destiny lies as the new Stone Voice.
ISBN 978-0-15-206292-7 (hardcover)
[1. Fantasy. 2. Orphans—Fiction.] I. Title.
PZ7.T56355St 2009
2008025114

Printed in the United States of America
10 9 8 7 6 5 4 3 2 1

Special Thanks To

My editor, Kathy Dawson

My writers group:
Matt Coyle, Murray Hagen, Cathy Worthington

My special Sunday friends:
Ron Nicolosi, Natasha Starbuck Smith, Fred Starbuck Smith, Glynis Elwell, Tommy
Doucette, Sonny D'Angelo, and Gail Mowat

and Alexandra Piñon, for vetting my Spanish

And Very Special Thanks
(and every kind of love)
to my parents,
Ruth Carnes Tocci and Valentino Tocci,
for their never-ending support and encouragement,
even when I did really stupid things.

This book is dedicated to the memory of

Miss Judy Wiggin,
my fourth and fifth grade teacher,
who taught me the magic of words.

Chapter One

The Infant Stone Voice

As usual, Lilibit woke that morning before the sunrise. Not as usual, however, she lay in bed and stared at the ceiling.

She had no choice. It would have to be the Temper Tantrum.

This was not a decision she made lightly. She had tried Logic. Reasoning. Charm. Humor. Cajoling. Whining. Insolence. And Bribery. She was now Desperate. It would have to be the Temper Tantrum. And she knew that to get her way, this could not be a normal temper tantrum. This would be a Gut Stone Tantrum.

It would not be pretty.

She lay in her bed making her plans, plotting her strategy, planning her war.

The opening volley of this battle had been fired the night before when the Stranger arrived and the Aunties sent her to bed. Even though she wasn't a bit tired.

After creeping back to the top of the stairs, she lay on the floor. She peeked out between the rails and watched the whispered conversation of the grownups below. In her hand she clutched Tosh, the nosy stone.

Only Lilibit knew that beneath Tosh's façade of mottled gray stone there hid a yellow crystal center of vanadinite. And Tosh had another secret. He liked to eavesdrop. So when Lilibit pressed Tosh to her ear, she heard her Aunties and the Stranger as if she were sitting between them.

The Stranger was tall and stern-looking. His skin was dark and his hair was darker. It hung in a thick black braid down his back. His pants were made of brown rawhide pulled tight over thighs that looked more like two tree trunks than legs. A tan leather shirt stretched over his barrel chest and a forest green cloak hung from his shoulders. His hands rested on a tall gnarled staff, its knobby surface worn from untold years of use, but Lilibit didn't think he used it to walk. He was strong, she could tell; the whole house buzzed from his presence.

He smelled of leather and pine trees and grass after the rain. His name was Keotak-se, but to Lilibit he looked more like the big oak that grew in their backyard, so when she talked about him to her stones, she called him Mr. Tree.

He stood looking down at the Aunties as they sat in the parlor. "We can wait no longer." His voice was low and deep. Tosh quivered in her ear. "We must leave tomorrow."

Auntie Shalla nodded sadly, but Auntie Wolla put up a proper fight.

"She's too young, Keotak-se! She's not even seven!" Auntie Wolla's voice chirped with distress. "And she's so small for her age!"

Auntie Shalla patted Auntie Wolla's arm as she looked at Mr. Tree. "I too thought we would keep her here until she was twelve. That was the decision of the Council when you first brought her to us. Since the death of her parents, we have been the only family she has known. Does the Council think it wise to move her again before she is the proper age to send a child to Kiva?"

Lilibit pricked up her ears. The Aunties never talked about her parents. Whenever Lilibit would ask, all the Aunties would say was "a big brown bird left you on the front porch." And they would never tell her anything more, no matter how many times she asked.

Lilibit didn't think the Aunties were her real aunts. Their hair was black like hers, but their skin was dark brown and tanned, like Mr. Tree's. Lilibit's skin was a pale gold. And her eyes were different too. The Aunties' eyes were round, like almost everyone else's in the neighborhood, but Lilibit's eyes were slanted, like she was laughing all the time, even when she wasn't.

She pressed Tosh hard against her ear and hoped that, maybe this time, the grownups might let something slip.

"Her voice grows strong," Mr. Tree rumbled. "The soil echoes with her words. Even from Kiva, the Flame Voice can hear her speaking to the stones."

This startled the Aunties. After a quick glance at each other, they looked up the stairs toward Lilibit's bedroom, but they couldn't see Lilibit as she hugged the floor, safely hidden in the darkness on the landing.

"If the Flame Voice can hear her, then so can the Enemy. They seek her day and night. She is young, it is true. But the time has come for her to be moved to Kiva." He turned to look at the top of the stairs. Lilibit didn't think he saw her, yet his eyes seemed to look directly into hers.

"Where she will be safe?" asked Auntie Shalla.

"Where she will be safer." His voice offered no promises. "Where she can be trained to protect herself."

Lilibit held her breath as it grew quiet in the parlor. Auntie Wolla sniffed a few times, yet it was Auntie Shalla who finally spoke.

"There are things we must see to before we leave. If tomorrow we were all to disappear from Hazeltown at the same time, it would be noticed."

Mr. Tree nodded. "This is true. She and I will leave tomorrow. You two can follow when your tasks here are completed."

The Aunties quickly looked at each other and then back to Mr. Tree.

"Perhaps Wolla should accompany you, Keotak-se." Auntie Shalla sounded concerned. "To help look after the child."

"No." Mr. Tree did not encourage discussion. "We will travel faster if it's just the two of us."

"But —" started Auntie Wolla.

"No." His eyes narrowed as he glanced between the two women. "For the love of the Stone, women. I have lived ten centuries. I have fought against the hordes of the headless dreads, have faced the assassins of Chee-tola. I have traveled through the Labyrinth of the Flame. I am the last of the True Stone Warriors. I think I can handle a six-year-old child."

The looks on the Aunties' faces echoed Lilibit's words.

"We'll see about that," she whispered to the stones as she crawled silently from the landing back to her bed.

Chapter Two
Stopover

What do you call it when a pair of crows crash into each other?

In the back seat, Todd turned away from the window, ignoring the large black bird that followed the car.

A two-caw accident! With a rawk, the bird answered its own riddle.

Todd bit back a snort of laughter. Crows always told really stupid jokes, but they still made him laugh. "That's so lame!" he whispered.

"Stop talking to the birds, Todd," said Ms. Burbank from the front seat.

Todd slouched deeper on the vinyl bench. Looking up, he saw the caseworker's eyes in the rearview mirror as if she were peering through a floating window from another dimension.

"Yes, ma'am." Todd turned his shoulder against the window and away from the bird outside.

"You're a big boy now. You're eight years old." Ms. Burbank's voice was not unkind. "You're much too old for those sorts of pretending games. That's what caused all that bother at the last home where we placed you."

Bother? Mrs. Jenson thought he was an extraterrestrial spy and made him wear tinfoil on his head whenever he left his bedroom. Mrs. Jenson read the *National Enquirer.* Todd folded his arms across his chest and stared at his sneakers.

I bet if I had curly blond hair instead of straight black hair, thought Todd, *Mrs. Jenson wouldn't have kicked me out. Maybe if I had blue eyes and freckles instead of brown eyes and brown skin, I could have stayed.*

Maybe if I didn't talk to the birds . . .

"We're lucky there's an opening at Dalton Point." Ms. Burbank interrupted Todd's thoughts. "It's up in the mountains and you'll have a bedroom all to yourself."

"Yes, ma'am."

"But you need to behave yourself. No more nonsense about talking birds, do you understand?"

"Yes, ma'am."

As the car wound its way up a mountain, Todd watched the houses and even the telephone poles disappear. Barren canyon walls broken by rocky glens rose alongside the narrow road. Todd straightened and looked out the window. It had been a long time since he'd been in a place with so few people.

They turned on to a long gravel driveway and rode in silence. The car slowed as it got to the last bend, and as it rolled to a stop, Todd saw six kids: four boys and two girls wearing jeans and T-shirts. They stood in a line, their arms crossed over their chests, glaring at him. Something nasty started to rise from his stomach into his throat. He swallowed hard and pushed it back down as he opened the car door. The paper bag with all his clothes spilled onto the gravel as he stepped out.

The tallest boy broke formation and bent to pick up a large duffel bag before walking toward the car.

Todd put out his hand to greet him, but without a word, the taller boy elbowed him hard. As Todd stumbled, the boy pushed past and climbed into the back seat. He glared straight ahead, ignoring everyone.

"Come along, Todd." Ms. Burbank's hand touched Todd's shoulder lightly. "We'll get you settled in."

Todd turned to see the remaining five children staring at him without a hint of a smile or welcome. Ms. Burbank bent to whisper into Todd's ear.

"Remember," she hissed, "no talking birds."

Todd gritted his teeth and nodded his head as he followed Ms. Burbank into the house.

Chapter Three
The Runaway

The room was rosy with the light of early dawn as Lilibit crawled under her bed to pull out her tatty pink bib overalls. Her closet brimmed with starchy dresses and lacy pinafores, but she always wore the same pink bib overalls, the one with the eight pockets.

The talky stones always went in the top left pocket. Tosh went in the top left pocket too — not because he was a talky stone but because he liked to listen. The quiet stones went into the top right pocket. They didn't say much, but Lilibit always kept an ear open, because when one of the quiet stones spoke, it was usually pretty important. Frando stayed in her lefthand pocket by himself, partly because he was too big to share a pocket and partly because he was a bit of a bully and did not get along well with the other stones.

They were still working on that issue.

Veranda and Winnie ("the Girls") lived in her righthand pocket. These were Lilibit's favorites: two egg-shaped quartz stones polished smooth by countless decades of ocean waves. They reminded her of the Aunties. They were a little bit bossy, but they could do lots of special things and sometimes they remembered stuff that Lilibit forgot. The bottom two pockets on the legs she kept empty in case she found any new stones during her travels. Lilibit considered back pockets pretty stupid since they weren't any good for storing stones in, not even pebbles, because they hurt when you sat down. Lilibit couldn't figure out how anyone ever used back pockets.

Grownups were weird.

Lilibit's bare feet made no sound as she pattered across the gleaming hardwood floors in the predawn glow. Her purple panda backpack hung heavily on her shoulders and the weight of its contents pressed hard against the small of her back. As usual, the kitchen was sweet with the smells of drying herbs, fresh bread, and homemade cheese. Lilibit giggled as she packed her provisions for the mission. She didn't waste a thought on any possible punishment. The Aunties never got angry. They just tutted and huffed and fussed. And Lilibit knew she could always wheedle them out of their miffs.

The soft green smell of the morning dew met her as she walked out the back door from the kitchen. She wiggled her bare toes in the mud and grass and stopped to pat Caddock, the massive mottled boulder that guarded the backyard.

"I'm off to have an adventure, Caddock," Lilibit whispered to the stone. "I don't know when I'll be back, but if I find any friends for you, I'll bring them."

The rock buzzed briefly in response.

"Oh, Caddock, don't be silly!" Lilibit giggled and patted it farewell before climbing over the back fence and dropping onto the path beyond.

Lilibit knew exactly where she wanted to go. In the east, her mountain, the one that looked misty and blue in the morning, called to her, as it had for months. She didn't know how long it would take her to walk to her misty blue mountain, but she knew that was where she wanted to go. She made up a song about her stones and their mother and she sang it as she pattered along the path through the woods.

> "The grass, it is so cold,
> My feet, they are so hot,
> The Stones, they warm my toes,
> The Earth, it warms my heart;
>
> "Though I'm all by myself,
> I'm never all alone.
> For deep inside my pockets,
> I've always got my stones."

The song may not have sounded very good to grownups, but under her toes, the Earth hummed along.

The path opened out on Willow Creek Road. She trotted down the street and, with a sigh, paused before the Lin Su house.

Now, as far as the grownups in the neighborhood were concerned, the Lin Sus' house was very grand and impressive.

Lilibit was not impressed.

As far as the grownups were concerned, the Lin Sus' yard was a major disappointment. Lilibit was not disappointed, but she was disturbed. When the Lin Sus purchased the house a year ago, they'd torn up the luxurious green lawn and replaced it with an "architect-designed" rock garden. The neighbors might sniff and roll their eyes at the foreignness of the landscaping, but what bothered Lilibit was the large gray stone they'd placed near one of the bedroom windows. The stone, a twisted and contorted lump of pumice, was more than half Lilibit's height, but like a sponge, was so riddled with air holes, it weighed no more than a few pounds.

Four times now, Lilibit had walked by the house and heard the stone screaming. Four times now, she had dragged the stone away from the window as far from the house as she could manage. Then, gathering soothing stones from here and there amid the rock garden and adding several from

her knapsack, she made a circle of friends around the screaming stone.

Today the stone was back under the bedroom window.
From inside, Lilibit heard a baby crying as he echoed the
pain of the screaming stone.

Lilibit veered off course to rescue the stone. Again.

As she wrapped her arms around the stone, she caught
the vision of a soft warm island in the middle of a bright
aqua sea and felt the stone's pain as it longed to return to the
arms of its mother there among the enveloping black sand.
She hummed to the stone, a gentle promise that one day it
would return to its faraway home. After dragging the stone
away from the house, she gathered those grownup stones
that knew who they were and would whisper comfort to the
lonely baby stone and snuggled them together.

Lilibit was purring soothingly to the sobbing stone when
she heard voices from the house, sharp staccato voices speaking angry words she couldn't understand. She saw Mrs. Lin
Su's head in the window of the house, yelling at her, her finger jabbing toward her like a lizard's tongue. Lilibit patted
the sobbing stone a rushed farewell and ran like a squirrel
back to her path.

She ran down Willow Creek Road and took the corner
onto Phillip Terrace at such a tear that she slammed into
what, at first, seemed to her to be a brick wall. Her next

thought, as she bounced back and fell on her behind, was that sometime during the night someone had planted a towering oak in the middle of the sidewalk.

From flat on her butt, Lilibit looked up and sighed. It was Mr. Tree. She rolled over to get to her feet, but Mr. Tree reached down and lifted her by her purple panda knapsack until her eyes met his and her bare feet dangled in the air.

"Put me down!" Lilibit squeaked with rage, her fists and feet flailing in the air.

Mr. Tree did not speak. This enraged Lilibit even more.

"You listen here, Mr. Tree!" she said. "If you don't put me down right now, you're going to be very sorry!"

Mr. Tree did not smile, but Lilibit felt he was laughing at her.

Fine! she thought. *I warned you!*

Then from out of her left pocket, she pulled the Temper Tantrum.

Gripping Frando between her fingers, she whipped the large stone at Mr. Tree's head with a movement so quick most grownups wouldn't have even seen her hand, never mind the stone.

Yet, with a swift twitch, Mr. Tree moved his head and the stone sped past his ear. Lilibit glared as she gave a silent order. Frando stopped in mid-air then veered around, aiming right for the back of Mr. Tree's head.

As if by itself, Mr. Tree's staff leaped from his hands, spun behind his back, and struck the stone to the ground.

Well, so much for the Temper Tantrum. Evidently Mr. Tree had a couple of tricks of his own.

Her pockets weren't exactly empty either. She reached in and pulled out "the Girls." She did not throw these stones, but holding one in each hand, she glared into his face. Then, with a squeak of defiance, she slammed them together.

Suddenly, an icy gust of wind blew out of the east, building power as it buffeted the two of them. Leaves and branches flew off nearby trees. Trash barrels ricocheted off lampposts and a hail of dirt and sand pounded the cars parked in the early morning hush of Phillip Terrace.

Mr. Tree stood without moving, his eyes staring calmly at the girl. Then he lifted his staff and with one swift motion, stabbed the ground with a resounding crack. As quickly as it had started, the wind stopped. Grains of sand fell gently like an early snow.

"That will be enough," Mr. Tree said at last as he lowered Lilibit to the ground. "I did not walk from beyond the mountains to play silly games with a child."

Lilibit decided to change tactics. She'd never met a grownup who could stop the Temper Tantrum. Brushing the sand off her clothes, she eyed him warily.

"Well, Mr. Tree," said Lilibit in her most grown-up voice, "I'm sorry that you came all this way, but if you'd asked me first, I could have saved you the trouble. I'm not going to Kiva."

She stooped to pick up Frando where he'd landed in the gutter. "It doesn't sound like it's going to be the least bit fun," she added.

Mr. Tree did not blink.

"Thank you anyway," she said, belatedly remembering her manners.

Mr. Tree stood. Lilibit fidgeted. They both waited. Finally, Lilibit decided that she had waited long enough.

"Thank you anyway," she repeated, "and goodbye." She walked about a half dozen steps and then peeked behind her to see Mr. Tree standing calmly as if he were planted in the middle of the sidewalk on Phillip Terrace. She walked another dozen steps before risking a second glance behind.

Mr. Tree had disappeared.

Lilibit walked backwards, her eyes searching everywhere, trying to figure out where Mr. Tree might have gone. She gave a little yelp as she collided with him again when he reappeared behind her on the sidewalk. Once more, Lilibit ended up on her butt.

"Oh, for all the stars in heaven!" she exclaimed, sounding just like her Auntie Shalla. "If you're going to move like that, you can at least look where I'm going!"

"Where you are going," said Mr. Tree, "is back to your Aunts' house. Would you like to walk there, or shall I carry you?"

Picking herself up off the ground, Lilibit wrapped the shreds of her dignity about her. "I will walk." Like any good general, Lilibit knew when a strategic retreat and regrouping might be necessary to achieve ultimate victory, and as she marched back to the Aunties' house, she was already planning her next coup.

Stopping at the curb at Willow Creek Road, she reached up and grabbed Mr. Tree's hand. The Aunties always told her to hold their hands when they crossed the street, so Lilibit assumed Mr. Tree, like all adults, needed her help to cross a busy street.

Lilibit scrambled over the rear fence and landed with a splat in the backyard. She turned back to see how Mr. Tree was managing, only to find him standing beside her on the grass. She sniffed and marched defiantly into the house.

Inside, Lilibit discovered the Aunties in a tither. Mrs. Lin Su was there, with a police officer.

"Oh, Lilibit!" Auntie Wolla said with a sigh. "What have you been up to this morning?"

"It is not just this morning!" Mrs. Lin Su trembled like a mosquito. "She is always vandalizing my garden! She tears apart my landscaping over and over again, but today I caught her in the act. You evil child!"

Auntie Shalla moved to place herself between Lilibit and the shrieking Mrs. Lin Su, but Lilibit would have none of that. She stepped around her Aunt and peered up into the angry woman's face, her head tilted in curiosity. This seemed to infuriate Mrs. Lin Su even more and she lunged toward the child as if to slap her.

Officer Garcia stepped in at this point, restraining Mrs. Lin Su with a word and bending to speak to Lilibit eye to eye. "Lilibit," asked the police officer gently, "can you tell me why you keep moving Mrs. Lin Su's rocks around?"

Behind her, Lilibit felt Auntie Shalla's body tense as she reached out her arm to draw Lilibit closer. Lilibit would have told the officer about the weeping stone that wanted to go back to its island home, but it was difficult for a six-year-old to put the feelings she heard from the stone into words. She thought hard for a moment and then settled for the words that would make sense to the grownups.

"It's making the baby sick," she said.

As one, the Aunties' eyes darted to the suddenly rigid form of their neighbor.

"What?" gasped Mrs. Lin Su.

Lilibit tried to find better words, but since she wasn't quite sure how she knew this, she gave up with a shrug.

"Well, well, well," Officer Garcia said as he shook his head. "You know, I wasn't sure if we were dealing with a hardened criminal or just a malicious vandal . . ."

The Aunties held their breath, but Lilibit saw the smile hiding behind his eyes and grinned back.

Officer Garcia chuckled as he straightened, reaching out to tousle Lilibit's hair. His smile stopped, however, when he looked at Mrs. Lin Su. Her hands grasped the back of a chair as if the bones had been removed from her legs.

"It's just a case of an overactive imagination," he said, watching her pale face. "I'm sure she won't do it again. Right, Lilibit?"

Lilibit opened her mouth to argue the point, but Auntie Shalla silenced her with a squeeze on her shoulder.

"Lilibit will be going off to school soon, Officer Garcia," said Auntie Shalla. "We can assure Mrs. Lin Su it will not happen again."

Auntie Shalla's eyes locked with Mrs. Lin Su's, who nodded blankly, her eyes unfocused. She then turned and walked out of the house without saying another word.

Mrs. Lin Su waddled quickly down the street and through her front door. She barked at the nanny to move the baby out of his bedroom. While the woman scampered to obey, Mrs. Lin Su dialed her husband at his office, hysteria working her voice into a squeaky whisper.

Minutes later, a large gleaming car screeched into the driveway. Mr. Lin Su did not question why he must take his wife's favorite landscaping stone far away from their home.

He never argued with her when she got herself like this. At first, it was his intention just to throw it off to the side of the road into the nearest ditch. Twice he slowed down to pull over, but something pushed him onward and he found himself driving eighty miles to the ocean. He wrestled the stone out of his trunk, carried it to the peak of the cliff, and grunted as he flung it over the edge.

A strong gypsy breeze rose, caught the falling pumice stone, and sent it sailing over the rocky shore.

The man looked down, expecting to see the stone smashed against the craggy beach below, but instead it bobbed merrily on the waves. And then, as if propelled by some invisible sail, it floated west, homeward at last.

Mr. Lin Su returned home to find his son sleeping peacefully in his mother's arms, neither squirming with discomfort nor crying in pain. He stood and watched them for a long moment before calling the office and canceling the rest of his appointments for that day.

From the foyer, Lilibit looked at her Aunties as they watched the police car drive down the street. Mr. Tree entered from the kitchen where he had stood, still and silent, unnoticed by the visitors.

"That was unfortunate. We must leave now," he said.

The Aunties turned to Keotak-se and nodded sadly.

Lilibit's eyes darted from her Aunties to the tall man.

"No!" Lilibit folded her arms and plopped to the floor. "I won't go!"

Auntie Shalla moved to the stairs. "I'll finish packing her things."

Auntie Wolla lowered herself to speak into Lilibit's eyes.

"You will like Kiva," she told Lilibit as she pulled her to her feet. "There will be other children there to play with and lots of aunties and uncles to take care of you. Auntie Shalla and I shall come there too, as soon as we are able. Now you be a good girl and obey Keotak-se. He will take you there safely."

Lilibit read nothing in Keotak-se's face as he glanced down at her. She stuck out her lower lip as she met his gaze before turning and stomping upstairs.

Chapter Four

The Road

An hour later, Lilibit sat in the passenger seat of a 1928 Dodge sedan as it rolled eastbound down the interstate.

"Nice car," Lilibit offered conversationally.

Mr. Tree was silent for a while and Lilibit thought he was ignoring her. She looked out the window and watched her misty blue mountain roll slowly past.

"We might have taken horses all the way, but traveling by car will create less notice," Mr. Tree said at last.

Lilibit stared at him, thinking he was trying to be funny, but he seemed to be serious. If puttering down the interstate at forty miles an hour didn't get them noticed, driving in an antique automobile that looked like it was just transported from another century certainly would. Lilibit watched as nearly every passing car slowed to look at this relic.

After a few minutes of this, Lilibit decided to explore the back seat. Climbing over the bench, she plopped into the back and began running her fingers over the upholstery, her fingernails traveling up and down each ridge in the leather. Within minutes she'd squirmed her way over every inch of the interior and now worked her way back to the front by wriggling under the passenger seat. Her head and shoulders appeared on the floor next to Mr. Tree and he watched her bemusedly as she lay on her back and began to intricately fold and unfold an old gum wrapper she had found.

"Are you in discomfort?" he asked.

Lilibit looked up at him, puzzled. "No. Why do you ask?"

"Why do you not sit quietly on the seat that was given you?"

Lilibit stared at Mr. Tree as she pondered this question.

"I did," she answered. She returned her attention to the gum wrapper.

"Get up and sit on the seat."

Lilibit opened her mouth to argue, but something in Mr. Tree's voice made her think twice about that. With a huff and a flurry of twisting limbs, Lilibit was again on the seat next to him, though her bare feet were where her head should be and her long black hair fell over the seat to where her feet belonged.

A long stubborn silence, then the dam broke. "Where is

Kiva? How far is it? How long will it take to get there? Are we more than halfway there yet? What is it like there? Do they have television? Can I have a dog?"

Mr. Tree blinked twice, perhaps befuddled by this onslaught. There was another long pause before he spoke.

"Kiva is many miles away. Today we drive east eight hundred miles to the End of the Road. We shall not rest until we reach the End of the Road. Then we will ride horses to the Valley between the Four Mountains. We should be at Kiva by tomorrow evening. At Kiva, there are homes created by the Earth and food given by the Creator."

A shiny little car leaned on its horn as it screamed past on the right. Mr. Tree stared coldly at its taillights as it passed. Lilibit squirmed up to look out the window just in time to see the shiny car begin to sputter, gray smoke pouring out from under its hood.

"And there is no television," Mr. Tree added.

"No television?" Lilibit flopped back onto the seat and waved her toes out the window to the shiny car that was fuming in the breakdown lane. "Do I *have* to go?"

It was the same question she had asked the Aunties a hundred times already, so she wasn't surprised to receive the same short answer.

"Yes."

"Why?"

Now the Aunties knew better than to start the never-ending game of why-because, so Lilibit was secretly pleased when she got a real answer to that question.

"Because Kiva is the place where all neophytes go to learn to serve the Stone."

Intrigued, Lilibit's toes stopped fidgeting.

"What's a . . . knee-fight?"

"A neophyte is a young man or woman" — his eyes flicked toward her before returning to the traffic — "or child who hears the call of the Earth Stone. At Kiva, they learn the skills they need to become stone warriors."

"What do stone warriors do?"

"They serve and protect the Stone Voice."

"And what's a Stone Voice?"

Mr. Tree took some time before he replied. Lilibit wondered if she had used up all her questions. When he finally spoke again, his voice was curt and flat. He almost sounded angry.

"A Stone Voice serves as the eyes and ears of the Earth Stone." He glanced sharply at her before continuing. "The Stone Voice is not only the servant of the Earth Stone, she serves the People as well. She must be humble and obedient, wise and strong."

"She?"

"There have been instances of male Stone Voices, but usually the Stone Voice is female. And when the new Stone Voice rises, she will grant special stones to her warriors.

Those found to be worthy of the Stone will wield great power."

It was quiet in the car despite the rumble of the motor. Lilibit kicked her heels against the bench seat as she digested his words. Finally, with a flurry of movement, she squirmed herself upright. Kneeling in her seat, she turned to face Keotak-se.

"And then can I have a dog?" she asked with a glare.

Mr. Tree let out a large sigh and shook his head. "We shall see" was all he would say.

Lilibit flopped back onto her seat with a huff. "We'll see" was on her list of the most annoying things grownups said. It was right up there with answering a question with a question and saying she will understand when she gets older.

She pulled out Veranda and Winnie from her pocket and began playing with the two white stones on the dashboard. She hummed to them quietly and in the pauses between her songs she listened to their replies.

Mr. Tree watched her with interest. With a sniff, she turned her shoulder on him, her nose in the air. These were *her* stones. They were talking to *her*.

From deep within her top right pocket, a stone began to sing. Quite loudly. Lilibit pulled out all the quiet stones but it took her only a moment to find out who was making that racket. Branken was singing so loudly, you could almost *see* him humming. This was surprising. Branken was normally such a quiet stone. In fact, he spoke so seldom, she sometimes forgot to pack him along. She pulled him out and placed him against her cheek.

There was a frown between her brows as Lilibit listened to Branken. "Are you sure?" she hummed. Stones don't speak with words, but Branken's reply was definite.

She looked closely at the stone, then stood on the seat so she could reach Keotak-se's face. Placing the stone on his cheek, she almost dropped it; Branken's song became so loud, he was almost shouting. Again, she pressed him against her own cheek, listening one more time just to be certain, but there was no mistake. Branken was emphatic.

"Branken wants to stay with you," she said, tucking the stone into the pocket of Mr. Tree's tunic.

Lilibit sat back down and gazed out the window. She didn't know what to make of this. She'd never had a stone want to stay with someone else before. But that's what Branken wanted. From her seat, she heard him singing. Singing for Mr. Tree.

"Thank you," Mr. Tree said after a long pause.

Lilibit looked at him closely. His face seemed a little paler than its normal weathered brown color. He reached one finger into the pocket of his tunic to stroke Branken almost reverently. Perhaps even fearfully. With unusual awkwardness, he pulled his hand away from the stone and gripped the steering wheel so tightly his knuckles gleamed white.

Several minutes passed.

"Thank you," he said again. His voice and manner returned to their normal stoniness, but Lilibit thought he was really grateful.

"Then can I have a dog?" She was never one to let an opportunity slide by.

"We shall see," he replied.

Lilibit sighed and again looked out the window. There was a long silence as the road passed beneath them.

Chapter Five

The Institute

In a cold gray room in a cold gray tower in a cold gray city, countless computers retrieved immeasurable amounts of data, and in reviewing and cross-referencing the information, searched for those details that correlated with their programmed parameters.

Parameters met. Factors aligned. Details linked. Report generated. Data transferred. Awaiting assessment.

His name was Andrews, not that it mattered. He staffed the fourth cubicle on the third floor in a windowless dungeon, and between the hours of midnight and ten in the morning, the cubicle was his entire identity.

He was nearing the end of his shift when the data was dumped into his review queue. He was tempted to archive it for tomorrow so he could leave on time. If it weren't for the electronic trail attached to all such activity, he probably would have rejected it back into the data banks so it would

wash up on the shores of some other poor slob's worksta-
tion. He sighed and opened the report.

Oh great, he thought. *This one needs to go up.* This
meant filing a report, attaching the data, forwarding it upstairs, and then standing indefinitely at the desk of his
supervisor, waiting for the report to be reviewed. Again he
considered "accidentally" hitting the delete key and heading
out the door on time. He sighed as he thought of the
monthly lease payments on his new Z-300 and opened an
incident report.

Baxter watched Andrews approach his desk. Baxter
had ambitions, and they exceeded being a low-level supervisor in the Information Analysis Department. He faith-
fully carried every nugget of data with potential to *his*
superior in the hopes the next one would be the stepping-
stone to his inevitable advancement. He nodded blandly at
his subordinate and assigned the appropriate clearance to
the report. He watched as the fool sprinted back to his
station, eager to log out and return to the banality of his
life outside the Institute. With a few decisive keystrokes,
Baxter eliminated Andrews's references and added his
own credentials. He printed out the report and carried it
up to Syxx.

Syxx sat at the immense, bare ebony slab that made his
desk. Directly above the desk, a vaulted skylight focused a
shaft of light onto it — but there was something unworldly

about that material and the light did not reflect back but instead was absorbed into a void. Nothing marred the clean blankness of his realm. No phone, pencil, or scrap of paper disfigured the unbroken domain of his office. He sat staring without emotion at the array of forty monitors mounted on the wall behind his desk as they flashed data and reports and telecasts in an unremitting stream. His pale bald head gleamed in the eerie light. His back to Baxter, he did not acknowledge his presence as the report was placed on the inviolate tableau of his desk.

Baxter stood patiently. He understood that the length of time Syxx kept him waiting was directly proportional to the lack of respect Syxx felt Baxter deserved. Baxter was not offended by this. He used the same tactic with his own subordinates, but perhaps the day would come when Syxx would stand waiting at his desk while Baxter basked in the aura of authority.

Perhaps sensing this impertinence, Syxx turned and met Baxter's eye. Baxter quickly stifled the thought. It was said that Syxx could read minds, and staring into those uncanny eyes, Baxter did not doubt it.

An unpleasant smirk touched Syxx's cheek as he picked up the report and flicked a quick glance at the single sheet. Baxter held his breath. Syxx looked at the report a second time. Baxter felt his pulse gallop. Syxx slowly raised his eyes and smiled. A frozen, lifeless smile that stopped Baxter's racing heart cold. Baxter forced himself to remain standing and not faint like a sickly schoolboy.

"Well done, Baxter," said Syxx. It was the first time Syxx had ever used his name and Baxter felt himself able to breathe again, perhaps a bit too shrilly. "I will note this in your file."

Baxter walked stiffly out of the office, restraining himself from running out the door. Trembling and a little dizzy, he blindly passed the Director of Security.

The Director approached the ebony slab. Syxx gestured to the printout lying on the desk in solitary state. He picked it up and with great interest read the police report filed by an Officer Garcia regarding a seemingly insignificant vandalism complaint. The Director smiled humorlessly and nodded as Syxx spoke.

"You know what I expect."

Chapter Six

Incident at Lambert Oasis

Keotak-se studied the rearview mirror. The child had not spoken for many miles. She lay in the back seat arranging her stones in a variety of positions that seemed to amuse her, for she occasionally chuckled for no apparent reason.

She stopped now and returned her stones to her pockets and her knapsack. Then she flung herself like a salmon over the bench and landed with a flop in the front passenger seat.

"Mr. Tree, I have to go number one."

This appeared to have some significance to her but of what Keotak-se did not know.

After a long pause: "I really have to go number one," she repeated, squirming in her seat. "Bad."

"Where is number one?" Keotak-se asked slowly.

Lilibit rolled her eyes. "Number one? Sit potty? Go pee?"

Keotak-se attained enlightenment. "You need to make water?"

"Is that where water comes from?" Lilibit paused in her squirming, momentarily diverted. "Is that where the oceans came from?"

Keotak-se chose not to answer, but that question held Lilibit rapt and silent for the several miles it took for a dilapidated gas station to emerge out of the expanse of the wasteland.

They had left the interstate some time ago for a little-used stretch of an ancient highway, a relic of another time long since abandoned by the rest of the world in favor of the high-speed freeways. With a thump and a crunch, the sedan left the roadway, rolled past the pumps, and came to a slow stop on cracked asphalt and gravel.

The late summer air hung heavy with dust and petroleum, yet as Keotak-se stepped out of the car, he could taste the tang of the desert sage that lurked obstinately just beyond the grasp of civilization.

A grizzled old man stepped out of the gloom of a ramshackle garage. He acknowledged Keotak-se with a nod, but his eyes were enthralled by the car.

"'E got no gas," he said with a grunt.

"We need no gas," Keotak-se replied. "We have need of your commode."

The grizzly man pulled his glance from the car to answer Keotak-se. "Don't know whatya talking of, but 'e got none of it."

Keotak-se sighed. Men's expectations of self had so diminished in recent centuries. He saw a man who might have been a great warrior, a man among men, but all that remained was a fossil of a soul that wasted his chance on a discarded roadway.

"The child needs to make water."

It was then that the grizzly man first noticed the girl barely seen peeking over the hood of the car. He smiled at her.

"Sorry," he replied with real regret. "Out of order. Has been for near on four years now."

The child hopped from one leg to another. "Tree!" Her voice squeaked with desperation.

"Well, we not got many trees 'bout here, but if you're none too picky, you can go behind the shed out back," offered the grizzly man.

Lilibit bolted around the back of the building and disappeared behind the shed. Keotak-se chose a spot that gave the child her privacy yet allowed him to see her if she tried to run away.

Behind the shack ran an open concrete culvert. *In the city they call this a river,* thought Keotak-se with disdain. Here in the desert they called it a wash, and at this time of year, a turbid stream of water and refuse moved quickly down its cement spine. Beyond the wash were countless miles of barren wilderness creeping to a ridge of gray mountains on the horizon.

Lilibit walked reluctantly back toward Keotak-se. He could see her racking her brain to think of some delay, when he heard a faint buzz in the distance. The Stone Warrior turned swiftly to face the north. There on the horizon, he saw a cloud of machines rising over the outlying mountains.

In three strides, Keotak-se crossed to Lilibit and, with an arc of his arm, swept her up. Crossing to a pile of discarded tires, he deposited the child inside the squat tower made of aging rubber. Lilibit squeaked in protest as Keotak-se planted himself in front of the tires and, turning to face the approaching enemy, brandished his staff.

"Stay." His voice was terse, his attention focused on the horizon.

"Now, now." The grizzly man hobbled up to the Stone Warrior, amusement crinkling his eyes. "It's not but a bunch of helicopters. It's probably just one of them military exercises. Nothing to get in a twist over."

Keotak-se spared only a sliver of a glance at the old man, but it was sufficient. Whatever the grizzly man read in that look, it chased the grin off his face. He watched the helicopters arrowing toward his little service station and wiped a drop of sweat from his brow.

"Well, my Uncle Vernon always did say that prudence

was the better part of luck. I'll just be over there if'n you need me."

With that, the grizzly man scurried to his garage, closed the door, and prepared to watch the events from a point of relative safety.

Keotak-se's focus was disturbed. He knew the enemy. He knew what he must do. He was ready for the battle. His stone, Hakuya, hung at his neck and Keotak-se felt the power of that stone resonate through his bones. But Branken trembled in his tunic pocket and from that stone Keotak-se felt strange dimensions added to his powers. His eyesight was keener. Even though the enemy was still nearly a mile away, he could see the markings on their machines; he even saw their grim faces, partially obscured behind dark, menacing goggles. His staff felt foreign too, its power amplifying, surging to a pitch never felt before. He was tempted to throw away the new stone so he might face the enemy without distraction, but he knew the truest way to tap the power of an untried stone was to face a foe in righteous battle.

On the far side of the wash, the enemy halted and hovered like a swarm of hornets. The wind from the propellers buffeted Keotak-se's cloak, but he waited unmoving. Ropes like the legs of spiders dropped out of the hatchways. Black-garbed figures repelled down the lines, dispersing in synchronized maneuvers, fanning out to surround the isolated oasis.

Keotak-se did not wait for the enemy to attack first, but recognizing their intent, struck the butt of his staff on the earth three times. The staff hummed faintly as a surge of light and energy pulsed, rose to its apex, and awaited the Stone Warrior's command.

Grasping it in both hands, Keotak-se aimed the staff toward the closest of the helicopters. With a blast of light and a crackle of power, it shot an arcing beam of energy toward its target. With a deafening bang, the chopper exploded in a blaze, showering the troops below with a flurry of flaming debris.

Strings of small detonations streaked across the barren sands, marking rapid-fire bullets shot from one of the choppers. The Stone Warrior stood unmoving as the lines of gunfire swiftly approached. Suddenly, the staff in his hands began to spin swiftly, faster than the eye could track, like a glowing baton. The bullets ricocheted harmlessly into the gravel. Two more pulses from the staff and two more helicopters dissolved into balls of inferno.

But there were more coming.

Lilibit fumed. She thought she'd been behaving quite well. It was true she'd been thinking about misbehaving all morning, but she hadn't actually gotten around to it yet, and therefore scowled with a quite righteous anger at being dumped into a stack of tires. The sound of a helicopter exploding startled her and she raised her head to peek out.

"Keep down," Mr. Tree barked, the end of his staff gently prodding her head. Lilibit puffed a snort of disgust as she settled back into her hideaway.

Chino swore long and softly under his breath as he ran to flank the western boundary of the offensive field. Nothing in their mission briefing had prepared them for a defense of this caliber. Every time he took a job with the private sector, he always regretted it. Give him a sweet little drug cartel or a neurotic despot of some colorful Third World country. These private corporate missions, they never tell the mercenaries all the details, probably because they figured you'd want more money if you knew all the facts.

Chino and his squad sprinted down the ravine, leaped the narrow dirty stream, and emerged on the far side. Then they deployed behind a shed to the rear of the service station and waited.

His ear jack cackled with sharp directives from the Institute's squad commanders overseeing the assault from the far side of the ridge. Chino ordered the remainder of his squad to fan out and secure the western perimeter. His rifle at the ready, he waited behind the shed for his next set of commands.

Without warning, a figure raced around the corner of the shed. On instinct, Chino spun around to face his assailant, but pulled up his weapon as he identified the intruder.

The "Mission Objective" had come to him. The girl's eyes locked with his and she froze.

Nothing in her short life could give Lilibit any conception of the danger rising around her in the oasis. It didn't occur to her that the assault was directed at her or that disobeying at this moment could be disastrous, if not fatal. She'd seen only that, at last, Mr. Tree's attention was diverted and this was her chance to teach him a lesson. She was not to be picked up, dragged about, and then dumped like a bag of groceries.

However, it was Lilibit who was learning something new. Fear. She looked into the cold eyes of the gunman and felt more frightened than she ever had before.

In one motion, the man shouldered his rifle and grabbed Lilibit by the neck, crushing her against his chest.

Lilibit's arms flailed as she reached into her pocket to fetch the Girls, but she had barely pulled them out when she felt the chokehold on her neck loosen, and she dropped to the ground, gasping, her stones falling to the earth.

Twisting around, Lilibit saw the grizzly gas station man wrestling with the black-garbed killer. Spinning with a vicious sweep, the dark man struck the old man's head with the butt of his rifle and the grizzly man collapsed, bleeding, onto the gravel.

Lilibit wasted no time. She ran.

She hadn't run more than a few steps when a spray of gunfire riddled the ground at her feet. She veered, headed for the wash, and tumbled down the embankment into the ravine. Scrambling under a scrub of underbrush, she huddled down, covered her head with her arms, and hid.

Chino smiled. Mentally he was already spending the substantial bonus he was about to earn. He alone had a clear view of the crouching child. He shouldered his assault weapon and withdrew a cruel-looking tranquilizer pistol. Aiming at his target, he pulled the trigger.

The report of the pistol surprised him. It should have been a muffled whistle, not a resounding crack. He glanced at the gun in his hand, thinking it sounded more like a .44 caliber Smith & Wesson. Blood dripped onto his weapon. Puzzled, he reached to feel the back of his head. He felt something wet and his fingers dripped red. When he turned, he saw the dying old man clutching a relic handgun.

I was right. A Smith and Wesson forty-four, Chino thought with satisfaction as he fell and died.

Lilibit hugged her knees and listened to the firefight rage above her. She knew Mr. Tree would be angry when he found out she hadn't stayed in the tires, but that didn't frighten her as much as the empty eyes of the men with the guns. She uncurled herself and was poised to dash back to the tire dump when she felt a piercing stab in her shoulder.

Lilibit reached back and pulled out a black metal barb. She gazed at the needle with eyes that wouldn't focus. She turned to run but she couldn't remember where or why. Her feet stumbled and her legs felt like willow branches. She took a few steps before toppling into the stream. Her mouth filled with water and she coughed, flailing her arms weakly. The world was growing dim and murky when her arm came down hard on a large scrap of lumber floating in the gully. She managed to pull herself onto the board before everything went dark.

From the far side of the mountain, the Director of Security listened as the reports came in from the field. Syxx had mentioned that the Mission Objective would be accompanied by a bodyguard and that this guardian would have unexpected defensive abilities, but the Director had underestimated these powers, with disastrous results. Three choppers were down, five operatives confirmed dead, and eighteen others were not responding. It wasn't the loss of equipment or life that concerned him; it was his ability to conceal these losses from the Public. The Director gave the order to withdraw.

The next offensive would have to be more subtle. He was already devising his next stratagem as he delegated cleanup duties.

This battle may have been lost, but this war was far from over.

Keotak-se watched as the men retreated over the ravine, scaling the ropes into the remaining helicopters. He did not revel in victory. He knew they would return with stealth and the journey would now be increasingly perilous. When the enemy had withdrawn to a safe distance, he relaxed his stance and turned to check on Lilibit, only then discovering the child missing.

As he scanned the barren desert for any sign of her, he wasted no time on anger. The blame was his. His misjudgment in handling the child might be fatal for her.

The ground at the oasis was windblown and well-trodden, but Keotak-se could see the trail of Lilibit's escape. He followed her tracks around to the back of the shed, where he found, next to the corpses of the grizzly man and the mercenary, two small egg-shaped stones of quartz.

The stones were Lilibit's. His knuckles bared pale as he clenched the stones in his fist, as if by sheer force of muscle he might will the child back to safety.

Lilibit's trail ended in the wash, where it disappeared as it crossed with the tracks of the retreating enemy.

The withdrawing choppers were miles away and Keotak-se could not hinder their escape without destroying them, and with them Lilibit, whom he assumed had been taken by the enemy. As he placed the two quartz stones in his pocket, he felt Branken, the stone Lilibit gave him earlier, trembling with energy. This gave heart to Keotak-se because he knew the stone's lifesong would continue so long as Lilibit lived.

Kneeling on the gravel, Keotak-se grasped his staff with both hands and intoned loudly, "CHEE-ot-say. Toh-GEE-na. Sha-be-KAH."

As he cried out the last syllable, it modulated into the caw of a great bird. Where a moment before stood Keotak-se, the last of the True Stone Warriors, there now poised a giant condor, its eyes red with anger. With one massive sweep of its wings, the condor launched into the air and followed the retreating enemy.

The official report had it that old Randy Lambert died in a gas line explosion.

The locals, sparse and scattered though they were, knew better. They knew something big had happened out at the old Lambert Filling Station. Local legend held that aliens came down from outer space and grizzly old Randy died single-handedly defending the Earth from extraterrestrial invaders.

Yet, for centuries to come, in the annals of Kiva, this would be known as the Battle of Lambert Oasis. The opening skirmish in the War of the Staff and the Stone.

And Randy Lambert would be canonized in that history as the first warrior to fall in battle.

Chapter Seven

Popokelli

Lilibit's body was wet and cold yet her mouth was dry and raw. Her head ached and the world bobbed and dipped in a strange manner. She opened her eyes slowly, blinking in surprise to see that the world had grown dark with dusk.

Her makeshift float had stopped before the mouth of a large concrete conduit. A grill of vertical bars prevented the larger flotsam from clogging the gully, and pieces of debris bobbed and bumped against Lilibit's raft, scratching her legs and bruising her arms.

For a long moment Lilibit lay, her head so fuzzy she barely recalled who she was, never mind where. Then, with a start, she remembered the battle at the gas station. She jerked her head and her body lurched sharply. The sudden movement upset the little raft and she toppled into the shallow stream. Coughing up mouthfuls of water, she waded to the embankment. There she sat with her arms wrapped around her legs. She wept quietly — wet, cold, hungry, alone, and too frightened to call out.

She froze as the sound of a melodious tooting filled the gully. Looking up, she saw a small figure the size of a large doll sitting on the lip of the culvert on the other side of the stream playing a crude flute. As she watched, he stopped piping, then bounced down the gravel embankment.

He looked like a little man but was no more than half her own height. His face was colored with broad blocks of red, green, and blue. His white hair was cobbled into stiff little tufts, each tuft topped with a colorful bauble. His clothes too were patterned with bright colorful blocks and stripes, like a clown. Only his hands, with their exceptionally long slender fingers, seemed un-doll-like. His large black eyes glistened and blinked. He beamed a broad toothy grin at the child.

"Hello! How you are? Across may I come?" The little man's voice was high-pitched; his speech, a rhythmic singsong. "Lost are you be? Face of you, glum!"

Not being able to think of a thing to say, Lilibit just nodded. With that, the little man jumped the ravine in one astounding bound and landed next to Lilibit. His arms waved like laundry in the wind as he tried to keep from falling on his behind.

"Popokelli was I. How you do did? You to me look like one lost little kid!"

Despite her fears, Lilibit giggled. "My name is Lilibit. I . . . do . . . did . . . fine." She paused. "Except I want to go home. I want my Aunties."

Popokelli stared closely at the girl. "Eyes of you leak-ed," he said with a solemn pout. "Nose leak-ed too. If me took you to Aunties, what give to me, you?"

It took Lilibit a moment to understand what the little man asked. "I don't have anything to give you. My Aunties can give you something, though. When we get there, they can give you cookies?"

"Hmph! Pockets of you are bulging and full! Give of what pockets hold then take you I will!" Popokelli gave her a sly wink.

Lilibit patted her pants, noticing for the first time that the Girls, Veranda and Winnie, were missing, but she had no time to do more than glance around for them before answering Popokelli. "All I have in my pockets are some stones I picked up." She shrugged. "I can't give them to you. They go where they want to go."

Popokelli pouted and he plopped next to Lilibit. He placed his chin in his hands and stared at her, sulking.

Lilibit looked back at Popokelli and thought hard. Popokelli's large black eyes grew even larger as, one at a time, Lilibit pulled out each of her stones. She held them against her cheek, listening, before replacing them back into her pocket. She shook her head at Popokelli, shrugging apologetically.

After a long morose silence, Popokelli leaped up. Grabbing Lilibit's hand, he announced, "Your Aunties' house will you and I find! I cookies no want but stones may change mind!" He tugged Lilibit to her feet and pulling her by the hand, led her up the embankment.

Lilibit and Popokelli walked along the streets of the town. Those people who noticed them at all saw only a small dirty girl carrying a clown doll. However, most passed them by unaware, too busy minding their own minutes to take notice of a lost child. Several times she tried to speak to the people striding by, but Popokelli pulled at her hand and hissed a warning, so she stopped trying.

Popokelli seemed to know where he wanted to go. He took them along a maze of side streets and even once through a dry sewer pipe. He finally stopped in the back lot of a noisy building. Lilibit saw no one among the cars parked outside, but inside she heard loud music and people talking shrilly.

Lilibit wanted to go inside and ask the people to take her to her Aunties, but before she got to the door, a man stepped out from a shiny black car parked near the building.

The man wore a gray suit and had a shiny hairless head, but his eyes made Lilibit shy away. His eyes were empty, like two dark, bottomless caves. She turned to run, but his arm reached out and his hand grasped her shoulder.

The hand was cold as death. Spears of ice pierced her neck. Her spine stiffened and her body grew rigid. Freezing pain impaled her brain. She couldn't breathe. Yet those eyes tormented her the most. She felt them slicing through her mind, chasing the very soul out of her body.

The world grew dim as she fell to the ground. She felt the frenzied hands of Popokelli pulling at her pockets, stealing her precious stones. Yet it seemed he didn't find what he was looking for, because the last thing she heard was Popokelli's voice raised in a tantrum.

"Not here! Not here! Lied you to me! Curse you! Curse you! I spit on your knee!"

The man in gray laughed coldly and kicked Popokelli, who scurried away cursing. He then bent to pick up the limp child.

All went black.

Chapter Eight

The Passing of the Stone Voice

Keotak-se stood at the crest of Red Rabbit Ridge and looked into the Valley of Kiva. Below him, he could see the People plowing the fields, tending the animals, working, as they had all their lives. As had their ancestors for centuries before. Working to create a haven with which to nurture the Infant Stone Voice.

More than a month had passed since Keotak-se left Kiva to collect the Infant Stone Voice. Summer was waning and the evenings grew cool and the People awaited their return. Keotak-se stepped onto the path that would take him into the Valley.

Even from this distance, he could see the People pause in their tasks to watch his descent. He saw their heads turn with wordless questions and he read their despair in the answer.

Keotak-se strode silently past the questions in their eyes

and entered the Hall of the Flame Voice, blinking as his eyes adjusted to the gloom.

On the floor near the western wall sat a woman, ageless and still, her eyes fixed on flames rising smokeless from the firepit in front of her. Silver strands ran through her long black braids. Those streaks of gray and the knowledge in her eyes gave only the faintest of clues as to her true years.

Keotak-se waited until she looked up before crossing to stand in front of her. He wasted no words on greetings or excuses.

"Gil-Salla, the Enemy has taken the Infant Stone Voice," he said with a voice robbed of all emotion. "Her stones grow faint; her Voice is stilled."

The woman dropped her eyes back to the flames. Her face was impassive but the palms of her hands twitched as they brushed the mute soil. Then Gil-Salla stood. Crossing to the opening of her hall, she released a wail, telling the People of the Valley the news they dreaded.

The Infant Stone Voice was lost.

Chapter Nine

Milestones

"Todd!! Todd!!"

Todd could hear the other kids looking for him. But he wasn't coming down from the tree where he was hiding. Not just yet.

He wasn't a reject like them. He had a father. And he knew his father was coming for him. It was only a matter of time. And then it wouldn't matter if he was the newest and the smallest.

He pulled his cherished pocketknife from where he kept it hidden sheathed inside his pant leg. It was shining silver and its handle was colorful with stonework. He still remembered what his Dad told him when he'd given Todd this knife.

"You are a warrior, Todd," he'd said, his voice deep and important sounding. "You are the son of warriors and the grandson of warriors. And someday your sons will be warriors too. Now, a warrior does not make war but protects with his strengths those weaker than himself. It is a great calling. And to follow this vocation, you must acquire many tools. Here is your first. A knife worthy of a warrior."

Todd barely remembered the solemn manner with which his father had handed him the knife. He had been much too fascinated by the beauty of the weapon to pay attention to his father's words, but they came back to him now as clearly as if he were there in the tree with him.

He slid the knife back into its hiding place. He wasn't a reject. He was a warrior. His father had said so.

A large black bird settled on a nearby branch.

"Find my Dad!" Todd hissed at the raven. "Tell him where I am! Tell him to come get me!"

The bird *rawk*ed apologetically, ruffling its wings in sympathy, but didn't leave the tree.

"Go!" Todd swung his fist at the raven. The bird flitted off the tree, and Todd, losing his balance and his grip, crashed to the ground.

The force of the fall knocked the air out of him and the world flashed white. When his breath returned in choppy gasps, he rolled onto his stomach. He was pulling himself together when a grip on the back of his neck yanked him onto his feet.

"Did you hear us calling you?" One of the bigger boys shook him by the shoulders while two others stood nearby sneering. "Well, did you?"

When Todd wouldn't answer, the boy shook him harder, then pushed him back down on the ground.

A second boy stepped forward, knelt, and yelled into Todd's face. "Listen, you little weirdo. I don't know what butterfly factory they let you out of, but here at Dalton Point, we have rules. Rule number one: no wandering off by yourself. And rule number two" — he turned to share the joke with his buddies — "no talking to birds."

The others laughed, and one boy picked up a rock and hurled it at the raven. With an indignant squawk, the bird flew off.

"Listen!" The voice of the kneeling boy became less mean. "It's just a stupid bird. You're too old for stupid games like pretending birds can talk. Grow up."

Todd watched the bird disappear over the mountain without even a backward look. "Stupid bird," he muttered, wiping his eyes with his sleeve.

And many years would pass before Todd allowed himself to once again hear the words of the raven.

Five Years Later

Chapter Ten

The Lost Years

"Five years!"

Ed the bartender nodded but Baxter knew he wasn't listening. Ed never heard anything except the rap of an empty glass on the counter. It was one of the things that made this place so popular with employees from the Institute. Here, in the dark corners of Hattie's Bar, they drank away their paychecks and hid their fear under bold talk and booze. And no one heard them because nobody listened.

Except today.

"Since what?" A low throaty voice made him turn to stare. She was thin and pale with almond-shaped eyes that disappeared in the dim light. She wasn't pretty, but Baxter, with his retreating hair and advancing gut, knew that he was no picture of manly beauty himself. He smiled and moved to make room for her at the bar.

"Charon Woo." Her straight black hair barely moved as

she swayed her head. "That's Charon with a C. Five years since what?" she asked again.

It had been so long since anyone had actually listened to him, he wasn't quite sure how to continue. "Well, I work for the Institute," Baxter started, then paused.

Everyone knew what the Institute was: the Nil and Voight Medical Research Institute. NAVMRI. Once Baxter had been thrilled to get a job there, but that was a long time ago and now he felt as if his soul were being sucked right out of him. He wanted out but he couldn't find the exit.

"Yes, I know." Charon's whisper brought his thoughts back. He wondered if she read minds. "I've watched you for a while. I've often wondered why someone with your potential would waste his time with a dead-end organization like the Institute."

"It's not a dead end." Baxter felt compelled to defend it. "But sometimes it seems like someone keeps moving the ladder."

She laughed, but he wasn't sure if he liked the sound.

"Oh, come on. Rumor has it that the Institute has a one-trick pony, and without it, it couldn't get funding and it'd collapse like an overhyped IPO."

"Hmph." Baxter set the empty glass on the counter. Within seconds, it was replaced with a fresh drink.

"What gets me" — his words slurred a little as they exploded from him — "is they wouldn't even have that pony if it wasn't for me. I was the one that found her. And what do I get? A note in my personnel file, and five years later, I'm still stuck in the Information Analysis Department."

"You deserve so much better."

"Yeah." He emptied the glass into the back of his throat.

"You know, I heard that Acheron Biotechnical is looking for someone like you. You should check it out."

It took a moment for her words to cut through the fuzz of the alcohol. He blinked his eyes and looked at her closely. "You work for them?"

Her smile told him yes.

"You're a long way from home," he said. Acheron's offices were two hundred miles away in Ravage City.

"Acheron's in trouble." What she told him he already knew. "For the last five years, NAVMRI has landed every grant and contract that we've gone after. Acheron's board has heard rumors that the Institute's success is because of a secret research subject they have. Acheron wants it. And they're willing to pay a lot to get it."

Baxter shook his head. "I don't think it's the research subject that's getting us those grants. It's the Operations Chief," his voice dropped and he looked warily around the bar. "Syxx."

"Six?" Charon chuckled. "Is that his name or his IQ?"

"Shh!" Baxter hissed, his fingers icy with fear. "You haven't heard of *Syxx?* He's been the Operations Chief at the Institute for the last five years or so. He's the one who knew about the research subject. And he's the one who gets everything he goes after. He's not just ruthless, he's" — Baxter shot a look at the bartender's back. Suddenly everyone seemed like an Institute spy — "creepy."

"So? What can he do to you? Fire you?"

Baxter's voice was barely a mutter as he spoke the words that he hadn't ever dared to speak aloud before. "Nobody leaves the Institute. At least not for the past five years."

Her laugh tinkled shrilly. Baxter now knew for a fact that he did not like that sound at all.

He jumped as if he'd been shot when her hand lightly touched his, her fingers nudging under his palm. He looked down and saw what seemed to be a thick roll of hundred-dollar bills. His hand snapped back as if he'd been burned, but Charon was quicker and grabbed his wrist. With unexpected strength, she forced his hand back down to the bar, but he kept his fingers extended, his hand creating a cage over the money, his palm resisting its touch.

"Get us research subject seventeen-seventeen," she whispered in his ear, "and Acheron will make you very, very happy."

And then, like an icy breeze, she was gone.

Baxter sat without moving, barely breathing. There was

more than just cash underneath his sweating hand. It was his ticket out. His palm itched as he weighed a future with Acheron Biotechnical against his fear of betraying the Institute.

And crossing the ominous Syxx.

Slowly Baxter's fingers closed around the bills.

Chapter Eleven

Trouble in Maircott City

Todd's scalp was buzzing. This was not a good sign. He scrubbed his fingers through his hair, trying to rub away his uneasiness. It didn't work. He broke into a run.

Normally it took him ten or fifteen minutes to get from the middle school he attended to the elementary school where the rest of the kids went. This afternoon he made it in five.

He rounded the corner at a dead run, his book bag slapping painfully against his back. From out of the alley that ran alongside the dry cleaner shot eight-year-old Nita. She stopped as she reached the sidewalk, looking back and forth, hopping with indecision. Then she saw Todd and she jumped up and down, her arms waving in panic.

Nita was so frantic, she was speaking in Spanish. "Todd! *¡Ven aquí! ¡Apurate! ¡Ellos estan matando a Donny!*"

"In English, Nita!"

"There is no time for English!" she cried, grabbing his hand and dragging him into the alley. *"¡Ven aquí!"*

It took Todd only a second to grasp what was happening in the alley. Donny sat curled up against the wall, his head hidden behind his arms, his shirt torn and bloody. One boy had eight-year-old Devon pinned with his arms behind his back while three other boys threw stones at Donny.

Todd shrugged off his book bag as he ran. It flew behind him as he tackled the biggest boy and the two of them scrabbled in the gravel. Todd was on top for the moment, but he knew it was only because he had surprise and momentum going for him. It took only a couple of seconds for the other boys to react and Todd was quickly outnumbered.

"¡Ayúdenos! Help us! *¡Por favor!"* Todd could hear Nita calling out in the street.

Somehow Devon broke free from the kid holding him and started swinging at the back of the boy straddling Todd. The bigger boy shrugged him off like a fly. Devon, too small to be much help in a fight, was thrown against the wall.

"Boy, we could use the cavalry right about now," Devon muttered as he rolled to his feet.

"Do you think so?" Todd snapped. An elbow pressed down against his cheek. He turned his head and bit it. A satisfying yelp was heard from one of his attackers.

"Police! Freeze!" A deep voice echoed down the alley.

The boys' response was immediate. They broke and ran. Within seconds, only Todd, Devon, and Donny were left in the alley.

Little Devon recovered first. He ran over to where Donny still lay huddled against the wall.

"It's okay, Donny." Devon's gray eyes were dark with worry. He patted Donny's arm as if Donny were the younger boy. "Don't cry. They're gone now."

But Donny wasn't crying. His eyes were glazed and unblinking. His mouth opened and closed, but he made no sound as he rocked back and forth. Gently Todd helped Donny to his feet.

Even though, at twelve, he was a year younger than Todd, Donny was already three inches taller, but his size didn't hide his childish mind. When he was happy, Donny acted like a four-year-old. When he was frightened, like he was now, he barely functioned at all.

Todd knew from experience that, with time, Donny would recover. This wasn't the first time this kind of thing had happened. He just hoped that this wouldn't be a major setback. Sometimes it took Donny weeks before he'd try talking again.

"Where's Marla?" Todd glanced around. "And Jeff?"

"Over here!" Marla's voice came from the street.

Marla, Jeff, and Nita stood at the opening to the alley. At

twelve years old, Marla was just beginning to look a bit less like the plump little black girl she had once been and a whole lot more like a young woman. She had always been somewhat popular at the elementary school, but when Todd had started eighth grade at the middle school last month, he'd been surprised at how much the older boys noticed her. At the moment, with her hair pulled up into a bushy black ponytail and biting her lip sheepishly, she looked more like the little kid she really was rather than the grownup who she sometimes pretended to be.

"Where were you two?" Todd felt justifiably angry. "You know you shouldn't leave the little kids alone." That Donny was the tallest and the second oldest was irrelevant; he'd always be one of the "little kids."

"I'm sorry, Todd." Marla shot Jeff a glance that was both apologetic and accusing. "I had to go looking for Jeff."

"And where were you?"

"I had things I had to do." Jeff wasn't apologizing. He stared back at Todd defiantly. Eleven years old, Jeff had bright copper curls, twinkling green eyes, a charming smile, and the personal ethics of a coral snake. Whatever he'd been up to, Todd was sure it wasn't for the greater benefit of mankind.

"Jeff's in trouble!" Nita cried gleefully. "He cut class!"

"Where'd you go?" Todd asked.

"None of your business." Jeff answered.

Todd moved toward Jeff, hands clenched into fists, intending to make it his business, but Marla stepped between them.

"Not now, Todd," she hissed. "We're going to have to run if we're going to catch the bus."

Todd didn't push the issue, but he kept glaring at Jeff until Devon's voice broke the standoff. "Where's the police officer?" Devon looked up and down the street.

"Oh, that was me." Jeff smirked. He deepened his voice menacingly. "*'Police! Freeze!'*"

"I'm guessing you've heard that a couple of times before," said Todd.

"C'mon, guys." Marla grabbed Donny's arm and started jogging down the street. "We'll miss the bus."

They had been standing for five minutes in various degrees of guilt and discomfort. Mrs. Callow glared and sniffed and stared at the wall above their heads. Mr. Callow kept his nose buried behind his newspaper as he always did. The kids had missed the bus and had had to walk the three and a half miles back to Dalton Point. Todd, Donny, and Devon were a mess: their clothes torn and dirty, bruises and cuts on their faces and arms. Jeff, however, managed to look both innocent and benign.

"It wasn't our fault," Todd said at last, staring at his feet. "There were these kids picking on Donny —"

"Quiet!" Mrs. Callow quivered with anger. "Look at your clothes! Those were new last month!" Or as new as anything else they'd bought at the thrift store. "If you think we're replacing them, you're wrong. Do you know the rules about fighting?"

"We weren't —" Todd tried to explain.

"Quiet!" Mrs. Callow wasn't interested in listening to anyone except herself. "No supper for you three. And extra chores for all of you. Now go upstairs. I don't want to see any of you for the rest of the night."

They shuffled out miserably, Nita mumbling in Spanish, Donny still dazed and withdrawn. As they climbed the stairs to their rooms, the voices of the Callows drifted up after them.

"Mouthy brat." Mrs. Callow huffed as she rattled the pots on the stove. "Well, he's thirteen now."

The newspaper rustled. "Yup," Mr. Callow muttered. "I'll be glad when *that* one's gone."

Chapter Twelve

Gray Feather

The square of the hypotenuse is equal to the sum of the
squares of the other two sides.

But the diagram was of a triangle. Why are they talking
about squares? Todd flipped to the back of the book, desperate to find the meaning of the word *hypotenuse*. "Is there
anything on this planet more horrible than geometry?" he
muttered to himself.

"TODD!" Mrs. Callow's scream echoed up the stairs,
making the tip of Todd's pencil tear through his homework.
"GET DOWN HERE! NOW!"

"Well, that answers that question." He smoothed out his
homework and left his book open on his desk before not
rushing downstairs.

"GET OUT! GET OUT! GET OUT!"

Todd knew that this time Mrs. Callow was not screaming at him. He stepped into the kitchen and into a slice
of chaos.

A huge black bird was flapping and *rawk*ing all over the kitchen. Mrs. Callow huddled under the table and clutched her two gray tabby cats that hissed and whined in protest. Mr. Callow, hiding behind the open refrigerator door, swung his horseracing newspaper at the bird as it dove in and away.

Gray Feather again, thought Todd with a sigh. He recognized the raven by the one gray feather on its right wing. A flock of crows lived in and around the canyon nearby, but only the raven, Gray Feather, was bold enough to enter the house, stealing scraps of food and anything shiny it could find.

"Get that crow out of this house!" Mr. Callow roared.

Gray Feather stepped across the kitchen floor and peered into the open refrigerator, poking its beak into the jars on the door. It jabbed a hole in the plastic ketchup bottle, then began to peck at the drops as they hit the linoleum.

"It's a raven, not a crow," Todd said as he walked to the window. "Crows are smaller."

The bird flicked its wings and watched Todd as he pushed the window all the way open and took off the ripped screen.

"I don't care if you want to call it a crocodile!" spat Mrs. Callow from under the table. "Just get it out of my kitchen!"

"C'mon, Gray Feather," Todd said as he stepped away from the window. "Out you go!"

Mrs. Callow screeched again as Gray Feather hopped onto the kitchen table, staring at Todd in that unblinking way that birds stare, as if it was thinking about whether or not to obey.

"Out!" Todd repeated.

The bird *rawk*ed once, launched itself from the table, and took one circuit around the room. It headed for the open window, but not before making a detour to grab a silver utensil from the counter. With a triumphant caw, it flitted through the opening. Todd choked back a chuckle as he closed the window.

"My can opener!" Mr. Callow bleated as he came out from the corner. "It stole my can opener! The one the race-track gave me for being their guest of the month!"

Actually, thought Todd, *they gave it to you for being the sucker of the month and losing more money than any of the other idiots.*

"Give it back!" Mr. Callow grabbed Todd by the shirt and began shaking him. "Give me back my can opener!"

Todd's head rattled on his shoulders. "I didn't take it! The bird took it!"

Mr. Callow pushed him and Todd staggered back, knocking his butt against the table. He rubbed his hip. He'd have a bruise there tomorrow.

"He's your bird! Get it back!" Mr. Callow had a deranged look in his bloodshot eyes.

"He's not *my* bird!" Todd was pretty sure that Mr. Callow had completely lost his mind. "He's just a wild raven from the canyon."

Mrs. Callow pulled herself out from under the table. Her hair all askew, she stroked her cats maniacally. "They are your birds, you little freak! We didn't have all those crows in the canyon before you got here. And we never had a bird in the house! It's all because of you!"

"Me? I was upstairs doing my homework! How can you blame me 'cause some dumb bird flew in the window?"

"Don't you dare talk back to her like that!" Mr. Callow roared.

Todd turned in time to see the back of Mr. Callow's hand slam against his face. This time it was his head that hit the edge of the table. His knees gave out underneath him as his vision went white.

The room was unnaturally quiet as Todd knelt on the floor, leaning onto his hands, his head hanging weakly. The only sound he could hear was his own breath heaving. After a moment, he straightened and felt the bruise on his forehead. His hand came back wet, warm, and red.

Looking up, he saw Mr. and Mrs. Callow staring at him aghast. Mrs. Callow moved first, walking to the sink to pull a clean dish towel out of the drawer. She dampened it before handing it to Todd, who held it against the cut.

"Go up to your room." Mrs. Callow's voice was monotone. "We'll discuss this in the morning."

Todd pulled himself back to his feet and hobbled out of the kitchen. He stopped at the foot of the stairs and listened to Mrs. Callow huffing wordlessly as she cleaned up the blood and ketchup.

"I've had enough," Mr. Callow said, his voice low and angry. "Tomorrow you call Ms. Burbank. I want him out of here."

Anger built like a wave of vomit in Todd's stomach and pushed itself up and out. It wasn't fair. He was going to get kicked out. And it wasn't his fault. He hadn't done anything wrong.

He pounded up the stairs and down the hall. The entire house shook as he slammed his door shut. He punched the wall, hurting his knuckles a lot more than he did the plaster, and then collapsed onto his bed.

It wasn't fair.

Chapter Thirteen
The Broken Child

Todd heard the tires crunching on the gravel driveway long before he saw the car. He knew who was driving before it pulled into sight, and he knew why it was there before it rolled to a stop. He looked over at the other kids in the yard. They'd all turned to stare at him as soon as they'd seen the car. They knew who it was too. They'd all heard what had happened last night.

Ms. Burbank, the social worker, stepped out of the car and turned to open the back door. She reached in to unfasten the seat belt and lifted out a child, placing her unsteadily on her feet.

"Uh-oh," said Donny. "Girl broken."

Jeff snickered, but Todd knew that Donny wasn't trying to be cruel. Unfortunately his description was too accurate.

The girl could barely stand. Her black hair, what little she had, was short and patchy and looked like it had been hacked off by a lawn mower. Her scalp showed through in patches, and in those gaps, cruel scars were seen crisscrossing her skin. She was sickly pale, as if she hadn't seen the sun for countless months, and her arms and neck looked thin and bony where they peeked out of her jersey. Her right arm hung limply, and when she stepped, her right leg dragged sluggishly.

Yet it was the girl's face that was most disturbing. The left side looked normal; her brown eyes, despite their sad and vacant gaze, had an exotic slant. But the right side of her face was slack and drooping. She looked like she was wearing a mask with one half horror, the other half sorrow.

At first, her eyes were glazed and unfocused as she trembled on the driveway, but then her gaze sharpened and she stared hungrily at something behind Todd. He turned to see what it was, but there was nothing there except the fence with Blue Mist Mountain beyond it.

Wow, Todd thought. *Seriously damaged goods.* Most kids by the time they got to Dalton Point were in rough shape. Either they'd just lost their parents or they'd been raised in the foster system and shuffled around like library books. But this kid looked completely trashed.

Usually when a new one arrived, Todd had a little pity. But not this time.

This girl was the Seventh. His Seventh. And at Dalton Point, they all knew what your Seventh was. There could be only six resident kids here. A Seventh meant that one must leave. The oldest was going to get pushed to Hardwell, the juvenile facility — jail for those children guilty of the state's most unforgivable crime: being alone and unwanted.

Todd knew it wasn't the new girl's fault, but he still wished her dead. He barely remembered a time that he hadn't been tossed around like a tumbleweed, but since arriving at Dalton Point five years ago, he'd started to feel a little less alone, a little more a part of the world, or at least a part of the small group of castoffs collected here.

Not for much longer. Todd kicked the gravel, sending granite shards flying. Over the years, he'd watched the older kids get pushed out as younger children arrived. He'd always known that someday it would be his turn to leave.

"Marla" — Ms. Burbank's voice recalled Todd from his thoughts — "will you let Sarah take a nap on your bed until we get her settled? And Jeff, would you grab her bag from the back seat?"

Todd scowled. As the oldest it should have been his responsibility to get the new kid settled, but Ms. Burbank wouldn't even look at him, never mind speak to him. He stormed through the gate and up the steps into the dorm wing. The rest of the kids followed more slowly, Marla lagging behind to help Sarah.

Jeff caught up with Todd and grabbed his arm. "Hey, Todd! When you go, can I have your room?"

"Shut up, Jeff," Marla snapped. "And no, you can't have his room."

"You won't be in charge, Marla," Jeff said smugly. "You won't be the oldest. Donny's older than you, so he'll be in charge."

Marla gave his comment the snort it deserved. No one expected Donny to take charge. When Todd left, Marla would be the senior resident and they all knew it.

Todd shook off Jeff's grip and stomped up the stairs. The others followed him down the hall to Marla's room. Marla sat Sarah on her bed while Todd crossed to her closet and moved her shoes out of the way. When the closet floor was bare, he quietly lifted the floorboards, exposing an abandoned vent in the ceiling above the kitchen. They sat silently and listened to the conversation between Ms. Burbank and Mrs. Callow below while Sarah stared listlessly out the window.

"That boy should've been moved out months ago," Mrs. Callow said as she placed the kettle on the stove. "He's thirteen now."

She said the words *that boy* like they were poison. The others shot glances at Todd, but he forced his face to stay blank.

"I know," twittered Ms. Burbank, "but the County hasn't had any other suitable placements this year."

"Now, about this new one." Mrs. Callow sniffed. "I'm not certified for special needs. You know I only want residents who can take care of themselves. I don't have the energy to handle high-maintenance placements."

"She's fairly self-sufficient and there's no need to keep her in County Medical any longer," said Ms. Burbank. Todd knew what she meant: the County didn't want to spend the money to keep her in the hospital.

Mrs. Callow seemed to understand this as well. "It won't be as expensive to keep her here as in County Medical, but she'll cost more than the healthy ones."

There was a hint of relief in Ms. Burbank's voice. Mrs. Callow would foster a cobra if there was more money involved. "The County has authorized a higher allowance for this one. They don't expect her to last too long."

The eavesdroppers glanced at Sarah, who still sat motionless on the bed, her glazed eyes staring out the window, apparently oblivious.

"What's wrong with her? She's not contagious, is she?" asked Mrs. Callow as she bent to scoop a fat cat off the floor, coddling him protectively.

"No, no, no," assured Ms. Burbank. "She was in a car accident. Her mother died and we can't find any other relatives. From the ID we found in the wallet, we know the mother's name was Charon Woo. We don't know her real name, so we call her Sarah Woo. Not much use to call her anything, though, since she hasn't been very responsive to therapy."

"Must have been a bad accident, from the looks of her. Head injury?" asked Mrs. Callow.

"Now that's the strange thing," answered Ms. Burbank slowly. "She was barely hurt at all in that car accident. Her head injuries seemed to be caused by some exploratory brain surgery that went badly. We checked with all the neurosurgeons in the country, but there's no record of any child having that much cranial work done in the past year. We figure the mother must have taken her down across the border for some backroom surgery and it went wrong. County Medical thinks it'll do more harm than good to go back in and see what they were doing, but the CAT scan shows it's pretty much a mess up there. It's possible she'll survive, but at this point they figure she's got about six months before she'll deteriorate to the point where she'll have to be institutionalized."

"Why put her here, then?" asked Mrs. Callow. "Might as well stick her in an institution now as later."

"We're not done searching for her people yet. It's possible someone might turn up, and we don't want a repeat of last year's Elkin scandal."

Mrs. Callow nodded knowingly. "Well, we'd best get her

settled in, then. Now, what about the boy? He started seventh grade weeks ago."

Todd felt his chest tighten, and a knot in his throat made his eyes burn with hot tears. He gritted his teeth and wouldn't look at the others even though he knew they were staring at him. From the corner of his eye, he saw Nita's thumb edge up toward her mouth but Marla pulled it down before she could start sucking it.

"I'll be back on Monday for Todd. Can you find space for Sarah until then?" Ms. Burbank asked. "I do hate taking them to the Hardwell Center. Good things never happened to children at that place. But there just aren't enough other options."

"If you ask me" — Mrs. Callow snorted as she cleared away the teacups — "it's where a little freak like him belongs."

Upstairs Todd stood up and, without a word, walked out of the room, leaving Marla to replace the floorboards. The others silently watched him leave. Even Sarah turned her vacant eyes from the window to see him go, a faint flicker of thought glittering behind the haze.

Chapter Fourteen

The Last Supper

To a stranger, the silence at the dinner table might have seemed like everyone was upset Todd was leaving. Or perhaps people were angry at each other. Or maybe everyone was suddenly shy and no one could think of anything to say.

But the truth was there never was any conversation at the Callow dinner table. The Callows didn't hold with a lot of rude chatter during a meal.

Every night, Mr. Callow hid behind his horseracing paper and steadily shoveled food into his mouth. It didn't seem as if he could possibly have enough time to chew and swallow before the next forkful arrived, but that would remain a mystery since you rarely saw his face during the meal. Mrs. Callow, having "nibbled" away a four-course meal while preparing dinner, pecked at the tiny portion on her plate. After dinner, she'd spend an hour on the phone calling friends, complaining how could it be that she hardly ate at all but still couldn't lose any weight.

Eight minutes and forty seconds into the meal, Mr. Callow dropped his fork, lowered the racing sheet, let out a smelly belch, and pushed himself away from the table.

Right on schedule.

Mrs. Callow would then sigh and, after dabbing the corners of her mouth with a napkin, place her plate on the floor for the cats to eat. (She never served herself any vegetables since the cats didn't like them.) Then, without a word, she'd leave the table, leaving the dishes for whoever had been assigned that job for the night.

It would stay quiet for the next sixty seconds as the kids waited for the television to go on in the living room. That was their cue that they could speak since the Callows wouldn't come back into the kitchen for at least two game shows.

"Did not!"

"Did too!"

"Did not, did not!"

"Did too, did too, did too!"

Jeff and Marla had been glaring at each other all through dinner, and as soon as they heard the TV blast, they broke out into a hushed squabble that threatened to escalate into out-and-out warfare.

"Knock it off." Todd knew just how loud he could raise

his voice without being heard in the next room. "What are you two talking about?"

"Jeff stole my locket!" Marla hissed.

"Shut up, Marla!" Jeff spat back. "I did not!"

"My grandmother's locket just happens to disappear from my jewelry box around the same time that you just happen to have enough money to buy that MP3 player?"

"I spent all summer picking up soda cans to buy it. I didn't steal your locket." Jeff's voice rang with the kind of righteous indignation that only the chronically guilty can have when they are occasionally innocent.

"Keep your voices down." Todd shot a worried glance toward the living room. The last thing he needed was the Callows coming back in. "Marla, did you check everywhere? Behind your dresser?"

"Yes. And I always put it in the same compartment. I went to take it out to show Sarah and it was gone."

"Yeah, well, maybe it was the new kid who took it," Jeff said.

They all turned and looked at Sarah, who sat staring blindly, her meal untouched.

"Jeff." Marla's voice was icy. "She's been here less than two hours, she can barely stand on her own, and I've been with her the entire time."

"Whatever." Jeff shrugged. "I don't know where it is, but I didn't take it."

"Bird took it," Donny piped in unexpectedly.

"Donny, it was inside my jewelry box. No bird could have lifted the top. Somebody" — Marla glared at Jeff — "had to have taken it."

Jeff glared back but didn't reply.

"Bird took it," Donny repeated stubbornly.

"Donny, did you see the bird take it?" asked Todd.

Donny's mouth gaped as he searched for the words, but it seemed that question was a bit too difficult for him so he just shook his head.

"Did Jeff tell you to say that?" Marla scowled at Jeff.

Jeff met her scowl and raised her a sneer.

Todd looked from one to the other as he scraped the last bit of mashed potato off his plate. This argument was going nowhere. Todd didn't believe that a bird took the locket any more than Marla did, but if the Callows heard her accuse Jeff, they'd both be joining him at the Hardwell Center. The Callows didn't hold with stealing. Or tattle-tales. Or anything else that might interfere with their television watching.

"We'll look for it tomorrow," Todd said as he took his empty plate to the sink. "If we can't find it in your room, then we'll try to find Gray Feather's nest. Maybe he's got it."

He doubted that they could find the nest, but since he didn't think the locket was there, he would just be killing time looking for it. And this would be his last weekend for exploring the canyon. Kids didn't get to go off by themselves when they got to Hardwell. Free time was spent caged in a paved yard behind high fences. He rinsed off his plate as he ran away from that thought. Monday would come too soon and his life would become nothing but steel and concrete and boredom.

Marla stepped up beside him at the sink. Her anger had morphed into tears and she hiccupped on a sob. "My grandmother gave me that locket before she died. She was the only one who ever cared about me."

Todd stiffened, worried that Marla might break down and start talking about her real family. No one ever talked about their lives before Dalton Point. He didn't know why; they just never did.

"My mother —" Marla started.

"I'll clear the rest of the table." Todd cut her off before she could embarrass herself.

Picking up the serving dishes, he looked back. Marla leaned over the sink, shaking. Her fingers gripped the counter while she pulled herself together. When she turned around, her face was gray but she was in control. She took a deep breath but wouldn't look Todd in the eye. Instead, her eyes snapped over to the table behind him.

"Puddles! Get down!" Marla waved a dish towel at the fat gray tabby that had jumped up and was sniffing at Sarah's

untouched plate. The cat meowed indignantly before leaping back to the floor.

"Sarah" — Marla stabbed a piece of meat loaf and held
it to the girl's mouth — "do you want to try some of this?"

Sarah stared out the window and ignored the fork waving near her face. After trying a few more times, Marla gave
up with a shrug, but as she moved off to finish the dishes,
the girl suddenly grunted.

"What is it, Sarah?" Marla asked.

"If you're holding out for dessert, kid," Jeff said as he
dumped his plate into the sink, "give it up. It ain't happening."

But the girl just pointed out the window, her grunting
sounding almost like a sentence. Marla glanced out the window into the darkening backyard.

"No, we can't go out now. It's getting dark," Marla said as
she rinsed off the silverware. "Maybe tomorrow."

Todd watched Sarah as he dried the dishes and put them
away. The spark of awareness that had been in her eyes faded
with the daylight as the backyard dimmed into blackness.
She was a bit of a mystery, and along with the rest of the
disappointments he was dealing with, he was a little sorry
that he wasn't going to be around long enough to figure the
new kid out.

Chapter Fifteen

The Midnight Pledge

The autumn breeze coming off the mountain poured through Todd's bedroom window. It tasted sweet. The house was silent and the world was dark. Usually the smell of pine would send him into a deep and calm sleep but not tonight.

He pulled out his knife from under his pillow. Tonight he didn't take it out of its sheath as he usually did but just let its weight rest on his fingertips, its leather sleeve smooth and familiar.

Maybe he should run away, disappear into the night, and start a new life. Maybe try to find his father who may have been looking for him all these years.

Waves of emotion hit him like punches in his gut. Gloom. Loneliness. Fear. He clenched the knife in his fist and doubled over.

"Loser!" he hissed to himself. "Reject! Nobody wants you. Your parents walked away from you and now the

Callows are kicking you out. You're nothing but yesterday's garbage!"

With a choked sob, he swung his arm and the knife whipped out the window, disappearing with a faint thud into the dark of the backyard.

Todd bit his pillow, not wanting to wake the others. He cursed himself for crying; for being such a baby. He was thirteen now and he'd always known that Dalton Point wasn't going to be his forever. He forced his breath to slow and the choppy gasps faded to heaving sighs. He rolled onto his back, not sure if he wanted the oblivion of sleep or if it would be better to stay awake as long as possible, savoring his last days at Dalton Point.

The caw of a night bird jarred the silence. Todd remembered his knife. Quietly he rolled out of bed and headed down the stairs. Going outside after curfew was against the rules, but then, having a knife was against the rules as well, and as angry as Todd was, he didn't want to lose this last link with his father.

The night was overcast and no stars shone through the haze, but a sliver of a moon gave just enough light and Todd had very sharp eyes. In a few minutes he'd found his knife over by the wood stile fence near the hose spigot. He slid it under the waistband of his pajama bottoms and was heading back to the house when a scrap of movement caught his eye.

A white wraithlike figure appeared from around the

back of the house. Todd held his breath and watched as it moved closer. It was a small ghostly figure that moved with an awkward, almost drunken gait.

Todd sighed as he recognized the new girl hobbling around the backyard in her nightgown. She headed out the gate and toward the path that led up to Blue Mist Mountain.

Todd shook his head with disgust and started back to the house. *Let her go,* he thought. *She's not my responsibility.* But Todd knew this wouldn't fly. He had the soul of a shepherd and all his instincts weighed on him to keep the flock together. With another sigh, he turned back to the gate and headed up the path.

It wasn't difficult to catch up with the girl. Her progress was slow and stumbling as her weak leg dragged behind her. She was only a few yards along the mountain path when Todd reached to her.

"Sarah," he said wearily, "you can't be walking around at night by yourself. It's against the rules."

If the girl heard him at all, the only effect of his words was to cause her to totter faster. Todd heard her breath panting in her throat.

"Sarah," said Todd, and reached out impatiently to grab her arm.

Like a wounded wildcat, the girl fought against his hold, grunting incoherently, pulling him off balance. Startled,

Todd released her arm, but with a few quick strides, stepped in front of her.

He didn't try to grab her again, but instead spread his arms to block her path. The girl made tortured attempts to speak, but all that came out was a series of unintelligible mutters and growls. Yet Todd could tell that she wanted to go up the mountain. And she wanted it badly.

And try as he might, Todd couldn't ignore that plea.

"Okay, I'll tell you what," he compromised. "Tomorrow we'll all go up the mountain together. How's that?"

She looked to the trail and then back to Todd, a flicker of understanding in her face. She nodded jerkily and didn't fight him when he reached out to take her hand and lead her back into the house. Yet her eyes stayed fixed behind her on the mountain that loomed above Dalton Point.

Todd hoped by morning the girl would have forgotten that midnight promise, but he doubted it.

Chapter Sixteen

The Trail of Stones

It was Saturday and normally there were chores before they could call the day their own. This morning, however, Todd looked forward to staying in bed since he'd done all his Saturday chores on Friday afternoon.

But for Todd, sleeping late was not his fate.

Something was quietly disturbing his rest. He fought the urge to wake up, but it was useless. With a sigh, he opened his eyes a crack to let in the early light.

He blinked once or twice to focus his eyes before letting out a piercing scream. Even if he'd been expecting the face that hovered inches from his nose, the sight of the new girl's mangled grin that close up would still have been frightening. Todd rolled away from her, falling to the floor with a thud and a tangle of blankets.

She grunted conversationally, almost as if to say, "Good morning. Can we leave now?"

"Oh, for the love of crows!" Exasperated, Todd rubbed the sleep out of his eyes. "Sarah, don't do that again! Ever!"

He looked up as Sarah made a strange gurgling sound, her face split with a twisted grimace. It took him a moment, but then he realized that the little brat was laughing at him! After the week he'd had, this was the last straw. His temper flared. But as she looked at him with that goofy half smile, he started to grin. His grin turned into a chuckle. He shook his head as he pulled himself to his feet.

His howl brought Devon and Nita, always early risers, scurrying into the room. They stood in the doorway, dumbfounded at the sight of Todd laughing with his Seventh.

"I think Todd has lost it," Devon whispered.

Nita looked even more confused. "Maybe it's under his bed?"

Todd sighed. "Get the others up," he said. "We're going hiking this morning."

Nita shrugged at Devon before darting off to rouse the others.

An hour later, the seven were dawdling up Blue Mist Mountain. At this hour of the day, you could see where it got its name. The morning fog really did look blue in the first light of dawn.

They walked slowly because of Sarah, but Nita and

Devon scampered ahead and back again like puppies, happy to be out on an adventure. Donny ambled at the head of the pack, content virtually anywhere, so long as no one was hurting him or being mean to him. The simplicity of his mind never led him to ask why they were hiking. He was told to get up and walk and walk he would.

Jeff sulked along in the rear, listening to music on his MP3 player. The bass of the percussion leaked through his earphones as he grumbled behind. They would have been on the trail earlier, but Jeff had dawdled. It wasn't until they threatened to go without him that he finally got out of bed.

Marla and Todd walked together behind Sarah, watching her. More than a couple of times, she stopped to pick up a stone from the path, holding it against her cheek while she hummed to it. Sometimes she placed it back on the ground with a pat and a smile. And sometimes she put it in her pocket and carried it along. Once she paused by a large boulder and pulled out three stones from her pocket and clustered them around its base. Giving the big rock a friendly pat, she gurgled happily to herself before continuing up the mountainside.

Devon and Nita picked up on the new game and began looking for stones to give to Sarah. Usually she placed them on her cheek for a moment before gently finding a home for them along the path, but the game was won when she pulled the stone from her cheek and placed it in her pocket.

The sun was still rising when they reached a clearing near the peak of the mountain. They unpacked the lunch from the backpacks Donny and Todd carried. Nita and Devon watched, fascinated, as Sarah took out her stones and, gurgling and humming, arranged them on the ground near where she sat.

Todd lay on his back and watched a brilliant white cauliflower cloud blossom over a distant mountaintop. The sun was warm on his face and the air was sweet. For the moment, he forgot all about the Callows and Monday morning and Ms. Burbank and the Hardwell Center. He fell into a peaceful doze.

A wet splat landed on his arm. Remembering how he'd been woken up that morning, he opened one eye just a crack, checking things out before committing himself any further.

Nita knelt beside him, pressing one of her leaf and mud "bandages" on his arm. Behind her, Devon stood grinning, his arms and face already plastered with Nita's "cure-all remedy."

"Thanks, Nita," Todd mumbled, looking down at mud dripping off the leaf onto his jeans.

"You got a mosquito bite," Nita explained. "And this

one" — she splatted another leaf onto his cheek — "will help you wake up so you're not sleepy all the time." Nita's leaf and mud remedies could cure anything from a bad mood to an algebra exam. Or so she claimed.

He sat up and saw Jeff standing on top of a large boulder with his earphones on, playing air guitar. Donny sat on the ground by his feet, watching with rapt enthusiasm, a lone groupie. He too had muddy leaves plastered over his arms and face.

Looking around, Todd found Marla, frowning as she looked up the embankment.

"Where's Sarah?" asked Todd.

With a jerk of her head, Marla indicated the slope rising behind him. Turning, Todd sighed as he saw the girl awkwardly climbing the slope toward the peak of the ridge.

Todd knew it was pointless to call out to her, but he did anyway. The results were no more than he expected. She didn't stop or even acknowledge his voice. With a resigned shrug, Todd stood and began to scale the mountain after her.

She reached the peak first and grinned crookedly down on him before turning toward the valley beyond.

It was just as Todd reached the summit that the trembling started.

Todd had felt a few earthquakes over the years, but there was something different about this one. It was like the very rocks beneath his feet were flexing and writhing. He looked over to where the girl stood. The ground cracked and crumbled at her feet.

"Sarah!" he shouted. "Get over here! Now!"

Sarah looked puzzled by his yelling but not at all unnerved by the chaos. He ran to reach her but another, more violent tremor sent him spilling back down the slope.

Below he heard the others shouting. Todd didn't know whether to go back to them or to help the girl. In the next moment, however, he was too terrified to consider moving at all.

On the ground in front of Sarah, a fissure opened. The ground screamed as it wrenched apart, and a huge shaft of rock like a broad, rough-hewn finger of stone rose from the mountaintop. She stood, not moving, while the earth made that horrible sound and the obelisklike stone climbed higher and higher.

When it finally stopped, it stood some thirty feet above her. The sudden silence was almost more frightening than the noise had been. A cloud of fine silt descended upon the mountaintop.

Todd rubbed his eyes and peered through the settling dust to see Sarah reaching out to pluck something that glittered on the obelisk. He wanted to cry out to stop her, but the words caught in his throat. Her hand grasped the stone and pulled it from its crevice. For a moment, the world was still as she smiled down at the prize in her hand. Then, without warning, the girl began to scream.

Todd rolled to his feet. The others below could only hear her tortured screams echoing through the canyon, but Todd could see her body twisting in pain as she clutched the stone. He leaped toward her, intending to wrench the stone from her fist, but as his hand tried to close about her wrist, an invisible blow to his chest sent him flying back. He scrambled to his feet, helpless to do anything but watch her suffer.

In the midst of an agonized contortion, the girl froze, her body arching. Her eyes, glazed with pain, stared at the midday sky. She shuddered and twitched. Then, with a sigh like a spent balloon, she curled into a ball, her body huddled around the fist that still clenched the stone.

Todd crawled over to her and found that whatever it was that had pushed him away before was gone. He lifted her as he would a load of laundry and carried her to where the others waited below.

The others watched silently as Todd came down the slope, and as he started walking back toward Dalton Point, they followed.

Beneath their feet, the People of Kiva felt a faint purr.

Men tending livestock, women working the fields, old

men telling tales, children playing in the hills, all heard the hum of the stones.

The Earth was singing.

For ten centuries, the Earth Stone had been silent. Ten centuries since Korap, the last Stone Voice, had fallen into corruption. Seduced by the Deceiver, Syxx, she had betrayed her calling, and now the Earth's delicate balance was askew and extinction of all things living was imminent. Climates fluctuated, earthquakes and tidal waves wreaked havoc, diseases ravaged the pure of spirit while the decadent thrived and all that was once held as precious diminished. All the elements of creation, carefully nurtured over the eons, hung on the cusp of destruction, and without the guidance of a True Stone Voice, all would soon be lost.

The People of Kiva left their tasks and quickly headed down to the Crescent Courtyard. The totem that stood outside of Gil-Salla's hall was silent. The bear on the bottom slept. The thunderbird perched on the top with its wings spread, and its beak, turned toward Red Rabbit Ridge, was lifeless. Only the owl in the center seemed awake, but she merely blinked her eyes and said nothing as the People entered the Hall of the Flame Voice.

Gil-Salla sat on the dirt floor near the far wall, her hands splayed out on the soil, the soles of her bare feet pressed firmly against the earth. Her eyes were closed and her breathing, slow and heavy. She did not move or speak while the People entered the hall and formed a circle three rows deep. They sat as she sat, with their hands and feet splayed, hoping to hear the words of their silent star.

With the People came the Others Who Watched and Waited. The Knowing Crows flew in through the chimney hole and made their own circle in the center of the hall. Dogs, wolves, squirrels, and rabbits padded in through the door and grouped themselves around the crows.

When all had assembled, Gil-Salla opened her eyes, looked up to the sun streaming through the chimney hole, and spoke.

"A new Stone Voice rises."

A silent breath of excitement flooded the hall. Five years had passed since the last Infant Stone Voice had been lost to the Enemy. No one knows when the Creator will bless the People with a Stone Voice. One may rise once in a life span or not for a dozen life spans. In these, the dark ages of the People, few Stone Voices survived infancy, murdered by the assassins of Syxx the Deceiver, servant of the Decreator.

A new Stone Voice meant a new chance. The People rejoiced.

Gil-Salla clapped a command and the crows flew up the chimney hole while the wolves and squirrels scrambled out the door. They raced to the four corners of the land, seeking news of the new Stone Voice.

Keotak-se alone thought otherwise.

He did not believe in the coming of a *new* Stone Voice because around his neck he felt the faint trembling of Branken, who for five years had lain still and dormant.

In his heart, Keotak-se knew Lilibit was alive.

He rose silently and left the hall to complete his mission.

The Ebony Slab shivered.

Deep beneath its austere veneer, a faint crack formed unseen by human eyes, yet Syxx was aware of that fissure and knew that he, the Deceiver, had himself been deceived. The child had survived.

Before the sun set, eighteen corpses lined the bottom of a rude grave in the middle of a barren desert. Among them, Baxter's sightless eyes gazed at an impassive sky before being covered by a blanket of earth.

To deceive the Deceiver is never a good career move.

Chapter Seventeen

And from the Ashes

It wasn't the burden in his arms that weighed Todd down as they hiked back to Dalton Point. Sarah was so thin, she didn't weigh much more than a couple of bags of groceries. But Todd's scalp was buzzing again and he couldn't free his hands to rub away his alarm.

Looking at the girl in his arms, he was surprised at her profile. Still curled in a ball with the disfigured side of her face pressed into his shirt, he could see only the undamaged side. He realized she had once been a pretty child. What had happened to her?

The quake had cast a pall over their spirits. Devon muttered softly to himself as he walked beside a silent Nita. Even Jeff's sulking was replaced by a quiet uneasiness.

A bend in the path revealed Naircott City below. They stopped and stared, stunned into silence.

The city was in chaos. Hundreds of thin gray columns of smoke rose from everywhere and a huge cloud of black smoke mushroomed from the industrial section. Even this far away, the sound of sirens wafted up the mountain.

Todd quickened their pace.

As they got closer to Dalton Point, the distant alarms grew fainter and the clearing was eerily quiet. The dust had long since settled, and even the ever-present birds and insects that normally hummed a constant harmony in the canyon were still. The children stumbled past the gate and stared.

Todd gently laid the girl, still unconscious, on a patch of grass and then turned to look at the wreckage of the Callow house.

The frame of the original house had imploded. The brick-and-mortar chimney rose forlornly from the rubble, an impudent finger ascending from the wreckage. The children's wing fared a little better, but the ceilings had collapsed in many places and splintered beams impaled the bedrooms where they'd slept only hours ago.

"Mrs. Callow?" Devon called as he started to run toward the ruins of the main house, his voice rising in panic.

Marla reached out and grabbed his arm and Nita's too, holding them both back. She shot a look at Todd, who flinched and forced himself to act despite the shock that numbed his brain.

Calling to Donny and Jeff to join him, Todd walked to the rubble and started to clear away the smaller debris.

Donny was already as large as a full-grown man and stronger than most. He grabbed a large beam and pulled it out of the wreckage. The three boys worked in silence. Marla joined them, but Todd told Devon and Nita to stay with Sarah. He didn't want them to see what they might find.

A gagging noise from Jeff alerted Todd that his fears were justified. Dropping the timber he was tugging, he sprinted to where Jeff stood green-faced, gazing blindly into the debris.

There among the broken timbers, they found the Callows dead in the living room, their lifeless eyes still focused on the blackened television.

As Todd stumbled to where the three youngest sat, he heard Jeff vomiting behind a shrub. His legs buckled as he sat and pressed the heels of his palms into his eyes, trying to push the image out of his mind. Donny stared at the corpses without understanding, as if waiting for them to wake up. Marla stumbled around aimlessly, as if looking for someone to comfort her, but then she stopped, realizing there was no one beyond Dalton Point who cared.

Silently they gathered around Todd and waited. He knew they expected him to tell them what to do. He shook his head as if to jump-start it.

"We'll have to wait for someone to come from the city with help. Until then, we'll need food and blankets to get through the night. Marla and Jeff, you two go into the dorm wing and see what you can scavenge. And be careful! The roof looks like it might still fall in. Throw what you find down to Devon and Nita, who can pile it over there." He pointed to a spot near the grassy area where Sarah still lay curled into a ball, not moving. "Donny and I will try to dig out the kitchen and search for some food and other supplies."

When night came, they built a small campfire and huddled around it. In the distance, the valley below was black. The quake had knocked out the power and the only lights seen were the glowing embers of homes and buildings still on fire. Occasionally the breeze turned and the sound of the sirens drifted hauntingly up the canyon and with it came an oily dark smoke that smelled of unclean things burning.

Todd glanced to where Sarah curled on the ground and was surprised to see her eyes open, staring at the fire. He could see from the furrow in her brow that her mind was working hard. In her eyes, there was a gleam of awareness that hadn't been there before. Todd watched her in silence and wondered.

Deep within her mind, the girl felt a responsiveness that had been missing for a long time. She stared into the fire — her memories patchy and elusive. She grabbed at them but caught only wisps of smoky dreams.

All that long afternoon she had lain without moving, her

damaged brain cells rebuilding themselves. Synapses seemed to rejoin with snaps, causing her entire body to twitch and spasm. Neurons revived with a gentle murmur, sending a buzz of warmth down her spine, making her sigh with relief.

Still she stalked through her thoughts for clues to refill the void of her mind. Elusive glimpses of faces and places, revealed out of context, only taunted her. She could not remember her name or her past.

"Sarah," she heard a voice speak gently. "Wake up. You need to eat."

The dark-haired boy, Todd, was offering her a wafer of food. She stared at it and focused on his words, trying to understand his meaning.

"Sarah?" he repeated.

She took the wafer, and as she nibbled it, she heard slurring words spoken by a slow raspy voice. Then she realized that it was she herself speaking.

"My name is Lilibit" — her voice broken and sputtering — "and I want to go to Kiva."

The others watched her in alarm as her eyes began to fill with tears. She cried harder and harder until her breath hiccupped painfully. Marla put her arm around her and wrapped her in the blanket until her sobbing subsided.

And then, at last, she slept. A deep and dreamless sleep.

Todd stared at the girl. Something in her words tickled

an old memory in the back of his mind. As they settled to sleep under the stars, he was determined to hear more about Kiva.

In the morning.

Chapter Eighteen

Dreams

"No time to sleep! Time to fly! No time to sleep! Time to fly!"

A strange voice cawed at Todd. Opening his eyes, he saw a large black bird sitting on his chest, its beak several inches from his nose. When the bird saw Todd was awake, it flapped its wings and repeated its call. "No time to sleep! Time to fly! Time to fly!"

As Todd sat up, the bird hopped off his chest and strutted around the clearing. It looked like the raven Gray Feather. He stared at it and then looked around to see if the others could see (or hear) the visitor.

He was alone with the bird in a strange clearing on the peak of a tall mountain. Below he saw a carpet of rolling clouds with an occasional mountaintop cresting through the mists. He looked around anxiously, trying to find the others.

Gray Feather cawed again, "Time to Fly! Time to Fly!" and launched itself into the air, heading into the rising sun.

Todd watched Gray Feather fly away. Suddenly he was no longer standing on the mountaintop but soaring alongside the bird.

"Where are the others?" he wanted to ask, but his voice croaked and cawed and caught in his throat.

Perhaps Gray Feather understood, for it dipped into the bank of clouds and Todd found himself following. The mists felt cool and soft against his face and he reveled in the freedom of flight.

As they broke through the clouds, Todd saw Naircott City smoldering far below. They traveled east over the mountains away from the town, rising and falling with the currents.

Something moved far below on the ground and Todd sank lower to check it out. Seven figures walked along a mountain path. Todd cawed in amazement when he recognized them: Donny striding in the lead, Jeff pulling up the rear; he knew each of the hikers. His wings faltered for a moment when he saw himself in the group, carrying a tall walking stick and scanning the horizon. He skimmed down and when his bird eyes met the eyes of the walking Todd, he felt the jolt of recognition from his other self. Then he flapped his wings and soared back into the clouds.

Gray Feather was once more beside him and together they soared over the mountains. Todd saw the cool wooded mountains drop away to flat barren deserts. They flew over small towns and quiet roads. Below them, a train chugged toward the east, but they passed it easily. They skirted a harshly lit city and soared along the path of a river that wound through cathedral canyons.

Then they ascended into another mountain range. Taller, greener, and it seemed to Todd, more alive. His breath quickened as he caught the outline of four mountains in the distant mist. There was something familiar about these mountains, something that called to him, that made him want to cry out.

Yet when he opened his mouth, all that came out was the croaking caw.

Frustration turned to awe as he watched thousands of birds fill the air. They were headed toward the mountains from all directions. Todd and Gray Feather joined them and were quickly surrounded by flapping black wings and deafening creels of joy. As they drew closer, his eyes greedily absorbed all the details. The four mountains were just the anchor points. A craggy rim of red stone cliffs stood like weather-beaten warriors, shoulder-to-shoulder, linking the four mountains. And beyond the cliffs, a glimpse of a valley, green and glittering.

They were almost to the foot of the mountains when Gray Feather began to drop. Todd tried to cry out, to protest, to demand that they continue up the mountain, but he seemed connected to the larger bird and together they descended. They landed in a rocky clearing near a noisy stream.

"Fly to Kiva! Fly to Kiva!" Gray Feather sang. And with that, it flapped its wings and headed back up to the four mountains. Todd leaped, wanting to fly, but he was once again just a boy, tied to the ground. He watched the birds fly low over his head heading to the mountains. His mountains. He fell to the ground sobbing.

"Todd? Todd?" a concerned voice softly spoke. "You hokay?"

Todd opened his eyes to find Nita gently shaking his arm. Beyond her, the others watched him uneasily. Jeff snickered, so Marla lightly punched his arm. The morning sun was just peeking over the mountaintops.

On the fence, Gray Feather sat motionless. Todd gazed at the bird. The others all turned to see what held his attention. The bird flapped its wings and launched itself into the morning.

"Just a dream," mumbled Todd, watching the disappearing bird. He shook his head to drive the sleep from his brain. "Where's Sarah?" he asked as he glanced around the clearing.

"Over there." Marla gestured toward the ruins. "I think we're going to regret her getting her speech back," she added with a dry whisper.

"My name is Lilibit!" the girl announced, her words slow and labored. She limped back to the clearing, her arms full of the foodstuffs she'd foraged from the house. She used her right arm mostly as a buttress to hold her stash in her left arm. Her lopsided grin was infectious as she dumped her booty next to the burned-out campfire and began to make a very sloppy sandwich. Nita watched with disgust.

"Cheese and peanut butter? Yuck!" she exclaimed.

Lilibit broke the sandwich into two pieces, handed half to Nita, then ate the rest in three bites. She returned to making herself another sandwich while Nita sniffed doubtfully at the offering.

"Well, it looks like her appetite's better, anyway," commented Todd, and wandered to where the spigot rose near the underground well. "Still got water," he said, and bent over to wash his head.

Todd watched Lilibit out of the corner of his eye while he dried his hair. Something was bothering her. Dropping her sandwich, she stood impetuously and took a few awkward strides toward the mountain. Then she'd pause, shake her head, and return to her sandwich. She did this three or four times, and it seemed to Todd that her feet wanted to get moving, but her mind didn't know which way to go.

He knew that feeling well.

They sat quietly around the cold ashes of the campfire, each wrapped in their own thoughts.

"I had a strange dream last night." At first, Todd thought he'd blurted out his own thoughts, but then he realized that it was little Devon speaking.

"I was walking alone along a mountain path when all of a sudden, a man was walking with me." Devon's voice was as cool and dry as the campfire ashes that he stared at. "He was dressed in white and he was shining so bright, I couldn't see his face. We walked along for a while and then I asked him where we were going. 'To Kiva,' he said. We walked some more and then I asked him how we get there and he said, 'Follow the raven.' I looked up and I saw two large black birds flying into the sun. I wanted to ask him which one to follow, but when I turned to ask, he was gone." Devon looked like he wanted to say more but then changed his mind. He shook his head instead. "Then I woke up."

"I had a dream too," announced Jeff smugly, "but I don't want to talk about it in front of the girls." He nudged Donny with his elbow. Donny laughed, having no idea what he was laughing about, but he knew his cue.

"Lilibit," Todd asked quietly, "what is 'Kiva'?"

Lilibit's brow was furrowed from listening to Devon's dream. "I don't know," she whispered. "I can't remember."

A thoughtful silence fell on the group. Lilibit rubbed her

temples as if the effort of remembering made her head ache, but then she spoke again and her voice was the clearest he had yet heard.

"At Kiva, there are houses made by the Earth and food given by the Creator. There are children there, and aunties and uncles to take care of them."

She looked as surprised by her own words as the others did. It was as if she had no control over whatever part of the brain they came from.

"Oh, and there is no television," she added.

"I'm out!" cracked Jeff, and nudged Donny again to provide his laugh track.

This time Donny missed his cue, too fascinated by the picture painted by Lilibit's words to be aware of Jeff's elbow.

"Let's go to Kiva," Donny said, as if it were as easy as walking around the corner.

Todd's dream was sharp in his mind. He almost felt they *could* just walk to the four mountains, but even if Kiva was really the place where he flew in his dream, the realities of life tied his feet to the ground.

"Where is Kiva?" Todd heard Marla asking Lilibit.

Lilibit looked at her bare toes wiggling in the dirt and answered quietly, "I don't know."

Another silence settled on the clearing.

"Todd," Marla asked, "why stay here?"

It seemed to Todd that everyone was in his brain today,

asking the questions he was asking himself, long before he was ready to say them aloud.

"There's nothing left for us here at Dalton Point," said Marla. "Maybe the quake will delay Ms. Burbank, but you know she'll be back to take you away sometime soon. And now that the rest of us can't stay here either, she'll separate all of us." Marla's voice cracked.

Nita hiccupped a sob.

"Thumb out of your mouth, Nita," Todd ordered absently.

Sheepishly Nita obeyed. If Nita was going to start sucking her thumb again, as she had when she first arrived at Dalton Point, then chances are they'd all start backtracking on the growth they'd made in the past few years. Jeff would go back to being the angry, violent brat he'd been when he first showed up, Donny would stop talking, and Marla might go back to her binge eating. Todd couldn't even remember what a mess he was when they'd dropped him off here five years earlier. Only little Devon had arrived without being trashed by life, but as Todd looked at him, he realized if they threw Devon into the system, it wouldn't take much time before he caught up and was as damaged as the rest of them.

Devon met Todd's eyes with his characteristic somberness. "I think we should stay together," he said quietly. "And if Kiva is real, I think we should try to find it."

"And what if Kiva isn't real?" asked Jeff with disgust. "What then?"

"Then we'll still be together," said Marla, "wherever we end up, but we can't stay here."

Todd felt their eyes on him, waiting for him to lead, but he didn't know what to do. Which way should they go? How would they get there? What would they eat? And where would they stay?

"We'll figure it out as we go," Devon said, nodding solemnly, as if he could hear Todd's questions. "We'll be fine. We just need to start."

Todd looked from Devon to each of the kids, all watching him anxiously. If they got caught running away, they'd be in worse trouble. Especially Todd. He knew they'd blame him the most because he was the oldest. And if they didn't get caught, then what? Kiva? His dream last night had been so vivid, but he couldn't tell now if he actually remembered someone telling him about Kiva a long time ago or if it was just the dream that made it seem like a real place.

Gray Feather returned with a *rawk* and perched on the fence, watching them. For a long moment, Todd stared at the bird, hoping it would speak again and tell him what to do. When he was small, he used to pretend the crows spoke to him, but he was thirteen now, almost an adult, and much too old for stupid kid stuff like that.

Todd let out a sigh, not even aware he'd been holding his breath. "Okay," he said. "Let's pack up."

"Todd? Got a second?"

Devon stood over by the stile fence, away from where the others were rummaging through the ruins and loading their backpacks. He kicked the ground with his sneaker and small puffs of dust rose, making him look like a short wingless angel floating on a cloud. But he was a dirt-smudged cherub who obviously had something eating at him. He muttered to himself and looked down as Todd walked over.

"What is it?" Todd heard his own voice sounding more curt than he'd intended, but he could tell that whatever Devon wanted to say, it wasn't going to be good and he really didn't need any more issues to deal with right now.

Devon's voice dropped even lower and he wouldn't look up. "My dream last night . . ."

"What?" Todd asked. "Did you make up the whole thing?"

"No, it's just that there was more to it than I told you."

Devon's voice was so soft that Todd knelt down so that he could hear. "The shining man said something else. I remember what he said, but I'm not sure what it means."

"Yeah? And?" Todd tried not to sound as impatient as he felt. "What did he say?"

Devon raised his head but closed his eyes, his face pinched as he tried to remember. His voice had a whispery echo to it that was kind of eerie. "'Seven shall travel the road to Kiva. Six shall reach the palisades. One shall fall, yet all shall rise to meet the dawning darkness.'"

Neither Todd nor Devon spoke for a very long minute, but it wasn't quiet. The insects chirped and the wind hummed and in the distance the birds cawed. Todd dropped back and sat on the cold ground, his elbows resting on his knees, his chin on his arms.

"Well, that's cheerful," Todd said at last.

Devon didn't smile.

"What does it mean?" asked Todd.

Devon shook his head but said nothing.

Only six will reach the palisades? Todd looked over at the others, who were still pulling together their gear. *One would fall? Which one?* Should they risk the trip at all if he thought that one of them wasn't going to make it?

"Well, it's just a dream, right?" Todd spoke more to himself than to Devon. "I mean, most of the time my dreams don't even make sense. Dreams don't always have to mean something."

"Mine do." Did Devon actually speak or was it just a breeze?

Todd looked at Devon intently. "Have you ever had this kind of dream before?"

Devon nodded miserably. "A couple of times. Before my parents went away, the shining man told me that they weren't coming back and that I shouldn't be afraid because I'd never be alone."

Todd didn't know the details about Devon's parents, but he did know that they were both dead. Most of the kids at Dalton Point weren't actually orphans. If they were, they'd have had a chance to be adopted. Most of the kids had parents who were missing. Or just didn't want them.

"Did you tell your parents about your dream?" Todd asked.

"Yeah. Dad just said that you can't waste your life running away from your destiny." Devon stared at the spigot, his eyes glazed. "And Mom said that you can't not do what you know you're supposed to do just because you may not like how it comes out."

"So they went anyway?"

"Yeah. They went anyway."

"So, what you're saying now is that you don't think we should go?"

"No." Devon met Todd's eyes. "My parents didn't chicken out and I don't think we should either."

"Then why bother telling me at all?" Todd asked.

"I thought it would be important for you to know." Devon bit his lip but didn't look away. "It's part of it. Having a dream, I mean. I've got to tell. It's important."

Todd stared at the canyon walls. "What's that part about 'dawning darkness'?"

"'All shall rise to meet the dawning darkness'?"

"Yeah, that part. What does that mean?"

"I don't know." Devon looked miserable.

Todd tried hard not to sound as frustrated as he felt. "So, what's the purpose of having a premonition if you don't know what it means and we're not to change what we were planning to do anyway?"

"I don't know," said Devon. "Maybe so that, whatever happens, whenever it happens, we're not surprised?"

"Wonderful." Todd rolled to his feet and looked around the clearing. The others were almost finished with their packing. There was no sign of Gray Feather. Todd could have used a little help in making this decision, but once more, he had no one but himself to do it.

Jeff walked up, grinning. He actually looked happy to be going. "Which way, O great navigator?"

The others, their packs on their backs, ambled over and waited. Todd grabbed his own pack, glanced at Devon, and straightened up.

"East." Todd pointed toward the path that led to the mountains and into the morning sun. That was the direction he remembered from his own dream.

Jeff took the lead and the others fell in behind him. Todd,

lagging to pick up the rear, took one last look at the ruins of Dalton Point.

One shall fall.

He turned his back on the clearing and headed up the trail that led from the canyon into the mountains beyond.

Chapter Nineteen

Puddle Town

Todd figured they'd walked nearly twenty miles that first day, but to their legs, it felt like they'd walked over a hundred. At every clearing on the path, Donny would ask if this was Kiva. The first time, Jeff sarcastically told Donny, no, this was not Kiva; it was Crap. After that, every time Donny asked that question, they'd make up silly names for wherever they were.

They hardly saw Gray Feather at all, but whenever the path took a rare fork, someone always seemed to catch a glimpse of a black bird flitting down a trail. It may not have been the same bird, but it was reassuring.

Todd watched Lilibit, but she seemed stronger today and she kept up with the others fairly well. On her back, she wore one of Marla's old book packs held together with safety pins. She'd insisted on carrying it despite Todd's reluctance to burden her. At first, all Todd allowed her to put in it was her blanket, but Lilibit was stubborn and insisted she could carry her spare clothes and jacket too. She tied her shoes to the pack as well, and then walked the entire day barefoot. Todd didn't argue with her, thinking she'd want her shoes soon enough on the trail, but her feet never seemed to bother her and she never put them on.

It was growing dark when the path opened into a clearing with a small waterfall that emptied into a shallow pool.

"Is this Kiva?" Donny asked.

"No," Nita answered gleefully. "This is Puddle Town!"

Devon and Lilibit laughed and Todd gave a small smile as he swung his backpack off his shoulders and placed it on the ground.

"Tonight," he announced, "we camp in Puddle Town."

Lilibit pulled her pack off her back and dropped it. Her limp seemed a little less noticeable as she stumped over to the pool and stepped in to cool her feet and legs. They all were hot and sticky from their hike and before long were paddling around in the pool, splashing and laughing.

They then changed into their spare clothes and gathered around the campfire Todd and Jeff built. Their eyes grew tired and the conversation lagged into a sporadic hum as they munched on the granola bars and peanut butter sandwiches they'd packed.

An hour later, huddled under his blanket, Todd learned

his first lesson about camping in the wild. Never bathe in a cold stream on a cold night right before you're about to turn in for the night.

"I'm sorry, Todd," Marla whispered miserably.

"What for?" Todd clenched his jaw to keep his teeth from chattering.

"I shouldn't have let the little kids go in the water. If I'd stopped Lilibit, then we all wouldn't be freezing now."

"Don't be silly, Marla. How were you supposed to know that it would be this cold up here at night? If it's anyone's fault, it's mine."

"I'm not cold!" piped up Nita.

"Me neither," said Devon.

Todd looked over and saw that Devon, Nita, and Lilibit had pooled their blankets and were huddled together. Marla picked up her blanket and moved over beside them.

"Wow, Lilibit!" Marla said as she curled up next to Nita. "You put out more heat than a wood stove!"

Donny knew a good thing when he saw it. He grabbed his blanket and joined them. Todd looked over at Jeff and caught his eye.

"No way!" Jeff said. "Too queer!"

Marla giggled from the pile. "Maybe it's queer, but it's warmer!"

Todd endured the cold for another two minutes before inching his way over to join the cluster. He felt Devon hud-

dle against his back. Next to Devon lay Lilibit. Todd was
amazed at how warm it was near her. She really was like a
smoldering ember of coal.

Jeff held out shivering for nearly half an hour before
Todd heard him move to lie down on the other side of the
cluster. Todd bit his lip to keep from chuckling but a snort
escaped.

"Faggot," Jeff retaliated sheepishly.

"Gaybo," Todd shot back.

The others giggled. Donny wanted to join the game.

"Retard!" he called out gleefully, which made them all
laugh for several minutes.

In the center of this cluster of giggles and warmth, Todd
felt Lilibit tremble. Raising his head, he looked over at where
she lay, wondering if she might be upset or in pain, but a
slight smile dimpled the left side of her face and she looked
very peaceful.

With a soft sigh, she fell fast asleep.

Chapter Twenty

The Hunters

"**S**he was checked out of County Medical on Friday by her social worker. You'll have to check with social services to find out where she was placed."

Naircott General Hospital was still in emergency status; earthquake victims lined the hallways. Still, you could see curiosity on the admission clerk's face. The Director's glance took in the key information from the file before the clerk pulled it away: the name of the social worker, Ms. Burbank, and her office address.

It was easy to find the social services office building and even easier to break into it. Within minutes, the Director was rifling through Ms. Burbank's desk. There was no problem finding the file on the child she called Sarah Woo; It was on top of the pile.

He winced as he paged through the documents. Syxx would not be pleased. For weeks, Naircott Social Services had been releasing bulletins seeking information about

Charon Woo and her supposed daughter, Sarah. The Institute's Information Analysis Department should have picked these up. Baxter and his accomplices must have buried them. There could be no other explanation.

The Director smiled as he remembered the fate of the traitors. Among the many perks of living in the service of Syxx was being able to eliminate weak links with impunity. Baxter had paid for his betrayal — a slow, painful, and final penalty that the Director had enjoyed inflicting. He paused to relish the memory.

There is work to be done, he reminded himself with a shake. He fingered through the file one more time, frustration growing. Quickly he paged through the other files but he found nothing else of interest. There was no mention as to the current location of the child.

Methodically the Director slid the hard copies of the files into his case while the contents of Ms. Burbank's computer were copied onto a memory card. Removing the card from the computer, he slid it into his pocket. From the same pocket, he removed a round metallic disk larger than a silver dollar, smooth and black. He placed it on the desktop and covered it with his hand. His thumb slid the switch built into the rim.

Within seconds, wisps of smoke began to rise from between his fingers. Then flames shot out from beneath his palm. Arms of fire crept along the desktop, consuming papers and machinery with equal speed. In less than a minute, the blaze had enveloped the room. He was surrounded by the inferno. Heat darkened his slate gray suit and singed his briefcase.

He laughed.

Yet another perk. The flames would not harm him. They danced around him and stroked his legs. And the Director reveled in the glory of the power of Syxx.

He needed no family. He needed no name. It was enough to serve Syxx.

The Director felt the floorboards weakening beneath him. It was time to go. The doors swung outward as he approached. The inferno escorted him down the hall. The building imploded with a whimper as he exited.

He did not look back.

Ms. Burbank's apartment building was in the area hardest hit by the earthquake. The Director stood before the rubble. The building was once a boring five-story box. It was now an intriguing one-story pile, but buried beneath its debris was the social worker. And she was the only one who knew where she'd placed the child. It was a dead end.

"Where is she?" asked a cold voice.

The Director was startled. From the shadows of a collapsed overpass stepped Syxx. Immaculate in black, the sun shone on him but did not reflect back. The Director had neither seen nor heard his master approach, yet he now stood beside him in front of the wreckage. How Syxx had appeared so silently, the Director did not know any more than he knew how his master had known where he was. It was another of the many traits that both thrilled and terrified the Director.

The Director did not make the mistake of thinking that Syxx had asked about the social worker. "On Friday, she was outplaced into a foster home. The social worker did not complete her paperwork, so we don't know which facility she was placed into."

"And the social worker?" Syxx asked.

The Director suspected that he already knew the answer, but he nodded toward the wreckage in response.

"The child is nearby. I can feel it." Syxx's gaze slowly took in the desolation and chaos that surrounded them, as if he could see through the wreckage to the bodies beyond.

He stepped toward a nearby pile and lifted a concrete slab with ease. A faint moan was heard. Light reached a man trapped beneath the rubble. For a moment, relief and joy could be seen in his face, then it slowly changed to terror as he read his fate in Syxx's eyes.

"No!" he screamed, his arms raised in both appeal and defense.

It was futile. Syxx breathed heavily, as if feeding on his terror, and then dropped the slab, crushing the man to silence. Syxx's chuckles faded before he turned back to the Director.

"Find her. Use all teams. All resources. The child must be found."

Keotak-se wandered the streets of Naircott, his eyes and ears alert for any sign of his quarry; yet the sun rose and set and still he had no success. A flock of crows perched in a leafless tree watched him approach. Keotak-se caught the eye of one and gave a soft caw. The bird flew down and balanced on the tip of his staff. For several moments, their eyes locked. Then the bird launched itself into the air, squawking loudly. The other birds took wing, cawing as they danced in the air, circling the first crow. They then parted, all heading in different directions, their caws fading as they flew.

Keotak-se stood as still as the trees around him and waited. Minutes passed and one or two crows returned to perch on the tree, squawking once or twice as if in apology before flexing their wings to settle quietly on a branch.

Then in the distance, a small cloud of birds noisily approached. The crows flitted around Keotak-se, diving and dashing at his head. Keotak-se motioned the birds to land, but they were too excited. Whenever one would try to touch down on the end of his staff, another would knock it off, much to the raucous annoyance of all.

Finally Keotak-se grabbed one crow and, holding it

against his chest, gave the ground a sharp rap with his staff. The birds gave one last squawk before fleeing for the safety of the tree branches.

The crow Keotak-se had caught settled smugly on his wrist. Keotak-se met its eye and asked a silent question. The bird broke off her self-congratulatory preening to chirp back soberly. Had it seen the girl? Keotak-se's memory was five years old, but the crow caught the image and recognized her nonetheless. It cawed gently, projecting back the image of a girl near a house in a canyon. But which canyon?

The crow turned its head northward toward one of the mountains, which loomed, misty blue, above the city. With a flick of Keotak-se's wrist, the bird flew off with a parting *rawk*.

As the bird settled into the tree, Keotak-se looked north toward Blue Mist Mountain and permitted himself a small smile, the first in many years.

Chapter Twenty-one
The Hunted

The next morning, Todd secretly watched Lilibit as they walked through the mountains. His curiosity burned. Who was she? Why did she play with those stones? And what was so special about that stone she plucked from the obelisk? Seeing the furrow in her brow, he guessed she probably wrestled with the same questions herself, so he held his tongue and wondered in silence.

She was smaller than Nita and probably younger, but even with her handicaps, she had a bossy streak as she decided the rules for the silly games the three youngest made up as they hiked.

Early that morning, Todd saw a long thick branch of dead wood lying along the path. He stopped to stare at it and the others glanced at him questioningly. There was something familiar about the branch. He picked it up and then grinned to himself. It looked like the staff he'd carried in his dream two nights earlier. Using his pocketknife, he nicked off the jutting knobs and twigs, then grinned again. It was silly to copy his own dream, but a tall walking stick would be a good thing to have on a long hike. He tapped it several times on the ground before jogging to catch up with the others.

Lilibit stood stock-still, staring at him. With her head tilted, her brow wrinkled, and her eyes unfocused, she looked as if the staff had triggered some vague memory that she couldn't place. The others kept walking but Todd stopped in front of Lilibit and waited for her to say something.

But she didn't speak. She just shook her head and started walking again, but she kept looking back at Todd. For the rest of the morning, she was quiet, her thoughts somewhere else.

The sun was high overhead when Todd began thinking about breaking for lunch. He was looking around for a likely place to stop when a flicker of movement on the horizon caught his eye. It took only a moment for him to identify it as a helicopter, probably from the Forestry Service on fire patrol, but its effect on Lilibit stunned him.

She froze and let out a pitiful whimper. Tearing her eyes from the approaching chopper, she turned to run. As she stumbled past Todd, he reached out and grabbed her by her waist, lifting her off the ground.

Her trembling surprised him. He felt as if she would shake apart in his arms. There was a look of animal panic in her eyes. Todd acted on instinct.

"Under cover!" he hollered. "Now!"

The others turned to see Todd carry Lilibit off the trail and scratch out a rude hiding place under the briar. Devon grabbed Nita's arm and the two of them scrambled under the shrub. Marla stood in the middle of the path looking bewildered, and Jeff rolled his eyes in disgust.

"Now what?" Jeff demanded.

The helicopter flew slowly toward them. Todd's feeling of alarm grew.

"Move!" he barked, his eyes fixed on the approaching chopper.

Plainly confused, Marla trotted over to Todd, who grabbed her arm and pulled her under the shrubbery. Donny followed Marla, grinning cheerfully, happy to be part of whatever the new game might be. Jeff, however, reveling in disobedience, turned to wave merrily at the approaching chopper.

The helicopter swept low and the wind from the blades ripped at Jeff's hair and clothes. Todd shielded his face as dust tore into their makeshift den. Peeking over his arm, he saw the markings on the helicopter and knew it was not a forestry vehicle. It was close enough that he made out the small logo on its matte black veneer, which read

NAVMRI. Through the smoked glass of the windshield, Todd saw two figures staring coldly at Jeff as he continued to wave gleefully.

Suddenly the helicopter rose and veered westward, apparently continuing its reconnaissance of the mountains. Jeff continued to wave as it disappeared over the eastern ridge. Then he turned to face the others.

"It's only a helicopter, butt-skulls!" He smirked.

Todd waited until the helicopter completely cleared the horizon before bursting out of the brush like a wounded bear. He was only an inch or two taller than Jeff, but his anger gave him unexpected strength. He grabbed Jeff by the jacket and bore him backwards, pinning him against a tree.

"Do you think this is funny? Do you think we're on a picnic? If you want to go to the Hardwell Center, fine! We'll leave you at the next road we cross."

Jeff looked frightened by the blast of Todd's anger, but he braved it out. "Oh, c'mon. It was just a helicopter. Even if they know we're missing, they're not going to send out helicopters into the mountains to look for us!"

Todd's nose was in Jeff's face. "Listen. If we're going to get anywhere, we need to be able to rely on each other. To trust each other. And if you're going to do the opposite of everyone else just because you think it's cool, then you're going to get us all caught."

Todd released his hold on the jacket and Jeff slid to the ground. Scavenging his dignity, Jeff brushed off his sleeves. "Yeah, right. 'Trust'! It's not about 'trust'; it's about obeying you no matter what you say. Just because you've got all the others kowtowing to you all the time doesn't mean I have to be another one of your peons!"

Todd felt the temptation to tell Jeff to beat it, to go back to Dalton Point and wait for them to take him to Juvenile Hall. Maybe it was Jeff who was supposed to fall, and that would take care of Devon's prophecy. Of all the kids, Jeff was the one that Todd would miss the least.

And yet some deeper instinct drove him to try to keep them all together. He couldn't see forcing one of them out just to satisfy some dream that might not even mean anything. He bit the inside of his cheek as he tried to get control of his temper.

"Listen. We're all going to need each other if we're to get to Kiva." Todd turned to look back at the others, who stood by the underbrush watching the fight with wide eyes. "All of us have to be on the same side or we're not going to make it."

"Todd . . ." Marla's voice was heavy as she gestured with her head to where Lilibit still huddled under the briar shaking.

Todd strode briskly back to Lilibit. She was curled into a ball again, sobbing.

"It's all right, Lilibit," Todd soothed as he lifted her out and tried to set her on her feet. "The helicopter's gone."

Lilibit's legs collapsed underneath her and she sat staring at the horizon, her breath choppy. Todd carried her to a secluded grove off the path, under a tree, where they ate their lunch in silence.

They'd finished eating and were packing their gear when Jeff stood up and walked over to Lilibit. "Here," he said roughly, handing half his granola bar to her. "You want the rest of my dessert?"

Todd was about to tell him where he could put his granola bar. That it was stupid to give Lilibit more food since she'd barely touched her sandwich. That this was a lame excuse for an apology for putting them all in jeopardy. But Lilibit's reaction cut him off.

Looking up at Jeff, she gulped back a sob and gave him a watery smile. She took the bar and nibbled at it listlessly, probably more out of consideration of Jeff's feelings than from any enjoyment of the food.

Jeff helped Lilibit to her feet and they returned to the trail. With his apology accepted, his cockiness returned and the incident with the helicopters seemed to fade into the back of their minds.

But Todd still seethed. He didn't talk much the rest of that afternoon. Jeff's defiance didn't bother him as much as the mystery of Lilibit did. His scalp prickled with a warning.

He ran his fingers through his hair, rubbing away the tingle. If only he could get rid of his qualms as easily.

The helicopter reconnaissance team had not thought much of the boy they had seen hiking alone out on the mountain, but to the Director, it was a deviation of significant note. A child does not cheerfully hike by himself in the middle of the woods, miles from the nearest port of civilization.

In moments, he cross-referred the surveillance photo with the county social services records and positively identified Jeffrey Terrance, eleven years old, resident of the Dalton Point Foster Care Facility. He dispatched an investigative team to that location, but he was certain he had a positive match.

As he reported his findings back to Syxx, it was agreed: the highest probability was that the girl was in the mountains.

All nine Reclamation Teams were dispatched.

To Keotak-se, the ground around Dalton Point was a book written in his native tongue. He saw Lilibit's arrival, her first thwarted attempt to reach the mountain, her successful attempt the following morning and her return, carried back down the mountain by a boy on the verge of manhood. Where they slept, what they ate, when they left, and the direction they walked were all written in the soillike words on a page.

Keotak-se felt a sting of grief in his heart for the evident pain the child suffered, but as he tracked the band into the mountains, his heart lightened as he read the signs of healing in her steps.

Keotak-se stopped and sniffed the air. He recognized the signs of the coming squall long before the clouds masked the sun and the air grew chill. He quickened his pace, running like a wolf over the terrain, pushing to reach the children before the impending storm.

Chapter Twenty-two

La Mesa del Tío

The sky turned gray and hard as the band trudged up the rocky trail. The light jackets, which they'd pulled from their packs, were little help against the biting winds of the mountaintops.

The hasty change in the weather surprised Todd. While Dalton Point was a thousand feet or so above the valley of Naircott, it was still pretty warm all year long. Now they were a few thousand feet higher and he hadn't expected it to be this much colder. And from the look of the sky, it would only get worse before it got better.

He heard Nita's teeth chattering as she trudged behind. Jeff grumbled constantly but the others were silent in their discomfort. Lilibit didn't seem to feel the cold as much as the others, but she seemed anxious and skittish, a deep animal fear replacing the sparkle that had grown in her eyes during the past few days.

"I just hope the snow holds off until we can find shelter," Todd muttered under his breath.

His words still lingered as a chill mist in front of his face when the first flakes of snow began to fall. He bit back his despair and threw back his shoulders.

"Huddle together as you walk. It'll be warmer," Todd barked. "I don't know how far we'll have to go before we can find a safe place to camp."

The snow fell quickly and heavily from the sky, and within minutes, it was calf-deep and showed no sign of letting up.

"This is ridiculous!" Jeff ranted as he trudged along. "I've never seen snow fall this fast or heavy before. Whose dumb idea was this, anyway?"

"Oh, stow it, Jeff," Marla snapped. "You're not helping."

"We need a warm place to stay the night," Todd heard Devon murmur beside him.

Todd bit back a sarcastic response. At the moment, Devon's habit of stating the obvious was more than he felt up to dealing with.

Nita stumbled and fell in the snow. Todd strode back to pick her up and hoisted her onto his back. As he plowed through the growing mounds, now with the extra burden, he wondered how much longer they could hold out against the storm.

They lost the path as it wound its way into a stand of towering pines, but they pushed forward. As they broke through into a clearing, they saw a forlorn little shack, windows cracked and the door slightly ajar, wedged open by a growing snow dune.

"All right!" Jeff gasped in relief, and they sped up to reach the shelter of the cabin.

They pushed open the door and walked inside, stamping the snow and cold off their jackets and legs. After the blinding white of the snowstorm, it took their eyes a moment to adjust to the dim light of the cabin and to absorb what they saw.

Jeff swore. Marla screamed. Nita clung to Todd, burying her face into his shoulder. They all stared.

At first, they didn't notice the dust and cobwebs covering the rustic one-room camp. They didn't see the musty mattress in the corner or the stacks of firewood next to the fireplace. They couldn't even absorb the large intricately carved table in the center of the room with its eight ornate chairs surrounding it.

Their eyes fixed on the sight of the remains of a man who sat at the head of the table. A desiccated skeleton. Dried remains of flesh drooped from his carcass. Wisps of skin and gray hair clung to his skull, which tilted back to rest between the post and rail of his high-back chair. Soiled, tattered clothes covered his corpse, and the remains of a solitary dinner lay in front of him on the table. It looked like he'd fallen asleep at the dinner table and passed away, quietly and alone.

They all jumped at the sound of the door slamming behind them.

Lilibit leaned against the closed door, having thrown her sparse weight against it to shut out the mounting storm. She alone seemed unperturbed by the skeleton. She walked to the table, tilting her head to one side as she looked at the corpse.

"Excuse me, sir," she asked as though he were just sitting reading the daily paper. "It's snowing out. Do you mind if we stay in here with you for a while?"

Todd and Marla exchanged glances.

There was a brief pause while Lilibit stared at the man attentively. She then turned and said earnestly to the others, "He says we are welcome."

Nita slid off Todd's back and walked over with Devon to look closely at their host.

"How long do you think he's been here?" Nita asked.

"Long enough to stop smelling bad." Devon edged closer and sniffed. "He smells more like leather than a dead guy."

"How would you know what a dead guy smells like?" asked Jeff, who stood as far away from the table as the room would allow.

"Well" — Devon shrugged — "he doesn't smell as bad as the possum that died under the porch last spring."

"Is this Kiva?" asked Donny.

Jeff moaned.

"No," Nita announced with a flourish of arms, "this is la Mesa del Tío!"

"And what does Mesa del Tío mean?" asked Jeff.

"It means 'Uncle's Table,'" answered Devon.

"I didn't know you spoke Spanish." Marla dropped her backpack to the ground but didn't take her eyes from the skeleton.

"Oh, I don't." Devon was already exploring the shelves against the wall. "But I can speak Nita."

Keotak-se stood motionless and unseen among the snow-draped trees as the helicopter slowly patrolled the storm-battered mountain ridge. He recognized the vehicle and understood its mission. He considered whether destroying it would draw the unwelcome notice of the enemy. He made his decision.

He tapped the end of the staff lightly on the ground and then waved it in a horizontal arc from the north, ending with it pointing at the approaching helicopter.

Abruptly a howling blast of icy wind rose from the north hammering the trees around where Keotak-se stood, his staff still aimed at the enemy. The wind grabbed the helicopter in its fist and slammed it against the cliff's rock face.

Keotak-se watched impassively as the machine dissolved in a blaze of black smoke and noise. Turning back to the trail, he continued to track the disappearing traces of the children's path.

Syxx stood before the glass wall in his tower office. Looking past the glittering city below, he could see the storm raging in the distant mountains. Behind him, the Director of Security waited to deliver the rest of his report.

"Do they think they can stop me?" Syxx's fingers curled and uncurled like claws. "I rule this land. The sky shall not thwart me."

"Air Reconnaissance Command reports reduced visibility and increased loss risk potential." The Director's face was blank, but Syxx could read his confusion. Unseasonably early snowstorms might seem random to some, but Syxx could detect preternatural interference and his anger raged.

Still, the Director seemed compelled to speak. "Air Reconnaissance Command requests permission to ground the remaining units and suspend the search until the weather clears." The Director's voice was as rigid as his stance. "They feel they shall be far more effective after the storm has passed."

Syxx's fury blazed red hot, but his voice was cold. "I am not interested in efficiency projections. Get your teams back out into the mountains and find the child."

The Director nodded curtly and exited but not before the door swung open and Dr. Nil barged into the room, fuming loudly. "Syxx!" she snapped. "Can you please tell me who authorized the deployment of all our field teams?"

With her whippet-thin body and her teased blond hair, Dr. Nil gave the impression of being very tall but was actually of moderate height. With her sharp tongue and abrasive manner, she was thought to be very powerful, but the truth was she was merely a puffed-up figurehead that Syxx exploited for his own ends. And with her numerous degrees and academic awards, many considered her to be a brilliant intellectual, but Syxx knew her to be an ignorant fool — all the more evident by her stupidity in addressing him in this manner. Yet even such a petty, annoying tool could still be useful. Syxx lifted the smiling façade over his anger and purred.

"Ah, Dr. Nil." Syxx gestured for her to sit in the chair opposite. "Back from your conclave? Did the committee appreciate your abstracts as much as they deserved?"

Dr. Nil twitched, the ruff of her anger ebbing as she settled in the chair. Her desire to flaunt her authority was almost as great as her need to gloat over her successes. "But of course, Syxx. I received a standing ovation. My findings on the Cortex Conundrum will be published next month."

"No less than I expected. Your efforts deserve it."

Dr. Nil smiled, and while she could easily be distracted, she did not often lose sight of her objective, particularly when that objective included throwing her weight around. "Enough of that. There appears to be a major field effort underway. Who authorized it?"

"I did." Syxx watched the woman closely. "At your request, I might add."

"Me? I was at the conclave. I made no such request!"

"True, but you did say that, since the loss of research subject seventeen-seventeen, you'd like to locate a similar specimen. I believe we can do even better."

As expected, Dr. Nil broke off her hissy fit mid-snap. The only thing greater than her self-indulgence and vanity was her greed.

"Better than the RS seventeen-seventeen?" She leaned toward him, her eyes wide with avarice.

"Actually, I believe that RS seventeen-seventeen is still alive. We are taking steps to recover her now."

"Alive? RS seventeen-seventeen? That horrible little slant-eyed brat?" Dr. Nil sat back with disgust. "Nonsense! I saw the autopsy results. She can't possibly be alive!"

Syxx considered the doctor carefully before answering.

There was no need for her to know how deep the deception ran throughout NAVMRI. Baxter and his accomplices had faked the child's death and then smuggled her out of the complex right under his nose.

No, there was no need for her to know the truth.

"Perhaps you're right." His voice was velvet soft. "And yet if I could obtain another specimen as viable as RS seventeen-seventeen, you would be able to complete your cortex research."

Dr. Nil lost herself in dreams of grandeur. "Yes, you're right. If that nasty child hadn't expired, I'd have been able to finish that research."

"And if I can find you another?"

"The successful completion of the cortex thesis will be my greatest triumph! Why, at the conclave, there was already talk of my being nominated for a Nobel Prize."

"You mean us, don't you?" a whiny voice squeaked from the doorway. Dr. Voight quavered into the room, seeming to try to assert himself while at the same time seeming to try to hide behind Dr. Nil's chair. Not an easy thing to do for a portly gnome like Dr. Voight.

"Of course, Stanley." Dr. Nil rolled her eyes impatiently. "Of course."

"Baxter's missing too," said Dr. Voight in a peevish tone, apparently continuing an earlier conversation. "That makes at least twelve employees that have disappeared while we were at the conclave."

"Baxter and the others were terminated," Syxx stated smoothly.

"Whatever for?" Dr. Nil raised an eyebrow.

"Security breach," answered Syxx. "They were found attempting to smuggle classified research material to Acheron Biotech."

"Well" — Dr. Nil raised her nose — "I certainly hope you adhered to corporate protocol and documented their exit interviews."

Syxx smiled nostalgically. "You must not concern yourself with that, doctors. Please be assured that I conducted the exit interviews myself. In fact, I found them most entertaining."

Perhaps it was something in his smile, but the doctors hurried from the room, showing no desire to know any more details.

When the blanket of snow concealed all traces of the children's trail, Keotak-se abandoned his ground tracking and took to the skies, but the mounting ferocity of the storm soon made even aerial tracking useless. He was forced to seek refuge.

Into the shelter of a mountaintop cave, a giant condor

landed, much to the chagrin of the other birds gathered there to wait out the tempest. When the condor suddenly turned into a man, the birds were not sure that this was an improvement, but as the man sat motionless at the mouth of the cave and made no movement to threaten them, they settled down to suffer out the weather together.

Keotak-se gazed over the snow-pummeled landscape. He only hoped the powers that sent this storm into the mountains also provided a reasonable shelter for the children.

Keotak-se buried his impatience and waited.

Chapter Twenty-three

The Father's Table

As usual, Lilibit woke first. She climbed over the sleeping bodies of the others, who mumbled complaints. While her strength and agility had improved, she seemed to get a perverse pleasure from bumping into the other kids when they still wanted to sleep. She purposely bounced a couple of times on Todd's legs, giggling when he mumbled, "Brat!" and swatted her off the bed before rolling over to enjoy his last few shreds of slumber.

Lilibit padded to the door, pausing at the head of the table as she did every morning.

"Good morning, Uncle Mesa!" she greeted the old man merrily.

She opened the door to reveal the wall of snow that had risen over the past three days to bury the entire cabin. They had carved tunnels into the snow, at first to get drinking water, then to create a latrine area, and finally just to play in.

Lilibit stopped at the opening to their winter labyrinth, her head cocked to one side listening.

"I think the storm stopped," she announced. She turned to look back at the mound of sleeping bodies sharing the moldy mattress in the corner of the cabin. She sniffed in disapproval when her weather report did not receive even a grunt in response, then climbed through the tunnels to that area they had designated as the Girls' Room.

They ate their meals at the large wooden table with Lilibit and Todd next to the dead man. Todd sat there because no one else would, but Lilibit apparently liked the corpse, including him in their conversations and passing on his responses to the others. At first, Todd thought she was making up his words, but there were occasions when she said things that made him wonder if she was concocting a story or if the old man really spoke to her.

Their first day in the cabin, they had discovered a rough wooden crate sitting in the corner. Inside they'd found dozens of cans of baked beans and brown bread but became frustrated when they couldn't find a can opener. Lilibit stomped up to the old man.

"Okay, Uncle Mesa," she had said, her hands on her hips. "We give up. Where'd you put the can opener?"

She'd tilted her head to one side as if listening to him for a moment before turning toward the fireplace.

"He says it's up here." She had stretched her arm up to reach above the mantel, but she was too short.

Jeff had snickered as Todd walked to the fireplace. Todd's fingers fumbled over the mantel, but when his hand came back down with a can opener, everyone just stared, amazed.

"Ha!" Jeff laughed. "Good one, Lilibit!"

Lilibit smiled, but seemed puzzled at Jeff's comment.

Walking over to Todd, Marla whispered, "That's just weird!"

"It gets weirder still," Todd whispered back. "Take a look at it."

The can opener hadn't been nearly as dusty as everything else in the cabin, and etched into its shiny chrome surface were the words NAIRCOTT TRACK AND CASINO.

"I think it's Mr. Callow's can opener," Todd said quietly. "It's just like the one Gray Feather stole last week."

"Okay," said Marla, "I am now completely freaked out."

This morning, Lilibit dominated the breakfast table with a long involved story about how Uncle Mesa had carved the tables and chairs for his seven children.

"For many years, the old man set the table for himself and his seven children. He'd prepare meals for them and then he'd sit and wait for his children to arrive. But they never did."

Todd watched Lilibit. It hadn't been more than a week

ago, she'd arrived at Dalton Point so badly maimed the doctors held out little hope for her survival. Now even her face had slowly healed so that her right side was almost the same as the left. Her voice was stronger too. There was only a hint of slurring as she told her tale about their Uncle of the Table.

"One day, Uncle Mesa called to his friends in the forest and seven little squirrels came to answer him. Uncle Mesa asked the squirrels to go to the homes of his seven children and invite them to dinner. As the squirrels ran to do the bidding of the old man, Uncle Mesa went back into his cabin to prepare the most sumptuous dinner he had ever made. Fresh cheese from mountain goat milk and wild berries of all kinds. A wounded deer walked into his clearing and offered herself to the old man to be part of the dinner, so there was fresh venison too. Besides that, there was —"

"Knock off with the food already, and finish the story!" Jeff pulled at his hair.

Lilibit sniffed before she continued. "Brown bread and baked beans!"

Devon and Nita laughed since that was what they ate for breakfast, having had the same dinner the night before and the night before that.

"That night," Lilibit continued, "the old man sat at his table with his gigantic banquet and waited for his children. The warm food grew cold and the cold food grew warm and still the old man waited. When morning came and still no one had come to eat with him, Uncle Mesa stood up from the table and walked outside and called to his squirrel friends. There was no answer. A passing blue jay heard the old man and flew down to the clearing. He told the old man that his children refused to listen to the squirrels and had killed them and ate them for their dinners.

"Uncle Mesa was furious! He bellowed with his loudest voice deep into the forest. Out came seven big bears in answer to the old man's call. Uncle Mesa asked the bears to go find his children and bring them to his table.

"That night Uncle Mesa made another scrumptious dinner. Besides the cheese and the berries and the venison —"

"— and brown bread and baked beans!" chimed in Nita and Devon.

"— he added warm potatoes and fresh bread and a nutty spread made of acorns —"

"Enough with the food!" bellowed Jeff.

"— and lots of other good stuff," added Lilibit with a smirk. "The old man waited all night for the bears to return with his children, but they never arrived. The next morning, the old man went out to the clearing and called for the bears. One by one the bears came out of the woods, looking rather ashamed of themselves. 'Well? What happened? Where are my children?' Uncle Mesa asked. The biggest, oldest bear answered, 'They would not come, even though we asked them quite politely!' The youngest, smallest bear then piped up, 'So we ate them!'

"The bears all apologized sheepishly, explaining that since his children were so rude and yet looked so delicious, it was pretty difficult to resist. They left the old man alone and heartbroken in the clearing.

"The old man went back into the cabin and put away all his good dishes. He took all the delicious food he made and threw it out for his friends of the forest to eat. He took off his fancy clothes and put on his rattiest work clothes. Then he sat down at the head of his empty table with nothing for his dinner but brown bread and baked beans on a rough wooden plate. When he finished eating, he laid his head against the back of his chair and fell into a deep sleep.

"Now the old man dreams and waits for the day that the raven will come and take his soul out of his body. When the raven comes, he will carry the old man up to the sky to *his* father's table. There his father has prepared the most delicious dinner on the most beautiful table filled with the most wonderful people, who will laugh and talk and eat with him. And then Uncle Mesa will be happy at last."

There was an appreciative pause before Jeff spoke. "Aren't you going to tell us what they'll eat?" he asked.

Lilibit's eyes twinkled as she opened her mouth to begin another long list of menu items, but Todd was quicker. He reached over the table and clapped his hand over her mouth.

"I think we get the idea!" said Todd.

They all laughed as Lilibit mumbled her laundry list of food into Todd's muffling palm. When she finally stopped, Todd waited a moment before gingerly withdrawing his hand.

"— and baked beans and brown bread!" Lilibit ended merrily, with much laughter from the others.

"Where did you hear that story?" Todd asked, shaking his head.

"From Uncle Mesa!" answered Lilibit as if it were obvious.

Marla leaned over to whisper in Todd's ear. "Either her memory's improving and she remembered that story from before or she has a very vivid imagination!"

While Todd was inclined to believe the latter, he did wonder. In the soft morning light, Todd thought the skull of the old man smiled, peacefully enjoying the laughter of the children gathered around his table. Todd shook his head as if to rid himself of the silly thought.

"And we're out here again, why?"

The sound of the helicopter drowned the voice of the man sitting in the cockpit, but from where he stood on the ground a half a mile away, Keotak-se read his lips.

"Because we've got orders. Now keep your eyes open," answered the man behind the controls.

"I doubt even an experienced mountaineer could have survived that storm. Does he really think a pack of kids could have made it?"

"We've got our orders," repeated the pilot.

Keotak-se watched the helicopter pull away, weaving its surveillance pattern over the mountain range. He was encouraged by their presence, since it meant not only did the Enemy believe Lilibit had survived the storm but that they had not yet located her.

Yet what heartened him even more than the helicopters was the song of Branken humming faintly around his neck. Gliding low over the terrain and with the advantage of keener and better-trained eyes, Keotak-se also searched, but could find no trace of the children.

Chapter Twenty-Four
Un Adiós al Tío

By the following morning, all their tunnels had dissolved into paths. If today was going to be as warm as yesterday, the mountains would soon be thawed enough for them to travel.

Todd felt the temptation to stay here at Mesa del Tío, but he knew the cans of food they'd found might last them only for another week or so, and winter would soon be full on them.

Closing the door, he turned to look at the others, who sat inside waiting for his direction. He was about to suggest they should start packing up when he heard the distant chatter of a helicopter.

Lilibit froze, then flew into a frenzy: running for the door then changing her mind and dashing around the room before darting under the table. She hugged one of the table legs in terror. The others watched her in growing fear.

Todd looked out the door and realized that the thawing

tunnels now appeared as branching fingers of paths in the snow, visible from the sky — and pointing directly to their hideout. The helicopter wove a search pattern across the southern sky, and Todd guessed they had only ten or twenty minutes before it would be close enough to detect their cabin.

"Pack it up! Now! We're moving!" Todd barked, the edge of panic in his voice spurring the others to action.

Marla grabbed the canned food and loaded it into Todd's and Donny's packs.

"Got the can opener!" Nita piped.

"Good girl!" said Todd. Nita beamed in pleasure.

Todd grabbed a coil of rope from behind the oak chest. He looked around to see what else they could take from the cabin. Jeff was scooping the dinner knives and Devon stuffed the ratty blanket into his backpack.

Todd ran to the door. The helicopter was still too far away to notice them, but it would be only a matter of minutes before it was upon them.

"Okay! Let's move out! Head into the woods; they won't be able to see our tracks from the air!"

Todd sent Donny first to wade through the waist-deep snow and break the trail. The others followed quickly.

Todd took one last look at the cabin and found Lilibit lagging behind. Surprisingly she seemed to have forgotten the threat of the approaching helicopter for the moment.

"Goodbye, Uncle Mesa, and thank you," Todd heard Lilibit whisper to the corpse. Taking a small glittering stone out of her pocket, she slipped it under his bony fingers. "I hope you like your new table."

"Lilibit!" Todd roared. "Now!"

Lilibit turned and raced out the door to catch up with the others. Todd stole a quick glance back at their lonely host before closing the door and hurrying into the forest.

For a long silent moment, the skeleton sat at the head of his again empty table, alone in his again empty cabin. A soft breeze pushed open the door and a flurry of snowflakes danced into the room. The skull dipped gently as if it were nodding off to sleep before falling with a placid thud onto the table. As if released from a spell, the bones of the old man lightly dissolved into a puddle of dust.

A raven flew in, a streak of gray on its right wing. It landed nimbly on the table and picked at the remains of the breakfast with a finicky air. Then it hopped to the head of the table and, finding the old man's shiny stone, picked it up in its beak and flew out the door and into the morning sky.

The gust from the raven's wings sent the puddle of dust flying into the air. Picked up by the breeze, he waltzed on the wind and out the door, never to dine alone again.

Chapter Twenty-Five

Into the Mether Rock

Todd ran to catch up. Lilibit's dash out the door had carried her past the others and now she plowed through the snow and ran ahead of Donny. Todd was astounded at the path she carved. They all knew that Lilibit gave off a lot of heat — they'd never lit the fireplace in the cabin; it had been warm just from her body heat — but that didn't prepare him for the sight of her blasting through the snow like a blowtorch. Jeff and Marla looked back at Todd as they ran, flabbergasted, yet Lilibit was too frightened to be aware that she was doing anything unusual.

Their path led to a streambed. Normally the stream would have been a gentle babble of water that they could have hopped with a leap or two, but with the extra feed of the melting snow, it was a chasm of rapids too treacherous to ford.

The group pulled up gasping at the bank. Looking back over his shoulder, Todd realized Lilibit had laid a trail so vivid, their pursuers would be able to track them easily, and with all their enemy's modern equipment, the kids would soon be overtaken. They couldn't see the helicopter through the web of pine trees towering above them, but they heard it getting closer.

Todd thought if they ran along the edge of the stream, they'd leave less of a trail. But which way to run? The others stared at him as he wavered. Downstream led them out of the mountains, but would their pursuers expect them to go that way?

A flicker of black skittered above the trees to his right. It wasn't Gray Feather, it was just a crow, but Todd had nothing else to go on. He pointed upstream and Jeff headed that way, the others following close behind, Todd in the rear.

Along the shallows, their feet grew numb from the frigid water but not even Jeff wasted his breath complaining. They didn't know who chased them or why, but instinct overrode their sense of body and they ran like a herd of gazelles chased by wolves. If they'd thought about it, they would have been amazed at their own stamina, but there was no time to think, only to run.

Still masked by the tree cover, Todd heard the buzz of multiple helicopters. He realized the enemy must have discovered their trail. And there were a lot more of them than he'd first thought. They couldn't hold up this pace much longer. He looked frantically for someplace safe to hide.

Suddenly, with a small yelp, Marla slipped, fell, and disappeared.

They'd been running in single file when Marla lost her footing on the icy stones and spilled into the rapids. Since they were behind all the others, Todd was the only one to see her fall, but even before he could call out to her, she was gone.

Todd yelled out to the others to stop. He rushed to the spot where he'd last seen her. There in the middle of the streambed, a small sinkhole had opened, about three feet across. The stream began cascading into a dark underground cavern. The streambed beyond the sinkhole quickly ran dry.

"Marla?" Todd's voice cracked as it echoed into the cavern. "You okay?" He froze, listening, but heard nothing but the babble of the stream running underground.

"Stay back!" Todd barked as the others moved to crowd around the opening. He didn't know how sound the earth around the hole might be. His eyes met Devon's; he looked pale and grave.

One shall fall.

"No!" Todd spat the word defiantly. Dream or no dream, he couldn't stand by and lose one of them, especially Marla. He shrugged off his pack and grabbed the rope he had taken from Mesa del Tío. Tying one end around his waist, he ran the rope around the nearest pine tree and, holding on to the other end, cautiously approached the hole. He turned to see the rest looking at him anxiously.

"I'm going down to find her. Jeff's in charge."

Jeff puffed back his shoulders in pride but then glanced at the others and realized just what being in charge meant. He looked back at Todd, a glimmer of panic in eyes. Todd shot back what he hoped was a confident smile, but he doubted it was all that reassuring.

Clinging to the rope, Todd lowered himself into the sinkhole. A sharp beam of sunlight lit his legs but nothing beyond them. Hand over hand he descended, calling out Marla's name, but got nothing but silence in response. The lower he went, the more he worried. *Could she have survived the fall?*

Then even his sunbeam failed him and the hole was nearly pitch-black. The rope was almost full out when his feet felt water. The current pulled at him and he flailed his legs, looking for some safe footing. Using his staff to push off from the streambed, he swung his body like a pendulum over the underground stream. He let out a little more rope and his feet found a rocky ledge. Standing on the bank, he let his eyes slowly adjust to the gloom.

The sinkhole's newly formed waterfall fed into an existing stream running through an underground cavern. He could see the roof of the cave about twenty feet above him, but he saw no trace of Marla.

"Todd!" Jeff hissed from above. "They're on the ground! They've got dogs!" Faintly Todd heard barks echoing down the mountainside.

"I can't find Marla!" Todd choked back the tremor in his voice. "We're going to have to go look for her! Throw down my pack, then send the others down the line!" Todd wiped away hot tears of fear before the others could see.

One by one they climbed down the rope as Todd anchored it. Jeff was the last one down. Todd untied the rope from around his waist and left it hanging.

Todd was groping the ground near the streambed, looking for any sign of Marla in the darkness when he noticed a glow coming from behind him — not from the opening in the roof. Turning, he saw something glimmering brightly from inside Lilibit's pocket.

"Lilibit?" Todd stared at the glow. "What's that?"

Lilibit reached into the pocket where she kept the stone she had plucked from the obelisk a week earlier. Though she frequently kept her hand in that pocket, she rarely took out the stone.

Now as she pulled it out, it glowed with a bright, warm blue light. Todd, after asking a silent permission with his glance, tried to pick the stone from her open palm.

An unseen force slammed his hand back away from the stone so strongly it felt almost as if his arm was wrenched out of its socket.

"You hold it," he said unnecessarily, rubbing his shoulder.

The sounds of the dogs grew louder. Todd peered into the stalactite-draped tunnel. He had no time to appreciate the peculiar eeriness of the cavern. He pulled the rope down into the cave, hoping he wasn't leading them into a dead end. With Lilibit holding her stone over her head, they followed him downstream, looking for some trace of Marla.

From the shadows, three towering gray figures watched the invaders creep into the depths of the labyrinth. Moving with a bulky grace, they stepped into the chamber. The tallest placed a quartz white hand on the wall nearest the opening in the roof and from his fingertips flowed a stream of crystal that traveled up the side of the cavern. It wove a web of stone over the breach, and as it solidified, it resealed the cave.

The sanctity of the chamber had been restored. There remained only one last factor requiring remediation.

Wordlessly the trio followed the trespassers.

The boots of the Director crunched over pristine snow. He had to examine the location himself. Syxx would not be pleased, but it was apparent the field teams had not exaggerated. The children had disappeared as if the earth had just swallowed them.

He suspected his search would be fruitless, but as he turned to walk back to his waiting helicopter, he ordered the

Reclamation Teams back into the air to continue searching the mountains.

Syxx would not be pleased.

A huge ugly bird perched on a low hanging branch and watched unblinkingly as the Director stomped near its pine tree. It flapped its wings as the Director passed underneath, upsetting the snowpack balanced on the branches. The heavy cascade of wet snow fell onto his head, unleashing the Director's precarious temper. He pulled out a .22 Luger and emptied a clip into the branches of the tree.

The ground team members still finishing their site investigation glanced at one another nervously and hurried to complete their work.

Within minutes, the site was deserted.

With a smug little squawk, the condor descended from the tree unscathed, and a moment later, Keotak-se stood where the bird had landed. Although the site was well trampled, he noted the rope scars on the pine tree and he could distinguish the children's footprints from the later traffic. A quick examination of the streambed showed him the exposed vein of quartz, which, to the inexperienced eye appeared to be the top side of a deep slab of bedrock. Yet Keotak-se knew of the forgotten legends of the mountains, and what he remembered stirred a strain of dread through his spine.

He knew of only one human who could speak to the People of the Nether Rock, but whether she still lived, he did not know.

"CHEE-ot-say. Toh-GEE-na. Sha-be-KAH."

The shadow of the condor passed over the deserted mountaintop, soaring to the wastelands that lay north of the mountains.

Chapter Twenty-six

The Stone Cage

For the umpteenth time, Todd held up his hand to halt the group and listen. Perhaps the extra sounds he heard were just the echoes of their feet clattering through the caverns, but Todd felt they were not alone.

His scalp tingled.

They followed the water downstream, calling out Marla's name with echoing whispers. The longer they went without any sign of her, the more anxious he felt. If she had walked away from the fall, she wouldn't have gone far, but if she had been injured, it was possible the current might have carried her.

They reached a point in the tunnel where the walls grew close together and the stream pushed through a channel so narrow not even Lilibit could have squeezed through.

Jeff groaned when Donny again asked, "Is this Kiva?"

"No, Donny," answered Todd. "This is a dead end."

With a sigh, Todd turned and led the group back upstream. Maybe Marla had wandered into one of the grottos that split off from the main cavern.

They had walked back only a few hundred yards when Todd froze. Something blocked the tunnel ahead. Brandishing his staff, he waved the others behind him.

For a long breathless moment, they waited for whatever it was to attack. When nothing moved, Lilibit raised her stone higher above her head. As if in response to their panic, her stone flared, clearly lighting the tunnel ahead.

There in the opening through which they had passed just minutes before now stood three imposing stalactites. They poured from the roof, puddling into stalagmites on the cavern floor, leaving bare inches between their stony girths.

Todd took a few hesitant steps forward and then sprinted to the newly formed pillars that blocked the opening. He struck at the stones with his hands, testing their existence, unwilling to accept their reality. With a groan, he turned and looked at the others, who stared in shock.

They were trapped.

Chapter Twenty-seven

Molly Coppertop

Keotak-se strode the deserted dirt streets of the abandoned village of Coppertop, a burlap bag hanging over his shoulder. He passed boarded-up storefronts and ruins of vacant shacks and did not stop until he stood at the opening of the derelict ore mine that was once the heart and soul of the town. When he'd walked far enough into the tunnel to escape the glaring desert sun, he paused, peering deep into the shaft. The echo of his footsteps faded into silence. Placing the sack on the floor of the cavern, Keotak-se stepped back, squatted on his haunches, and waited.

His ears were keener than most, but it was the change in the air that told him he was no longer alone.

"Keotak-se." A deep raspy voice creaked from the darkness. "Hmph. You don't change at all with the years. You know, when I was younger, I envied your longevity. But now I think that outliving everyone you once knew and loved may be the most dreadful curse of fate."

Keotak-se could not restrain a slight smile. "The years may slow your steps and bend your back, Molly Coppertop, but your tongue remains the sharpest blade."

In the near blackness of the mine, Keotak-se barely saw the hunched figure of an ancient woman shuffling toward him. Her near sightless eyes gleamed as an errant fragment of light struck them. She stooped over the bag and lifted out each of the sweetbreads and pastries, sniffing at them with a cracked smile before replacing them into the sack.

"If you're thinking to charm a lady with pretty words and sweet gifts, your efforts might yield more fruit from a younger sapling."

"The oldest oak bears the tenderest acorns."

The old woman barked a cackle of laughter. "Ha! With a tongue like that, Keotak-se, you'd have done better on the stage than wasting your lives dancing with stones."

Keotak-se's faint smile was warm but tinged with melancholy. He remembered Molly as a feisty young woman with bright red hair, a ready wit, and a sharp tongue. Only a glint or two of copper now showed through the mat of gray hanging below her shoulders. She still wore the colorful flowery prints of her youth, but now her clothes were torn and faded. A soiled, patched sweater hung loosely over her hunched shoulders.

It was nearly half a century since Keotak-se had last seen Molly and he alone knew why she'd chosen to stay behind when the town was finally abandoned. Near blind from a childhood accident, she loved the mines that did not treat her blindness as a handicap but as a strength.

And she loved Beryl, the Renegade from Nether Rock, whom she had stumbled across once while prospecting when she was barely more than a girl. He had strayed too close to the surface and was injured when a lantern ignited a natural gas pocket in the mine. Cut off from his people, he was preparing to surrender his Life Breath when Molly found him and nursed him back to health. The surface dwellers may have considered Molly's eyes too small and her nose too sharp, but Beryl saw a woman who had the copper of the mountain running through her veins and glistening in her hair.

They were an improbable pair: the blind woman of flesh and the voiceless man of stone. Yet they connected with a depth that defied the deficiencies of their contrary natures.

And when her people deserted the dying town, Molly retreated into the mines, content in her exile, rarely returning to the surface.

"I need your help, Molly," Keotak-se stated baldly. "A group of children have fallen into the labyrinth of the Nether Rock."

Despite the gloom, Keotak-se saw Molly eye him speculatively. "And since when does the Stone Warrior play nanny to a pack of brats?" Molly rasped.

Keotak-se said nothing, yet he knew the blind woman would see the truth.

"So it's true," Molly whispered, glancing around as if there might be spies of the Enemy even here inside her beloved mines. "A new Stone Voice is rising." She spoke it as a statement, but Keotak-se heard the question in her words.

Again Keotak-se answered her question by saying nothing.

Molly peered dimly at him. Keotak-se knew she saw just the blur of his silhouette yet perceived much more. She sniffed the air as if the knowledge she sought was a scent wafting from the shafts. She stood hunched for a moment, poised for flight, and then with a flood of motion, she strode down the tunnel with a speed and strength that belied her years, faultlessly weaving her way through the maze of tunnels.

From around his neck, Keotak-se pulled out Hakuya and stroked it once with his finger. The stone glowed warmly, illuminating Molly's retreating figure.

Keotak-se followed.

Chapter Twenty-eight

The Renegades of the Nether Rock

Marla woke. Or at least she thought she was awake. It was as dark with her eyes open as it was when they were shut. Her head throbbed, and when she raised a hand to rub it, she found a painful bruise on the scalp above her neck.

The slab of stone she lay on was cold and clammy. She sat up and closed her eyes, waiting a moment for her head to stop spinning and her eyes to adjust to the dark. When she opened them again, she froze, for there, dimly glowing in the darkness, a figure stood staring at her.

She knew it was a man, but a man unlike any she had ever seen or imagined. In the dark of the cave, his skin gleamed faintly with a weird, pale teal light. He was close to seven feet tall and his body looked like it was made of stone, like a raw, gleaming white slab of mineral that could bend and flex at will. His torso and arms were broad and powerful and his head was shaped like a hexagonal crystal, chiseled with a rough-hewn face. The top of his head where hair would be was a jagged edge as if he were a living gemstone broken off from a larger rock.

Terrified, Marla scuttled backwards. She gasped and held her breath as the man reached out his hand toward her, but when his finger tentatively pressed against the tip of her nose, she reacted in a way that surprised them both.

She giggled.

The sound had an immediate effect on the crystal man. He retreated from Marla with far more speed than grace, watching her warily from a safe distance. There was something so funny in his dismayed expression, Marla giggled again.

The crystal man responded with what, even on his stony face, could be described only as a foolish grin. Cautiously he slowly approached Marla again. Again he reached out with a hesitant finger and lightly touched the tip of her nose. When she giggled again, he abruptly sat down in front of her with a clatter of his stony legs and grinned at her.

Marla was intrigued. Gathering her courage, she reached out timidly to touch the nose in front of her. The crystal man watched charily.

The skin of the crystal man was hard and cold like a stone, but Marla felt it pulsing beneath her finger. She pulled back her finger in astonishment. The crystal man opened his mouth as if to laugh, but no sound came out. Marla smiled.

Marla didn't know how long the two of them sat there staring at each other. Time somehow lost its meaning, yet at some point, her body grew chilled from sitting on the stone and she stood.

"I need to find my friends," she said to the crystal man, and knowing he could not understand her words, she reached out and took his hand.

For a moment, he stared down at the small soft brown hand wrapped so smoothly around his large stony white fingers, puzzled. But then, with a slightly goofy smile, he allowed Marla to lead him out of the grotto. He couldn't know where they were going or what they were looking for, but for the moment, he was content to follow.

By the light of Hakuya, Keotak-se saw Molly halt before a natural opening in the mine tunnel wall. Here, decades ago, miners inadvertently had breached one of the subterranean channels that wove beneath the desert's surface. Molly let out a deep breathy whistle, then she waited as still as the stone.

Minutes passed before Keotak-se heard a creaking from the depths. Into the dim light lumbered a figure of dark stone towering nearly eight feet tall. His vitreous skin was dark gray and barely luminous from old age. Decades had passed since Keotak-se had last seen Beryl and it was evident he was reaching the end of his life span. In truth, Beryl had already lived far longer than most of his generation, hanging on to his mortality out of devotion to Molly, but the day would soon come when he passed back to the Stone and returned his body to the earth. When that day came, lost would be the only bridge between the People of the Nether Rock and the Overworlders.

"Greetings, Beryl," spoke Keotak-se, gesturing with his right arm the Nether Rock sign of welcome. Keotak-se knew his words were superfluous. The People of Nether Rock communicated primarily through thought. Body movements were used only in formal ceremonial communication. Sound was never used at all, yet over the decades, Beryl had learned to decipher many of Molly's words.

Beryl met Keotak-se's eyes and returned the gesture. Turning to Molly, the two of them began a series of motions and signals that they had developed over the years to communicate. It appeared to Keotak-se, however, that they spoke more through their locked eyes than through any gesture.

As abruptly as they'd started, the motions stopped. Beryl straightened to his full height and focused his eyes on a point far from the hollow in which they stood. Then, with a nod to Molly, he turned and disappeared into the murk of the passage.

"C'mon." Molly wheezed as she trotted after Beryl. "We're to appear before the Council of the Elders." Looking back over her shoulder, she shot Keotak-se a mischievous smirk. "We're the first Overworlders to appear before the Council in nearly two thousand years. A milestone of note even for you, Stone Warrior."

With a wry grunt, Keotak-se followed.

Todd sat on the bank of the underground stream, his head in his hands, unable to meet the others' eyes. Yet when he finally did look at them, their faces weren't accusing; they were merely waiting for his lead. Even Jeff held his tongue. All their hopes were on him, and their confidence crushed him even more than blame would have.

He was stymied. How the stone bars had appeared was not as important as how they were going to get past them. The rations in their packs might last a week, but unless Todd figured out how to escape, the food only postponed the inevitable. They huddled together against the cavern wall. Jeff tossed stones into the stream, occasionally glancing at him, his eyebrows raised in expectation.

Todd's keen ears pricked up at the sound of a distant murmur. Lilibit's hearing must have been equally sharp, for she too cocked her head before crossing quickly to the stalagmites, peering beyond them into the darkness.

"Douse your stone for a moment," Todd whispered. Lilibit slid it back into her pocket and the cavern went black.

Over the bubbling of the brook, Todd heard a far-off mumbling. He held his tongue, not knowing if it was friend or foe.

Jeff didn't wait to find out. "Help! Over here! We're trapped!" he yelled.

Todd started to tell Jeff to shut up but stopped himself. His leadership had got them into this mess, and at this moment, he wasn't feeling very qualified to tell anyone what to do.

"Jeff?" a faint voice answered. "Is that you? Where are you?"

Donny, Devon, and Nita began yelling too. Lilibit clapped her hands over her ears as the noise amplified through the caves. Todd shushed them with his hand, and after a moment, they quieted down. Lilibit pulled out her stone and its dim light returned.

Marla's voice echoed from somewhere deep within the labyrinth. Six faces peered through the gaps between the stalactites. Six sets of eyes saw Marla appear at the edge of the gleam of Lilibit's stone. And six mouths gasped as they saw the apparition that appeared behind Marla. Towering nearly seven feet, a figure of glowing white stone stepped into the light.

"Marla! Behind you! Look out!" Todd yelled.

Marla spun around, stepping around her new friend to

look behind him, then she paused and turned back to the others.

"Oh, him!" She grinned. "This is my friend."

She took his hand to lead him closer, but the crystal man hung back, panic plainly on his face.

"How'd you get in there?" asked Marla as she examined the stalagmites.

Todd ignored Marla's question. "What is that?" he asked in a terrified whisper. Only Todd and Lilibit still stood by the opening. The others stood far back from the pillars.

"It's not a *that!* It's a *who!*" answered Marla, a slight chill to her voice. She turned to smile at her new friend. "I think he lives down here," she added.

Lilibit stared at the newcomer. There was none of the fear that the helicopters caused, only curiosity. When the crystal man caught her peering at him, she grinned at him. Hesitantly he smiled back.

Seeing this, Marla grabbed the crystal man's hand possessively and stepped between them. "Can you get out of there?" she asked.

"No," Todd answered, his voice monotone in despair. "Both ends of this tunnel are blocked. These pillars just appeared after we walked through the opening."

Marla turned to the crystal man. "Can you help?" she asked, but while he stared back at her earnestly, he could not understand her words and she could not hear his thoughts.

Suddenly the cavern went dark, only the faint glow of the crystal man providing a dim light. All eyes turned to Lilibit, who had put her obelisk stone back in her pocket and now pulled out her other stones. She placed them against her cheek one at a time before laying them carefully on the ground. They watched her, puzzled, when a long finger-shaped stone made her pause. She sat motionless for several long moments, her head leaning to one side, her eyes focused inward. Then she replaced all the other stones carefully back into her pockets and pulled out her obelisk stone, which brightened obligingly. By the light of her stone, she picked up the finger stone again and placed it in her open palm.

It was an odd stone. One half consisted of pale white quartz and the other, dark luminous obsidian. Lilibit stared at the stone in her palm for several moments before closing her fingers around it. When she opened her hand again, the stone had split in two along the seam where the two minerals met. She looked up with a delighted smile.

Scrambling to her feet, she reached through the pillars and called to Marla to come closer.

"What?" asked Marla warily, walking toward the pillars.

"Here! Her name is Hesha-Tay," announced Lilibit, offering the quartz half of the stone to her.

"Lilibit! No!" The panic in Todd's voice echoed through the cavern. He remembered only too well what had happened to Lilibit when she first touched her stone.

But Marla had already taken the stone. It lay gently in her hand. She caught Todd watching her, an intent look on his face. Puzzled, she looked back at him and shrugged.

"Come here!" called Lilibit imperiously, gesturing to the crystal man with a smile.

The towering rock man could have crushed the tiny Lilibit with his hands, yet he approached her with the same wariness he might have with a hungry grizzly bear. He looked blankly at her hand when she extended the obsidian stone to him.

"Take it!" Lilibit said with exasperation. "His name is Oji-Tay and he wants to stay with you!"

The crystal man glanced at Marla, who looked from him to the stone in her hand and back again. After a moment's thought, she nodded for him to take the stone.

Marla spun around, her eyes darting back and forth. "Who said that?" she asked.

"Said what?" Todd replied. "No one said anything except Lilibit."

"You didn't hear that?" Marla sounded a little on edge.

"Hear what?"

"I heard someone say, 'Why does the small Overworlder

want to give me a stone?'" Marla looked up at the crystal man. "Did you say that?"

The crystal man's eyes grew even larger and his jaw dropped open.

"Wow!" Marla's voice was hushed. "I heard you speak! But not with my ears!"

"Weird," Jeff muttered in the darkness. "Just when you thought life had gotten as weird as it can get, we step over into weirder and weirder still."

Seeing Marla and the crystal man stare at each other, Todd could not argue with that.

Chapter Twenty-nine

The Council of the Nether Rock

It was not often Keotak-se felt dwarfed, but standing before the Council of the Fathers, all of whom stood between seven and eight feet tall, the Stone Warrior felt faintly diminished.

It was an assembly bordering on the bizarre. After the extensive formal ceremony of commencement, the Elders would communicate among themselves, then one Elder would address Beryl, who then signed to Molly, who then translated to Keotak-se.

Keotak-se gritted his jaw, biting back his impatience as the time-consuming formalities were adhered to. He did not know where the children were, but he knew the Enemy to be relentless and ruthless.

Molly leaned toward Keotak-se. "The Infant Stone Voice is a tad more important to the People of Nether Rock than you might think," she whispered. "The corruption of the old

Stone Voice has been a disaster for them. In the past ten centuries, their numbers have dwindled. Time was, there were more than ten million People of the Nether Rock living under all the continents; now there's less than two hundred thousand. Before the fall, there were more females than males. Now there's less than four hundred females. Beryl says the old Stone Voice has quarantined the Earth Soul, choking off Her vision of nature. And they say it's 'cause of the 'earth-blindness' that female babies in the Nether Rock don't thrive.

"'Bout two centuries ago the Elders started to isolate the remaining females to protect them and to encourage as many births as possible. These women are only allowed to raise their female children. All their male children are taken from them at birth to be raised by the fathers. Some females have borne as many as fifty offspring, trying to have one daughter that they'd be allowed to raise. Female children have become much too rare, and when a female child is born, it is often too weak to survive. Beryl says if things don't change, the People of the Nether Rock will die out within the next century or two."

Keotak-se would not trust himself to speak. He knew a corrupted Stone Voice was an abomination, but he was still learning how damaging the fall of Korap had been.

The Elder talking with Beryl bowed elaborately, signaling the end of the exchange. Then Beryl turned to Molly. Considering how long the Elders had spoken, Beryl's translation to Molly was unexpectedly brief.

Molly looked to Keotak-se as if she were presenting a coiled cobra as a gift. She spoke slowly and deliberately. "The Elders acknowledge that there's a group of children in the catacombs. They say to tell the Stone Warrior that they are safe and secure." Molly paused, weighing her words. "But if one of these children is the Infant Stone Voice, the Elders think the child would be safer here, in the Nether Rock."

Keotak-se hoped the Elders could not read the misgivings in his mind. The power of the Enemy above was vast and his own failure to protect the child in the past weighed heavily on his soul, and yet he knew what must be done.

With appropriate ceremonial gestures, Keotak-se directed his words to the Elders. "The Council speaks wisely. And yet if the child is to thrive, to attain the power needed to overthrow the corrupt Stone Voice, she will need to be trained in the Old Ways. Her survival alone is not sufficient." He paused, frowning. His next words might sting, but their truth must be heard. "Your true enemy is not the Overworlders. The Overworlders do not even know of your existence. But your true enemy knows of the Nether Rock. And of the plight of your people. Your numbers are too few. If the Enemy were to descend into the Nether Rock, your people would not be able to protect themselves, much less the child.

"In the Overworld, there is a Valley. The Valley of Kiva. There the People have worked for centuries to create a safe haven that will both protect and train the Infant Stone Voice. It is there that I would take the child."

Keotak-se bowed to the Council and nodded to Molly to proceed. Molly stared with dismay at Keotak-se before reluctantly translating to Beryl. The words of the Stone Warrior were blunter than the Council was accustomed to.

Beryl conveyed the message to the Council. Several of the Elders looked with great anger at Keotak-se, but most considered his words deeply.

Finally, the darkest of the Elders rose and bowed ceremoniously to each of the people assembled. He then turned and walked out of the chamber. One by one, the Elders repeated the ritual, exiting out the same door. When no one was left save Beryl, Molly, and Keotak-se, Beryl gestured to Molly. Her eyes brightened in anticipation.

"Looks like I may get to see a real Stone Voice before I die!" Molly cackled. "They're taking us to the children."

"Describe the terrain where the tracks ended." Syxx sat motionless as he listened to the report of the Director of Security.

"Terrain?".

Despite the Director's impassive expression, Syxx could see his confusion.

Syxx spoke slowly. The Director was the most competent of his current minions, but like all humans, he was innately defective. He curbed his temper as he spat out the words. "The composition of the ground where the trail disappeared."

"It was a streambed. Solid rock. Maybe quartz and granite." The Director did not know one rock from another.

Syxx steepled his fingers and stared at the ceiling. "Keep all units in full mobilization," he said at last, "with a particular focus on those areas where the mountain range meets the desert."

"It shall be as Syxx commands." The Director nodded a terse salute before exiting the office.

Syxx. It was the name he used in this time and place, but he had carried many different labels over the millenniums: Beelzebub, Cabaal, the Deceiver, the Seducer, Servant of the Decreator. To the People of the Nether Rock, he was known as Moltaine, and in those Nether Regions, that name was greatly feared.

Yet perhaps not enough.

Syxx had been too patient with the People of the Nether Rock. He knew how close their race was to complete extinction. His own machinations had pushed them there. For now it was merely a matter of time; they would soon be past the point of recovery. And yet that they might, in their current weakened state, present a threat to his plans had not occurred to him. This was an oversight that must be rectified.

Syxx smiled. Truly horrific violence is so satisfying and even more so when it serves a purpose. There would be nothing but pleasure in the forthcoming carnage.

Molly's breath heaved with the effort of keeping up with the long strides of Keotak-se and the Elders, but Keotak-se knew she would have choked to death before admitting weakness.

"Git a move on, 'Tak-se," she said, wheezing, when Keotak-se slowed his pace to meet her steps, "or will the Stone Warrior be left in the dust by the old woman?"

With an unexpected burst of speed, she pulled a few steps ahead of him, but Keotak-se heard in her panting how much the effort cost her.

Beryl fell back from the line of Elders weaving their way through the labyrinth. Without warning, he reached out and lifted Molly, who was not a small woman. He carried her as a child, with her face looking back over his shoulder. Evidently Molly was accustomed to this form of travel, since she did not seem startled. Looking back at Keotak-se, she took the opportunity to stick out her tongue while slapping

Beryl on his behind and yelling, "Git' up!" Beryl's shoulders trembled in silent laughter and he lightly smacked Molly on her behind as well. Molly's crack of laughter caused the Elders to look back in bewilderment.

The procession of Elders slowed their pace. From the frantic motions of their heads, Keotak-se knew that something was amiss.

The underground stream they followed branched off into a dark grotto. There stood two stalactites partially blocking the opening. Between them was a pile of rubble, apparently the remains of a third stalactite that had been reduced to pebbles.

Yet of the children, there was no sign.

Chapter Thirty

Escape from the Nether Rock

Bringing up the rear of the pack, Todd silently fumed. Why did he feel so insignificant? Was it the ease with which the crystal man had pulverized the stalactite that made him feel so inept? Or was it the adoring way Marla looked up at her strange new friend, holding his hand while he led them out of the labyrinth?

One day, he might admit to himself that it was both, but for now, he scowled and followed.

"Ulex says that there are caverns that run all over the entire world. He says that when we return to the surface, he'll be able to follow us underground." Marla was breathless as she spoke. It could have been from walking and talking, or it might have been just from holding Ulex's hand.

"So his name is *Ulex?*" Jeff asked. He hung back with Todd, staying as far away from their guide as he could.

"Kinda sorta. Ulex's people don't use their mouths to

speak; they talk telepathically. So they don't have names that you can pronounce. *Ulex* is just the word that I kind of hear whenever he refers to himself."

This was interesting and Todd would have asked her more about it, but Ulex stopped unexpectedly. In the dim light, Jeff bumped into Todd.

Ulex looked down and locked eyes with Marla. Then he pulled his hand out of hers and began running back in the direction from where they'd come. He ran with a speed unexpected for a creature so big and, within seconds, vanished into the dark.

"Ulex!" Marla's voice squeaked; her eyes were unfocused as she stared at the spot where Ulex had disappeared.

"Where'd he go?" Todd asked with a whisper.

"Something is invading the Nether Rock. They think it's heading for the Women's Chambers. All the men of the Nether Rock have been summoned to defend." Her voice cracked. "Ulex has been called too. He has to go. He says we're almost at the exit of the cavern."

"Anything else?"

Marla listened, then shook her head.

Todd took the lead. His feelings were mixed, but Marla's misery was real. He touched her shoulder in sympathy as he passed her. She shot him a broken smile and followed, looking behind more than she looked forward.

They walked for another hour, with the cavern getting

narrower and tighter. Donny and Todd had to bend to avoid hitting their heads. Finally, Todd halted the group and peered into the darkness ahead.

"Douse your stone," he whispered to Lilibit, who pocketed her stone with a shrug.

It took their eyes a moment to adjust to the darkness.

"Yes!" cheered Jeff when he recognized the glimmer of daylight ahead.

He ignored Todd's halfhearted warning and pushed past him to scamper to the end of the tunnel. The tunnel grew dark for a moment as Jeff's exit filled the opening. The others waited for Todd, who cautiously led them out.

Todd climbed out of a crevice between two stones that, from the outside, didn't look large enough to be even a bobcat den. The opening was at the rear of an orange grove that backed up to the mountains.

Jeff lay on his back, basking in the sun, smugly eating an orange. Todd shot him a dirty look, which he repelled with an impudent smirk.

Todd turned to help the others out of the opening. Marla hesitated, shooting one last look down into the cavern before climbing out to join her friends in the sunlight.

In the harsh morning light, Todd saw the pain on Marla's face. Awkwardly he hugged her and she broke into tears, sobbing as she gripped her stone and pressed it against the base of her throat.

"There's a battle going on below," Marla announced, her eyes cloudy with fear.

"He'll be all right, Marla," Devon said, a calm certainty in his voice that made the others turn and stare. He smiled reassuringly at them, then sat down exhausted, his lips twitching in one of those private conversations he sometimes had with himself.

It was morning. They'd been lost in the labyrinth of the Nether Rock for a full day.

"We'll rest here." Todd scrubbed at his scalp and looked at the sky. "I don't think we should travel in the daylight. We'll go tonight when it gets dark."

They curled up under the arms of an orange tree. The ripe fruit gave a sweet citrus smell and weighed down the branches to create a secret bower. They slept deeply, so exhausted that not even Lilibit stirred when the occasional helicopter passed overhead.

Chapter Thirty-one

The Battle of the Nether Rock

The Elders were mystified as to how the children had escaped from the grotto.

Keotak-se knelt to read the grit on the cavern floor. It appeared that a denizen of the Nether Rock walked among the seven children, apparently assisting in their escape. Why he should do so and how they managed to communicate mystified Keotak-se, but perhaps forces greater than he knew were assisting this Infant Stone Voice.

He would have left them then, but as he turned to take his formal leave, he was checked by the actions of the Elders. Acting on some message undetectable to the Overworlders, the Netherockians raced back down the tunnel.

Beryl waited only a moment before signing frantically to Molly, then sped after the disappearing Elders.

"Someone or something is invading the caverns." Molly stared after Beryl. "The sentries alerted the Elders. Beryl said they don't know who the invaders are, but they're heading for the Women's Chamber." Molly's face went white as she turned to Keotak-se. "If the attack is successful, it'll mean the end of the Netherockians."

Keotak-se was torn. He knew his primary duties were to find and protect the Infant Stone Voice, but he also suspected this attack on the Nether Rock was initiated by the same Enemy who knew the Stone Voice was in the labyrinth.

The thought of some greater power protecting the child gave him some small reassurance.

To Molly he said, "I will stand by the Nether Rock. I will help them defend."

Molly gasped as Keotak-se vanished, replaced by a small brown bat, which flapped a scant farewell before flitting down the labyrinth in pursuit of the Elders.

Keotak-se stood at the mouth of the legendary Crystal Cavern. A vast underground canyon two or three miles across, a dozen miles deep, and more than a mile high, it held the Nether Rock's most precious treasures.

It was said that no human had ever set foot in the Crystal Cavern. And lived. Keotak-se now knew why. With the light of Hakuya, he stared at the forest of crystal shards that grew thickly like tall, thin glass pine trees nestled side-by-side. They rose hundreds of feet into the air to create a labyrinth of razor-sharp hedges. To enter the maze would mean certain death, for the path was treacherous and with one false step an intruder would be sliced into pieces by the shards. There had never been a successful assault on the Crystal Cavern, and it had been centuries since anyone had tried.

Only the Elders of the Nether Rock knew the secret path through the labyrinth, for hidden deep behind its fortifications lay the Women's Chamber. It was there that the dwindling females of the Nether Rock lived and gave birth to their children. Most Netherockians left the chamber as infants, never to see it again. Few even saw the Crystal Cavern. Today, however, all the warriors of the Nether Rock, both young and old, assembled to defend.

Staff in hand, Keotak-se leaped from the mouth of the cavern twenty feet to the floor. Within moments, a dozen Netherockian warriors surrounded him. Mistaking him for an invader, they roared silently and brandished sharp crystal spears. He tapped his staff on the ground three times and it came to life, glowing brilliantly with the power of the Stone. The light temporarily blinded the warriors and they fell back, all four sets of their auxiliary eyelids slamming shut. But quickly adjusting, they regrouped and again closed in.

Unwilling to fight the Netherockians but unable to communicate with them, Keotak-se held his staff at the ready and his opponents at bay. The tip of his staff glowed brightly, and for several long moments, they stood facing each other in a tense détente.

Confusion replaced aggression; the warriors cocked their heads and listened to a voice that Keotak-se could not hear. Warily they stepped back and lowered their weapons.

Beryl strode into the circle, his skin dark gray with anger and dread. He glanced up to the mouth of the cavern, as if to assure himself that Molly had not followed as well, then turned back to Keotak-se. He pounded his spear on the ground and pointed up to the exit. Keotak-se understood.

"No. I stand beside the warriors of the Nether Rock. I will defend."

Keotak-se knew Beryl could not understand his words but his meaning could be read in face and gesture. Beryl, glaring at the Stone Warrior, might have tried again, but a rumble from deep within the catacombs turned his attention. Shoulder-to-shoulder, the Netherockians faced the opening. Keotak-se, his staff at the ready, waited.

Squeals and tremors mixed into a bestial clamor that terrified the Netherockians. The dark adults fell back as readily as the pale adolescents, panicked by the approaching attackers.

A hot blast of fetid air shooting out from the entrance to the cavern preceded the first surge of the invasion. Hordes of rabid rats, foaming white at the mouth, cascaded down the cliff. They slammed themselves in suicidal waves against the crystal shards and against the Defenders of the Nether Rock.

Keotak-se aimed his staff, its apex still glowing white, at

the first wave. With a blast of power that terrified his fellow Defenders, he incinerated scores of vermin. Yet no sooner had ten score been destroyed than ten times that number would teem into the chamber. They not only came through the main entry, but they worked their way through cracks and gaps thought to be too small to be a threat. The walls of the cavern throbbed as the invaders swarmed in from all sides.

The Defenders crushed the invaders with foot and hand. Seizing them, they smashed them against the crystal pinnacles. Small corpses littered the labyrinth and blood stained the crystals. At first, Keotak-se wondered if the rats, though numerous, could do much harm against the stone-plated denizens of the Nether Rock, but some greater intelligence seemed to be directing them. As they leaped to attack the Defenders, they aimed for their huge soft eyes and Keotak-se watched as one Netherockian after another fell in silent agony under the barrage of the rabid raiders.

From the corner of his eye, Keotak-se was aware of the approach of a young Netherockian. From his height and pale luminescence, Keotak-se judged him to be an adolescent, perhaps too young to be part of this battle. Yet he noticed a maturity and tenacity in this youth that his elders would do well to possess.

Like many of the others, this young Netherockian squashed vermin beneath his feet and crushed their bodies between his mammoth fingers. When an older warrior stumbled under a barrage of attacking rats and crashed into the nearby throng of stony shards, he leaped to his aid, stripping the vermin off his fallen comrade. Distracted, he was soon overpowered himself and within moments was enveloped.

Keotak-se strode to his side. Tapping his staff three times, he unleashed a blast that singed the young Netherockian's membrane but also incinerated his attackers. Standing shakily, the adolescent shook off his weakness and, with a wary nod of thanks to Keotak-se, returned to the battle.

There was something else about this young Netherockian. Hanging about Keotak-se's neck, Branken hummed frantically, as if to call out to this youth. Keotak-se, though engaged in battle, kept a close eye on him.

The young one also watched Keotak-se with a chary awareness. When Keotak-se swung his staff into the teeming horde like a scythe, the young Netherockian's eyes widened with interest. Picking up a long length of broken crystal, he held it in the same manner that Keotak-se held his staff.

Keotak-se felt his stone's power ebbing. He struck the stub of his staff against the ground and felt the spirit of the Earth Stone sing through its shaft. His hands tightened as energy surged to its peak. Light pulsed and the attackers perished into ash.

The eyes of the young one widened. Almost without thought it seemed, he struck the tip of the crystal shard against the ground. On the third strike, the crystal shard began to flare. The young one's eyes shuttered against its beam and he turned fearfully to Keotak-se.

Keotak-se quickly recognized the signs of a nascent stone warrior. He knew that this must be the denizen of the Nether Rock who had assisted in the escape of the Infant Stone Voice. And for Lilibit to have bestowed a Stone of Power upon him meant she must be healed sufficiently for her powers to be proliferating.

With a nod and a gesture, Keokak-se showed by example how to discharge the power of the shard. The young warrior nodded, turned, and aimed.

A deadly beam of pale golden fury burned into the swarm. The young warrior staggered backwards, caught his balance, and turned to face the old stone warrior. Keotak-se smiled. He still remembered both the wonder and the terror of first unleashing the power of one's stone.

Yet there was no time for either words or celebration; a disturbance behind them in the Women's Chamber recalled them to the immediacy of their situation. Wordlessly the two stone warriors battled side-by-side, standing firm while many other Defenders fell in their midst.

They stood fast, even as the tide of vermin finally ebbed.

They dealt with the occasional rat that remained, but the greater portion of their attention was focused on each other.

Keotak-se knew he had no words with which to communicate with the youth, so he took his left fist and struck his right shoulder, and then struck his left shoulder with his right fist. After dropping his arms, he repeated these gestures two more times. This was an ancient sign of the Nether Rock, a throwback to the time when the People of the Nether Rock were plentiful and Warriors of the Nether Rock were feared and revered, both above and below. This was the sign of one warrior greeting an equal with respect and esteem.

The young Netherockian's eyes grew large with wonder. It was so rare a gesture, he probably recognized it more from instinct than from experience. With awe on his stony face, he returned the greeting.

With that, Keotak-se gestured his farewell. He could not linger to decipher the mystery of this young stone warrior of the Nether Rock. At some point, this Netherockian must go to Kiva to train. If not, he must surrender his stone. That was a problem for the future. For now, Keotak-se must find the Infant Stone Voice.

He negotiated the Crystal Labyrinth, pausing to mourn the many fallen defenders. He would later learn that, while more than four hundred and fifty defenders died that day, only one of the precious females was lost. Yet for a population so stressed, this was still a holocaust, and throughout the Nether Rock, there roared a grief so great that in many places entire caverns imploded in anguish, wreaking a parallel havoc in the Overworld.

At this moment, however, the grief had a human face. There sitting among the carnage, Keotak-se found Molly — her sightless eyes pouring tears as she held the desecrated corpse of Beryl. Keotak-se found no words of comfort; he could only lay his hand on her shoulder as she wept.

She looked up to his face, but he knew she could see only a misty silhouette with the soft glow from Hakuya hanging about his neck.

"You'll be off to find the Stone Voice," Molly said, her voice dead with sorrow.

Keotak-se nodded. "You will need to see the healers of the Overworld. The bites you have received will need to be treated."

"I don't care if I survive. I've lived several hours longer than I wanted to."

And yet, with a flash of insight, Keotak-se saw that Molly might still have a part to play in the survival of both the Overworlders and the People of the Nether Rock. Lifting her to her feet, he led her out of the catacombs. It meant a delay in finding the Infant Stone Voice, but his heart told him it was a delay of future value.

Chapter Thirty-two

The Dream of the Wanderer

Todd dreamed.

He plunged toward the desert floor, the wind whipping at his arms and legs. He screamed, but no sound came out. A hot breeze struck him and pushed him, first to the side and then upward like a leaf. He drifted over placid meadows. While the feeling of flying gave him a heady sense of freedom, it bothered him that he had no control. At the same time, he felt a peculiar sense of relief. No one could expect a leaf floating on the wind to guide and protect those smaller and weaker than itself. And no one would blame an aimless feather for the aches and fears of a band of lost children. There was an odd bliss that went with being vulnerable and helpless. Slowly he floated toward four vaguely familiar peaks with a crest of red-brown cliffs connecting them.

"Kiva!" he whispered.

As the breeze carried him closer, the ridge of red stone

cliffs grew clearer. At first, the formations were intimidating. They looked like an army of sienna stone soldiers, rough-hewn, standing shoulder-to-shoulder, glaring at him. Yet there was something reassuring about them as well. Todd felt that if he could just get past those sentries, he would find safety on the other side.

He strained to push himself up and over the cliffs, but the breeze would not obey him and he choked back a scream of frustration as the wind dropped him onto the plains outside the Sienna Sentries.

Once more anchored to the ground, Todd scrambled to his feet and stared at the cliffs towering before him. He had to get over them and see what was beyond them. He sheathed his staff on his back and started to hike toward the base of the palisades.

Todd's body felt heavy, as if the air around him were thick and syrupy, but he plodded on. Then a wisp of mist reached out from the foothills and surrounded him. When the mist receded, he was no longer on the plains but inside a very large truck. It took Todd a moment to realize that the truck wasn't really that big; it was just that he was very small. He looked up and saw his Dad driving.

It had been so many years since he had seen his father, the memory had faded; yet here he was, just like that last time. Todd stared. His father's hair was black like his, except for one tuft of gray hair that he braided and allowed to

fall over his right ear. At the end of the braid was an ornament that looked like a small round spider web of silver.
Eight tiny chips of colored gems decorated the web and two
little down feathers hung off it. He had forgotten all about
that charm and now he couldn't draw his eyes from it.

"You must go to school, Todd," his father was saying.
"Don't worry, though; I'll come back to get you. You be a
good boy and behave."

Todd wanted to yell at him, to tell him not to go, that he
would never see him again, but all that came out of his mouth
was "Okay, Dad."

His father looked over at him, a strained smile on his
face. He was tall and thin and his face was tanned. Dark
circles framed his eyes, and as he drove, he kept glancing into
the rearview mirror, his brow furrowed.

Then they were at the school. One minute his father was
there, standing beside him; the next minute he was gone.
Todd walked through the empty halls of the school. No
matter how quietly he tried to walk, his footsteps echoed
like explosions. At the end of the hall, he saw a man who
looked like his Dad go through a door. Todd ran to the door,
but when he opened it, there was only the huge head of Mr.
Bensen, the principal, yelling at him. "BIRDS CAN'T
TALK, YOU LITTLE FREAK!"

Todd ran out of the room and opened another door.
"TEN POINTS OFF FOR BAD PENMANSHIP!"

screamed Mrs. Phlickson's head as she threw balls of crumpled homework at him. "SLOPPY, SLOPPY FREAK!" The balls stung him like rocks where they hit him.

He raced out of that room and pulled open the next door. "I'LL BE GLAD WHEN THAT ONE'S GONE!" yelled Mr. Callow's head. "THE LITTLE FREAK!"

He slammed the door closed. He was alone in the hallway once again. The hallway now stretched for miles in both directions. He ran down its length while voices screamed "FREAK!" from behind the closed doors.

A doorway appeared at the end of the hallway. Blinding light poured out from the cracks around the edges. Todd raced toward it and wrenched it open.

He was outside again at the base of the Sienna Sentries. He looked back, but the schoolhouse was gone — only grassy plains for as far as he could see.

The hair on his head prickled and his scalp tingled a warning. It was more of a scent in the air or a quiver in the earth rather than any sight or sound. His eyes scanned the horizon, but nothing moved.

Nothing moved. Not a bird or even an insect was seen or heard in the valley. Even the wind stopped dead, as if the entire earth held its breath.

A pinprick of black appeared like a faint flaw in the bright blue of the cloudless sky. The fleck grew into a black cloud, undulating as it approached. At first, Todd thought the dark mist was expanding, shooting out plumes of darkness into the spotless sky, but as it filled the horizon, Todd realized it was imploding, a Black Void that sucked in all matter, all life, all thought, all creation.

The Void paused and hovered before Todd and the palisades. Todd struggled to his feet and brandished his staff defiantly. Mocking laughter echoed against the façade of the Sienna Sentries as the Void churned slowly forward. A tendril of blackness snaked out to ensnare him. Suddenly a torrent of wind rose, pummeling Todd, sucking him toward the looming arm of the Void. He fell to the ground and his fingers raked the stone as he fought the pull.

Beneath the orange tree, Todd woke with a silent scream on his lips. His heart pounded in terror and his fingers were cut and raw from where they'd scrabbled the ground. He grabbed his staff and raised it in defense, but there was no enemy to be seen. The others still slept, except for Lilibit. She stared at him, her eyes wide, a vague echo of his nightmare in her face. She cocked her head at him, a silent question in her eyes.

"It was just a dream," he whispered. "Go to sleep."

Todd lay back down and shut his eyes, but it was hours before he himself slept again.

Chapter Thirty-three

Retreat from Tai-Kwee

Dusk was settling on the orchard when Todd woke again. He didn't feel all that refreshed, but at least the dread of his dream had faded.

Marla was already awake. She sat with her back against the trunk of an orange tree, a small smile on her face, her lips moving faintly in silent conversation. Todd sighed as he rubbed his eyes. Evidently Ulex was back on line.

The others slept, still recovering from their escape from the Nether Rock.

"Up!" Todd nudged Jeff with his foot, who grumbled and rolled over.

Todd sat up and yawned. Stretching his arms above his head, he cracked his fingers against a low-hanging branch.

"Ow!" He rubbed his knuckles grouchily and crawled out from their bower.

One by one, they emerged from under the tree. Lilibit wouldn't get up so Todd dragged her out by one of her feet.

She mumbled sleepily but didn't wake. She just lay on the leaves where Todd left her. Shaking his head, he reached back under to grab her knapsack.

"For the love of crows, Lilibit!" exclaimed Todd. "What have you got in there?"

That woke her. With a swift stab, she snatched her bag from Todd's grasp. "Just my stones," she muttered.

"That's got to weigh twenty pounds!" Todd cried. "You'll break your back!"

"They're not heavy." She pulled her chin up. "I can carry them."

Todd watched as Lilibit shouldered her bag as easily as if it were full of tennis balls. She glared up at him defiantly. Todd just shook his head.

They sat down to a breakfast of oranges and brown bread.

"Ulex says they stopped the invasion, but that many of his people were killed," Marla told them while peeling an orange.

Marla had been giving them updates from Ulex with tedious regularity.

"Ulex says there were other Overworlders down there during the battle," she added. "Ulex says —"

"Oh, will you shut up about Ulex already!" Jeff snapped. "If I hear 'Ulex says' one more time, I'm gonna vomit!"

Marla glared at Jeff. She looked over at Todd, who was

suddenly fascinated by the laces on his sneakers. He knew Marla expected him to back her up, but the truth was he agreed with Jeff. He was sick of hearing about Ulex too.

They finished their meal in a moody silence, watching the sun set and the horizon turn dark purple. They filled their knapsacks with oranges and then set out, walking between the rows of citrus trees, masked by the overhanging branches and the cloud-obscured moonlight.

They'd been walking less than an hour through the trees when Lilibit started an orange-throwing fight with Devon. As expected, Nita immediately rushed to Devon's defense and it didn't take more than a few moments for Donny and Jeff to join in.

Amazed, Todd shook his head. He was so tired, he was barely able to keep walking, but the others were diving in and out of the orange trees, ambushing one another. Since there were no homes in sight, Todd wasn't worried when Nita let out a high-pitched squeal when Jeff beaned her from behind.

When they finally reached the end of the grove, they were sticky and soiled from orange drippings and dirt. They stopped at a stream to wash, but a squeal of disgust from Nita brought them up short. There floating in the stream was a dead rat. After seeing the first one, it took them only a moment to notice a dozen more either floating down the current or washed up along the bank.

They all agreed when Nita declared that sticky was better than dead-rat water. They leaped over the stream, out of the protection of the trees and into the desert.

The moon broke free from its cloud cover as they crested the top of a steep hill. They didn't stop to admire the moonlit landscape. The desolate canyons and dunes, the patches of sage scrub and prickly palms; all looked eerie in the colorless light.

They trekked down the hill and into a vast desert valley. Todd felt exposed and vulnerable in the bright moonlight. He quickened his pace and urged the others to keep up.

Between looking over his shoulder and scanning the approaching horizon, Todd didn't immediately notice that Lilibit had wandered from the group. A movement out of the corner of his eye caught his attention and he sighed as he recognized Lilibit a couple of hundred yards away, moving at an angle from the others.

"Lilibit! Get over here!" Todd barked.

If Lilibit heard him above the hum of the desert wind, she made no sign. She continued to walk purposefully to the north. The rest of the group stopped and waited as Todd trotted over to her.

"Lilibit!" Todd called out again as he got closer.

Lilibit turned and looked at him with a grin that showed how completely oblivious she was to his frustration. Then she stooped and placed her hand onto the sand, and looking back toward the east, she waited.

She didn't wait long. Almost immediately the wind began to strengthen, pummeling Todd, stinging his face with thousands of sand crystals that needled his exposed skin like tiny bullets. Lilibit's hair and clothes flapped wildly in the wind, but other than her closed eyes, she didn't seem aware of the gale. Todd looked back and saw that the others, while watching in awe, were not in the path of the storm.

He fought his way to Lilibit's side only to find she was in the eye of the tempest. The wind was weaker here. He grabbed her wrist as if to break her hold on the desert floor, but her arm wouldn't move. She opened her eyes and turned to look at him with a dimpled smile. With a small movement of her head, she gestured to the east. A mounting dread rose from Todd's stomach as he looked eastward.

There, rising from the desert floor, moved a dune of sand. It rose to a height of several stories, a tsunami of silica heading straight for them. It crested as a wave and broke less than a hundred feet away, flowing to the point where they stood. Here the wave stopped, exhausting itself at their feet. The wind died down and the night grew deathly still. Slowly the stars reappeared in the sky.

The silence after the rage of the wind was, in a way, more frightening than the storm itself. Todd stood up. After assuring himself the others were safe, he looked to where Lilibit stooped, her hand still pressed flat against the desert floor.

On the sand, within inches of her hand, sat a stone. Todd stared at it, almost mesmerized. He held his breath as Lilibit reached out to pick it up and place it against her cheek.

She stood and, extending her hand, she whispered with a small smile, "His name is Tai-Kwee. And he wants to stay with you."

Todd couldn't take his eyes off the stone that lay in Lilibit's palm. It was a dark blue, like the night sky right after dusk, and mottled with white veins. Todd saw where it was rough-hewn on one side, but the side that faced up was worn smooth with a gentle indentation, like a thumb-shaped bowl. His fingers ached to touch the stone, to stroke his thumb along its tiny basin. His hand reached out blindly.

"No!" Todd pulled back as if burned. The stone fascinated him as much as it worried him, but there had been too much weird stuff happening lately and Lilibit and her stones were the weirdest. He didn't understand any of it and he wouldn't trust what he couldn't understand.

"No." He jammed his hands into his pockets, digging his fingers into his palms.

Lilibit's face fell. It hurt to see her disappointment but Todd just shook his head.

She dropped her eyes and looked at the stone. Lifting it

to her cheek, she listened for a moment and then with a small sad smile said, "Tai-Kwee says he'll wait. I'll hold him for you for now."

Todd's mind was in turmoil as they walked back to the others.

They walked eastward, their path running parallel to a spur of train tracks that ran along the far side of the canyon. Every time a train appeared, Todd made them crouch among the sage scrub and wait motionlessly until the cab pulled out of view. Since the rest of the train pulled flatbeds stacked with metal containers and had no people on them, they could walk alongside them and not worry about being seen. Some of the caravans pulled more than a hundred cars and took a half hour or longer before they pulled out of sight. The clacking of rails was comforting. They didn't feel quite so alone with the trains chugging alongside.

When the morning sun finally shone full in their eyes, they came upon an abandoned shack along the side of the tracks. There were holes in the roof and one of the walls had collapsed, but it gave them shelter from the wind and from any eyes looking for them while they slept.

Syxx sat in his darkened office, his fingers steepled beneath his chin, his eyes focused on the large gray rat that twitched nervously on his desktop.

Syxx was not pleased. The rat knew this but did not run when Syxx reached out and grabbed its head between his fingers. Syxx felt the rat's thrill of terror as its skull was slowly crushed. One short, shrill squeal and the rat was dead. He shook it once or twice, trying to catch that last sweet echo of death. Then he raised it above his head, opened his mouth, and swallowed it whole, sucking the tail through his lips like a fat strand of scaly spaghetti. He smacked his lips in satisfaction.

Syxx did not need to eat to survive, but the flavors of fear and death were irresistible to him, even in small servings. Yet this pleasant diversion could not distract him from the greater conundrum. Killing the messenger did not negate the message. The rats had failed. The Nether Rock survived. And the child still lived.

He called for the Director.

Despite all their vacillating and weaknesses, humans were still his most effective instruments for pure devastation. All you need do is seduce them with power, coddle their vanity, or deceive them into thinking that their own destruction is exactly the one thing they most desire. For such innovative, "rational" creatures, they were quite delightful in their corruptibility. Give him a dozen ego-bloated, power-hungry humans over a half million rabid rats any day of the week.

Syxx was smiling quite benignly when the Director entered his office.

◆ ◆ ◆ ◆

The sun was still a few hours from setting when they awoke. They ate a dawdling meal, waiting for dusk.

"I am so glad to see the end of these!" cracked Jeff as they opened the last can of baked beans. "If I ever see another can of brown bread, I'll scream."

Devon sneaked up behind Jeff and placed an empty brown bread can on his shoulder. The others broke up laughing as Jeff gave a mock scream of melodramatic horror and pretended to faint on the floor, but Todd's smile was a little twisted. He didn't know how much farther they had to go or how they would get more food.

A sudden silence drew Todd from his thoughts. Marla and Jeff looked at him with questions in their eyes, then glanced to where Lilibit sat arranging her stones, "listening" to them with her cheek. Todd knew what they wanted him to ask.

"Lilibit?" he asked quietly. "What are you doing?"

Lilibit looked up. Her smile faded when she realized they were all watching her. "Just talking to my stones," she answered, a defensive edge in her voice.

"Stones don't talk," Todd declared.

"Yes they do! Ask Marla! Doesn't your stone talk to you?"

Marla was a bit surprised to have all the attention redirected toward her. "I can hear Ulex with it. Is that what you mean?"

Lilibit looked at Marla doubtfully. Obviously Marla not being able to hear the voice of her own stone was something Lilibit was having trouble understanding.

"Well," she mumbled with a shrug, "my stones speak to me."

"What do they say?" asked Jeff with a smirk. "Do they like rock music?"

"I don't think so," answered Lilibit seriously.

"They don't like rock music because they're *stone*-deaf!" Jeff laughed at his own joke and Donny joined in after getting an elbow in his ribs.

Todd watched Lilibit as she went back to talking to her stones. He watched her secretly, not that it mattered. She was so focused on her stones, she was barely aware of anything else. Marla was talking with Ulex. She fingered her stone in her hand while her lips twitched. Like Lilibit, it would take a meteor crashing next to them to get her attention.

Todd stood and stretched, his shoulders creaking from sleeping on the hard-packed earth. He was looking around for a good place to bury their trash when a flicker of movement on the horizon caught his eye. A helicopter, looking like a flea in the distance, flitted around a mountain before disappearing behind the crest.

He watched that spot for a long minute, but it didn't reappear.

"Can we get going now?" Jeff kicked at the dirt grumpily.

"No." Todd, still staring at the horizon, felt Jeff's impatience like a fireball beating on his back. "We'll stay where we are until full dark."

Jeff grunted in disgust but didn't argue. Todd sat back down beside Lilibit, watching her fingers arrange and disarrange her stones. Tai-Kwee was one of the stones that lay there in the dirt, resting between half a dozen other stones. With an effort, Todd pulled his eyes away from them.

"Lilibit," he asked quietly, "what do you remember from before Dalton Point?"

Lilibit's fingers froze, suspended above her stones. One hand slipped into her pocket where she kept the obelisk stone while the other arm hugged her knees. She rocked softly back and forth, her eyes focused on a point beyond the shattered wall. When she finally spoke, her voice was hushed and slow.

"I remember things at the hospital. I remember the doctors and the nurses there. They were good. Not like the others. I remember the lady who took me to Dalton Point. She kept talking to me, but I couldn't understand what she was saying. I think my head was broken. I knew I should know stuff, but I couldn't remember what it was I was supposed to know. My head wouldn't work and it hurt when I tried. Then the lady took me to Dalton Point and I saw the mountain. I wanted to go up the mountain. I didn't know why; I just wanted to go. Then when we were walking, I started to hear the stones calling." She looked up and gave Todd a small secret smile. "They were glad I was there. Then the stones told the mountain and the mountain gave me my stone."

Lilibit smiled as she pulled her hand out of her pocket, revealing her obelisk stone. As she held it in her open palm, Todd was able to see it clearly for the first time. It wasn't a grayish brown as it had first seemed. Glinting in the afternoon sun, it had many colors — flashing purple and gold, blue and green, depending on how the light hit it. The colors reflected back up onto Lilibit's cheeks as she gazed at it.

"Her name is Ewa-Kwan." The simple joy in Lilibit's voice made the others stare. "And she stays with me."

Todd hated to interrupt her quiet delight, but there were too many questions needing answers. "Lilibit, what did you mean by 'not like the others'? Were there other doctors and nurses?"

Lilibit stared hard at Todd, but he could see she was thinking about something far away. Her eyes glazed, her brow furrowed, and her hand clenched hard at Ewa-Kwan.

Suddenly a wash of white filled Todd's head. He could still see, but his mind wasn't paying attention to his eyes. Instead, images flashed in his mind and Todd realized that these fragments were Lilibit's memories, pushed into his head by the frightened girl huddled in front of him.

Glimpses of a white room. Cold-eyed people dressed in white medical jackets. A chill of fear and loneliness and despair. And then a memory of pain so horrible that the vision dissolved. Todd's breath hacked in his throat and his heart pounded hard against his ribs. A glance at the others showed him that they were pale and gasping too. All of them had seen and felt Lilibit's memories.

"I can't remember." Lilibit's whisper was barely a breath. "I just know it was bad."

"And what about the helicopters?"

"I can't remember," she repeated.

Todd thought she might remember more if he pushed her, but she was so upset, he decided against it.

At sunset, he gave the order to pack up and they moved out of the shack. They hadn't seen Gray Feather, or any other bird, since they'd escaped from the Nether Rock, but since in his dream he'd flown into the morning sun, they hiked toward their fading shadows and the distant mountains that lay to the east.

Todd fell back with Marla. Nothing was said for a while as Marla talked with Ulex. Todd watched Lilibit plod along in a silent funk.

"Marla?" Todd kept his voice low. "What is it with that stone?"

Marla brought her focus back from Ulex. "What do you mean? You mean Ulex?"

"No. I mean the stone. What does it feel like? How do you feel when you touch it?" Todd found himself staring at Lilibit's pocket where he knew Tai-Kwee lay.

"Well . . ." Marla pulled her hand from her pocket, separating herself with an effort from her stone and from Ulex. "It's hard to say what's the stone and what's Ulex. The stone is warm when I touch it and it kind of hums. Sometimes, when Ulex isn't talking to me, I can sort of feel parts of my head working that never did before. Like I can remember things that I never knew."

It was quiet for a moment as Todd thought about all this. Marla slipped her hand back into her pocket.

"The cold hasn't really bothered me since I first held Hesha-Tay. And when we walk for hours and hours and everyone is so dead tired, I feel like I could keep on walking for another three days."

She pulled Hesha-Tay from her pocket and squeezed it between her fingers until her knuckles paled. "And I think if I ever lost this stone," she whispered, "even for a minute, I think I'd die."

They walked on, Todd navigating more on instinct than by any conscious thought. He couldn't stop thinking about the stone Tai-Kwee.

Was the stone a tool to be embraced? Or a trap to be avoided?

Chapter Thirty-Four

Occurrence in the Valley of the Wind Dancers

It was a heavy march that night across the desert. Small rockslides of gravel slithered beneath their feet as they plodded over one scrabbly hill after another. Then they crested a high knoll and stopped and stared.

Rows upon rows of stark windmills, arms turning like synchronized swimmers, lined the desert floor and rode up the slopes of the dunes and hills on all sides.

"Look! Wind Dancers!" Lilibit's voice echoed across the desert. She scampered down the slope and danced between them, her arms matching the spin of the blades. Nita and Devon ran down after her, laughing and flapping.

The sound of the wind rattling through the windmills was very unsettling to Todd as they passed between them. He rubbed his scalp. The hum of the Wind Dancers seemed to sing out a warning.

The desert sprawled in front of them. The lights of a small village glistened in the distance. The faint howl of a train whistle called a soft greeting to the little town. Todd changed their direction to skirt the town. Their new path would lead them over the train tracks and south of the village.

As they approached the edge of the windmill valley, Todd's ears picked up a new sound. Turning, he saw a white glow from the far side of one of the hills they had just crossed. As he watched, the light grew brighter, silhouetting the arms of the Wind Dancers as they spun frantically.

A blast of wind struck their faces. Todd counted nine helicopters in a menacing chevron cresting a distant ridge. Their spotlights brushed the desert floor in choreographed sweeps.

"Run!" The roar of the choppers drowned out Todd, but no one asked him to repeat himself. They ran for the village, hoping to hide among the buildings, but Todd realized they would never reach it in time.

"The train!" yelled Marla, pointing.

Looking back, Todd saw the lights of a train closing in on them from the west. It lost speed as it approached the town and Todd thought that if they reached it in time, it might be slow enough for them to jump on. Todd nodded and they veered to their right, racing down toward the tracks.

A rush of panic powered his legs but Todd was amazed to see Marla sprint into the lead. Marla, always a bit lazy at gym, had never been one for exercise, but now she ran like a deer. She leaped smoothly onto one of the moving cars and immediately started to run back along the line of flatbeds, bounding from one to the next as she worked to stay with the others.

Jeff reached the train next and grabbed at Marla's out-stretched arm. With a jerk and a heave, Jeff flew off his feet and landed in an ungraceful heap on the flatcar floor. When Donny reached for her arm, Todd was certain his weight would pull her right off the train, but with a sweep, Donny sailed past Jeff, bouncing off the side of the container that lay on the flatcar.

Todd ran alongside the train and scooped up Nita, lift-ing her to Marla, who hefted her easily and set her onto the train. Then he tossed his staff and pack onto the next car as Marla's car pulled away. Jeff ran past Marla, leaping over the gap between the cars to reach Todd just as he hoisted Devon up. Then Todd turned to grab Lilibit, only to find she was not there.

Looking back toward the searchlights, he saw Lilibit's silhouette running toward them, stumbling. Todd didn't know how she had fallen so far behind, but he did know that there was no way she would make the train the way she was running. With a hiss of frustration, Todd turned from the train to round up the stray.

Lilibit staggered and fell. Todd wondered if she was

hurt, but as he got closer, he realized she had collapsed in despair, her eyes blinded with tears, thinking she'd been left behind.

"For the love of crows, brat!" Todd pulled Lilibit to her feet. The helicopters were too close to waste any time worrying about feelings. "Don't just lie there!"

Todd was dragging her toward the train when an explosion rocked the desert.

One of the helicopters plummeted in a ball of flames. They shielded their eyes as it crashed into the desert floor, erupting in fire and fury. In the silhouette of the flames, they saw the figure of a caped man wielding a glowing staff standing to face the oncoming choppers. Lilibit froze, her head cocked as she gazed at the shadow of the man. When Todd realized that she wasn't running, he grabbed her by her waist and carried her toward the disappearing train.

Marla was still leaping from car to car, but she was approaching the end of the long caravan and he needed to run faster than he ever had before if he was to catch the last car.

"Here! Take it!" Lilibit's voice rattled from jostling.

Glancing down at her, Todd saw Tai-Kwee clutched in her hand. He tore his eyes from the blue stone and continued to run toward the train, but the image of the stone kept pulling his eyes back to Lilibit's fist. His breath was in tatters and the train was pulling away. He saw Marla on the last car watching him, uncertain as to what she should do.

Without thinking, Todd tore the stone from Lilibit's grasp. From the moment his fingers wrapped around it, he felt a rush of warmth starting from the palm of his hand, surging through his body. His legs ran effortlessly and with a rush of adrenaline, he felt his pace quicken. The train grew closer, and at first, he thought it was slowing, but after the cab passed through the small town, it had actually picked up speed and Todd was running faster than the speeding train.

With a final burst of power, Todd leaped onto the last flatbed car. Marla grabbed his shirt and pulled him from the edge of the platform. Panting, he released his hold on Lilibit, who scrambled away to catch a last look at the silhouetted figure of the man standing before the flames.

Todd was exasperated. You'd think at least she would show a little gratitude that he'd gone back for her, but his annoyance faded when she turned to look at him, fear and confusion in her eyes.

"Who is he?" asked Todd.

"I don't know," Lilibit whispered, her eyes glazed as she watched the fading glow of the helicopters. "I'm scared, Todd."

Marla looked as worried as Todd felt. Taking Lilibit by

the hand, he led her back up the caravan to where the others waited.

The glow of the wreckage was miles behind them, but Lilibit still stared in that direction. Todd could see her brow ripple as she worked to fit in what she had seen with the tatters of her memories. She sat alone at the end of the flatcar, her arms huddled around her knees.

Marla sat leaning against one of the containers, her eyes almost shut. Her lips moved faintly and her hand clutched her stone as she spoke with Ulex, miles away and fathoms below.

"Ulex can usually keep up with us," Marla said, her eyes not focused, "but the train is going faster than he can run through the caverns. And sometimes he has to take detours if the tunnels don't run exactly the same way we're going. He's getting farther and farther away."

"Can you still hear him?" Todd asked.

"Oh, yes!" Marla sighed with relief. "But I think it's going to take him a while to catch up."

Todd really wasn't sure what to say to that. A fierce seven-foot-tall rock man stalking them was a bit scary, and it didn't look like shaking him off was going to be that easy.

Jeff and Donny ran up and down the length of the train, jumping from car to car, hooting and howling into the night. Nita and Devon wanted to join them, but Todd had them stay on the flatcar that he, Marla, and Lilibit sat on. They had slept all day so it would be hours before they were ready to sleep again. They ran around the container, the roar of the wind and the clatter of the train drowning out their noise.

Todd also sat quietly, his fist grasping Tai-Kwee, his fingers exploring the planes and crevices of its façade. He was enthralled by his stone. He now understood what Lilibit meant about the stones speaking to her. Not in words or images but with emotions and a vast vision of the universe. Todd felt if he held his stone long enough, he could see all of creation, from its dawn to its zenith. Perhaps even catch a glimpse of the Creator if he could look deep enough.

Time stopped. That he was there and holding the stone were all he knew. He held the stone to his cheek and felt its song vibrating along his jawbone, up and down his spine, and into his skull.

It took all his resolve, but with a tug, he wrenched the stone from his cheek and placed it in his pocket. Looking around, he was dismayed to realize how long he'd been under the spell of the stone. The others had all returned from their racing around and were huddled around him sleeping. Only he and Lilibit were awake. Lilibit lay with her head against his knee, the midnight desert rolling past her unblinking eyes.

The train pulled through another small sleeping town.

Todd studied the darkened buildings with their backs turned on the noisy trespasser that rattled through their backyards.

In the back of a rickety old house, he saw a small window glowing warmly in the darkness. A face of a boy younger even than Devon looked out, watching the train pass. As he watched, the boy's eyes met his and they locked.

A hand reached down to pull the boy gently back from the window. Todd saw the boy turn his head up to speak to the face that belonged to the hand. He pointed out the window and Todd could almost hear their voices as he told his mother: "There's a boy on the train. I saw him . . ." "That's nice, dear. Now it's time for bed."

This town belonged to its people and the people belonged to their town. Todd felt a trickle of envy. Maybe they hated their dingy little town. Maybe they felt trapped or confined or bored, but at least they all belonged to this place. And this place belonged to them. All his life Todd had felt like a piece of litter blown around by the wind. Sometimes he landed in one spot long enough to delude himself that he might belong, but then the wind blew again and he would be tossed through the air. Without roots. Without home. Without identity.

The town passed by and the lights receded into the shadows.

He felt Lilibit staring at him. He looked down and saw her eyes, wide and knowing, watching him.

"Kiva," she whispered.

She stared at him silently for a long moment before pillowing her head more comfortably on his leg. Then she closed her eyes and slept.

Todd stared at the strange child for several minutes. Could she know what he was thinking? Would Kiva be the place where he belonged? A place that belonged to him?

Todd felt a tension in his chest loosen and ease — a tightness that had been there for so many years, he hadn't even noticed it until it was gone. Looking down at Lilibit's sleeping head, he rustled her hair gently. Then he leaned his head against the side of the steel container and closed his eyes.

With a small smile, Todd slept.

Chapter Thirty-Five
Little Pine

The squeal of the train's brakes woke Todd. It would soon be dawn and the train was pulling to a stop into a small sleepy town. They needed to get off before they were discovered.

Todd woke the others. They rubbed their eyes and stretched as Todd shouldered his pack and grabbed his staff. In the faint gloom of early morning, they jumped from the slowing train.

They scuttled around the back of one of the outbuildings that fringed the quiet, dusty town. Todd looked at the others and discovered a new problem.

"We look like crap!" he announced. It had been ten days since the earthquake and those days on the road had left their mark on them. Their clothes were filthy; their faces, muddy; their hair, matted. Not an issue when they were out in the desert, but if they were to pass unnoticed in the town, they needed to clean up.

Jeff snapped his fingers with the air of a carnival magician. "Follow me," he said as he strutted down an alley.

With a wariness born of experience, Todd nodded to the others to follow.

Jeff led them up and down hushed and deserted streets until he found what he was looking for. With a self-satisfied smile, he pointed ahead.

A modest motel slouched alongside the railroad tracks, a dozen or so cars in its gravel parking lot. Jeff dropped his pack and fished a couple of objects out of the pockets. Then he gestured for the others to stay put while he casually walked down the porch connecting the rooms. He chose a room at the end that had no car parked in front of it and tested the doorknob. Then he crouched and began to work on the lock. Todd was amazed at Jeff's nonchalance, but that quickly turned to dismay as a door farther down the strip opened and a man with a suitcase stepped out.

With one smooth movement, Jeff tipped an orange out of his pocket, tossed it in the air, and then caught it with a stab of his hand. A second ago, Jeff had been trying to pick a lock. Now he looked as if he was just some innocent little kid who had woken early and was playing ball by himself. With a seeming slip of his grip, the orange tripped from his hand and rolled down the porch toward the man just as he was about to close his door. With a smile, the man scooped up the orange and handed it to Jeff, who grinned his thanks.

Jeff waved goodbye to the car as it pulled out of the parking lot and continued to lob the orange until the car passed out of sight.

Jeff jerked his head, beckoning Todd and the others to join him on the motel porch. With a cheeky wink, Jeff went to the door of the room that the man had just vacated. A DO NOT DISTURB sign had somehow wedged itself into the door frame, preventing the door from closing all the way.

"Gee, I wonder how that got there!" Jeff smirked as he pushed open the door.

The travelers all quietly entered the room. Before closing the door, Jeff placed the DO NOT DISTURB sign onto the front doorknob. With a gloating grin, he turned to the others. "Checkout time is eleven A.M. I don't know about you, but I could use a shower."

Several hours later, damp, rumpled, but very much cleaner, the travelers walked down the main street of the small town.

But Jeff was not done demonstrating his innate aptitude for ingenuity and deception. He stopped in front of a neat little diner. Cardboard placards filled the windows advertising hamburgers, French fries, and shakes. The smell of the grill taunted them.

"Keep moving, Jeff," Todd said. "We have no money."

"Maybe not," Jeff responded, "but perhaps plastic will do."

With that, he pulled several small cards out of his pocket.

The others huddled around, either out of curiosity or out of a desire to hide Jeff's prizes from prying eyes.

"Those belong to the Callows!" Todd was appalled. "Where did you get them?"

"Where do you think? Loser!" hooted Jeff. "I found her purse in the rubble."

"We can't use her credit card; we don't have any ID!" said Marla.

Todd glared at Marla, wondering if that was her only problem with using cards stolen from the dead.

"We can use the ATM card and pay cash!" Jeff replied.

"I don't think we should use Mrs. Callow's cards. It's like stealing," said Devon.

"Thank you, Devon," exclaimed Todd, pleased that someone saw the immorality, if not the morbidity, of the situation.

Jeff rolled his eyes. "Listen, Devon, neither Mr. or Mrs. Callow worked. The only money they had was money the County gave them to take care of us. Any money in their account was for us. If they're not here anymore, then it's only right we appropriate it and use it to take care of ourselves."

A silence fell. One by one, the travelers looked to Todd, waiting for his decision. Todd was very uncomfortable, but he couldn't dispute Jeff's logic. Besides, he had no other ideas for feeding them.

"We don't know their password," he countered lamely.

Jeff snorted with contempt. "You don't think I didn't hack their password within a month of getting to Dalton Point? They used the cats' birthdays for everything!"

"Okay," Todd agreed after a long silence. "But we keep track of what we spend and we'll pay it back." Todd knew this was a weak sop for his conscience. Where would they get the money to replace it and to whom would they pay it back?

Outside a bank, they found a likely ATM. They huddled around Jeff, more out of curiosity than caution.

"Buggers!" Jeff cursed under his breath.

"What's the matter?" Todd felt a surge of panic.

"They've got a low limit on this machine," Jeff muttered. "I can only get out two hundred dollars."

"Two hundred? Do you think we need that much?"

Jeff shot Todd a look of contempt as two hundred dollars in neat twenty-dollar bills spat out of the machine. The other kids clapped as Jeff grabbed the cash before turning to bow, soaking up his adoring limelight.

"And now, my good children," he intoned pompously, "I shall treat you all to cheeseburgers and shakes."

"And French fries?" asked Donny with a grin.

"Only the good children can have French fries. None for Todd, however, unless his attitude improves." Jeff smirked a challenge at Todd.

The travelers laughed and cheered. Even Todd smiled, though he glanced around and rubbed his hair. Something about this situation did not feel right.

The technician, huddled into the corner of his cubicle, tried to avoid the four people he feared most as they crowded around his desk.

"Up." With the lift of an eyebrow, the Director of Security ordered the technician out of his own chair. The technician obeyed gratefully.

"W-w-w-e had a hit, s-s-sir," he stuttered breathlessly, peering around the partition. "It was at an M-M-M-fourteen style bank machine in the t-t-town of . . ."

The Director banished the technician with a withering glance. He ran down the hall like a mongrel with his tail between his legs.

"Little Pine Community Savings." The Director's fingers sailed across the keyboard, opening and closing windows with a speed he knew only Syxx and he could follow. "That's two hundred and eighteen miles east of their last sighting."

"Pull up the visual documentation," Syxx commanded coolly.

"This does not materially affect our discussion, Syxx," a female voice snapped sharply.

Syxx smiled warmly at Dr. Nil and Dr. Voight, who had entered the Information Analysis Department with them. The Director knew that Syxx needed the doctors to maintain the façade of the Institute. They were to be humored for a little while longer, but when their usefulness was at an end, so would end the patience of Syxx. The Director hid his anticipation.

"Recent expenditures are obscenely over budget and expense justifications are foully inadequate." Dr. Nil's long sharp nose twitched unpleasantly. Her unnaturally blond hair, pulled back into a severe bun, only emphasized the surgically enhanced planes of her austere face.

Dr. Voight had a round jolly face. If you did not look too closely at his eyes, you might mistake him for a favorite uncle. Only his eyes — dark, watery, beady, and lifeless — gave lie to his humanity. Emerging from her shadow, he opened his mouth to corroborate her statement, only to reconsider and dissolve into an intimidated huff.

"I can assure you, doctors," soothed Syxx warmly, "the end result will justify the expenditure." He nodded silkily to the doctors, oozing reassurance. "You will not be disappointed."

The effect of his voice on Dr. Voight was obvious. He nodded with a sublime smile, glancing up at Dr. Nil for her concurrence. Dr. Nil, however, was not so easily swayed and opened her mouth to continue her tirade.

"We have visual." The Director cut her off.

Dr. Nil sniffed at the interruption, but her curiosity prevailed over her desire to rant and she looked over the shoulder of the Director.

A series of grainy still images flashed over the monitor. The face of Jeffrey Terrance was seen, framed by a bevy of other faces, most partially obscured by the angle of the camera. The Director recognized each of the children from his files.

An imperious elbow shoved the Director away from the monitor. "Let me see that!" spat Dr. Nil, assuming the Director's seat at the monitor.

The Director shot a vacant look at Syxx, who returned the glance expressionlessly.

"It can't be," whispered Dr. Nil, her fingers dancing across the keyboard. The images on the monitor aimed and focused on a partially obscured face of a small dark-haired girl with large almond-shaped eyes. "There wasn't enough left of her to survive!"

With a spatter of finger action, the monitor revealed a dozen sequential close-ups, each showing the image of Research Subject 1717, AKA "Lilibit."

The silence in the cubicle congealed with tension. Finally, Dr. Nil spoke. "I stand corrected, Syxx. RS seventeen-seventeen's regenerative powers obviously require additional research." She stood and paced the cubicle, her fingers lightly tapping her temples in concentration.

"We examined the temporal and parietal thoroughly," she mumbled to herself. "We removed and dissected most of the frontal lobe and the entire occipital lobe . . . There was nothing in her DNA to substantiate any extraordinary regenerative qualities . . ." She paced distractedly while Dr. Voight watched anxiously and the Director and Syxx waited patiently.

"It must be in the brain stem," she announced at last. "It will have to be dissected."

"Removing the brain stem will certainly terminate RS seventeen-seventeen," objected Dr. Voight feebly. "Do you think it's worth the risk?"

"Nonsense, doctor. When our final results are published, the entire world will benefit. We are creating an entirely new field of medicine. Regenerative Medicine will completely revolutionize human physiology." Dr. Nil's voice rang with passion. "This will be a quantum leap in the evolution of mankind. I will be the supreme sovereign of the medical world."

"Um, don't you mean 'we'?" Dr. Voight's voice trembled.

"Oh, yes," Dr. Nil answered impatiently. "Of course, Stanley."

"And we must not forget those who doubted you," purred

Syxx into Dr. Nil's ear. "All your colleagues who questioned your brilliance? They must all be made to see the error of their ways. Can you imagine their chagrin when they hear about your success?"

Dr. Nil's eyes glazed with glory. "Yes! Yes!" she said breathlessly.

The Director hid a smirk.

"You may continue, Syxx," declared Dr. Nil. "I have complete confidence in your ability to reclaim RS seventeen-seventeen. Proceed. Regardless of the cost."

She turned and left the room, snapping commands into her cell-com as her heels clicked down the corridor.

Dr. Voight, pausing in her wake, turned to add his opinion but then thought better of it. With a gulp of air, he exited behind Dr. Nil with more speed than dignity.

The Director rose to return to his office, from where he would dispatch the Reclamation Teams to the town of Little Pine. Turning in the doorway, he looked back at Syxx, who stood transfixed by the monitor.

The screen still displayed a myriad of images of RS 1717. Slowly Syxx reached down to the keyboard to clear the images, but then a surge of rage poured from his fingertips and he gripped the keyboard in a fit of fury. The sound of splintering plastic mixed with the stench of melting vinyl. He slammed down the crumpled keyboard and left the office abruptly, brushing past the Director, who waited in the door.

Images of Lilibit flickered relentlessly on the monitor.

A barrage of red slime obliterated the city of Phoenix. It spattered the suburbs, leaving many of its streets unrecognizable under the bloody devastation.

With a quick swab of a paper napkin, Todd wiped clean the ketchup that had spilled on the map. Licking the remains of his hamburger from his fingers, he studied the paper with dismay. He hadn't expected Kiva to be listed on a map, but he hadn't really grasped the vastness of the area they needed to cover.

In his dreams, he flew into the rising sun, past deserts and rivers, canyons and mountains. But at what time of the year? He pulled at his hair. He couldn't match any of those vivid images on this lifeless map.

Lilibit squirmed under his arm and pushed her head in front of his to gaze at the map.

"Any ideas?" he asked without much hope.

"Nope," she answered simply. "I don't know how to read maps."

Todd snorted and shook his head as Lilibit scrambled back to her chair to finish her third grilled cheese and pickle sandwich.

"So?" asked Jeff around a mouthful of French fries. "Where next?"

"East," Todd stated, hoping he sounded more confident than he felt.

Jeff and Marla moved to look over Todd's shoulder.

"Yeah, but how far?" asked Marla.

"I hope we'll know when we get there, but I think we should move out." Todd rubbed the back of his head as he looked over his shoulder. "My hair feels funny. My scalp wants to get moving."

"Does what's underneath your scalp have any ideas as to how we should get there?" Jeff asked.

"Walk, I suppose," answered Todd. "Do you have any better ideas?"

"We could take the bus," Jeff offered. "We can pay for the tickets with the credit card."

"They'll want to see some ID," said Marla.

"Not if we order them online." Jeff grinned.

The small library in the town of Little Pine had only one public computer terminal. Todd and Marla watched as Jeff expertly navigated through all the screens. Within seconds, the timetables for the buses that ran to Phoenix scrolled down the monitor. The terminal was a twenty-minute walk away and the next bus left in an hour and forty minutes.

With the tickets purchased and waiting for them at the station, they decided to wait the hour in the library.

Todd and Marla sat next to Jeff as he surfed the Net. Donny was happily enthralled in a picture book of farm animals while Devon and Nita sat on the floor with Lilibit and initiated her into the wonders of the alphabet.

Lilibit labored over the writing on the page. She acted as if she had at one time known her letters, but the memory of them was just out of her reach. Sighing in frustration, she listened closely to Devon.

Marla nudged Todd with a smile and glanced down at Devon. Todd grinned back. Devon was a funny, quiet boy, but he had a nurturing soul and sometimes showed a surprising maturity.

Then Todd turned to Jeff. There were so many questions burning in his mind. Maybe this was a good time to get some of them answered.

With a quiet whisper, Todd asked Jeff, "Do a search on a company with the acronym NAVMRI. That's what was on the helicopter we saw on the mountaintop."

In seconds, the website of the "Nil and Voight Medical Research Institute" flashed on the screen. Jeff's fingers sailed through the public pages.

"Here we go," Jeff reported. "They're a private research institute working off corporate and government grants: 'researching healing, regeneration, and pain tolerance in humans.'" Jeff gave an ironic snort. "You got to love this . . . Look at the disclaimer at the base of their homepage: 'No animals are used in our testing and research.'"

Looking at Lilibit reading quietly, Todd understood their interest in her. Only a few weeks earlier, she was a broken husk balancing on the edge of survival. Now, other than when her choppily cut hair parted to show the scars on her scalp, she appeared much like any other child. But who had hurt her so badly? And why? And what did they still want with her?

"What more can you find out?" Todd asked Jeff quietly.

With a grin of pure mischief, Jeff responded, "You want me to hack into their network?"

"Can you?" asked Todd.

Jeff responded with a snort and the rapid staccato of the keyboard stuttered through the stillness of the library.

Minutes passed and Jeff's bravado began to fade. "They've got firewalls in place like I've never seen before. The CIA could take lessons from them!" he muttered to himself.

"How do you know what kind of firewalls the CIA have?" asked Todd.

Jeff responded with a cocky grin.

"Never mind," Todd added. "Don't answer that."

Another five minutes passed before Jeff slapped the desk with disgust. "It'll take me hours to get through their security, and I can't even be sure I haven't already triggered a dozen of their infiltration detectors."

Out of the corner of his eye, Todd saw Lilibit no longer studied her book. Devon and Nita watched her curiously as she sat back and began fishing through her pockets. She pulled out her stones and listened to them one at a time before finding one that seemed to answer her. Placing the others back, she stood and turned to Jeff.

"Here, Jeff." Lilibit smiled and extended her hand casually. "He wants to stay with you."

Todd, Jeff, and Marla froze with anticipation at her words. However, when Lilibit opened her hand to reveal her gift, Todd could not restrain a snort of laughter.

Revealed in Lilibit's palm was a scrap of mineral so meager it might have been brushed aside as a splinter of dust. It looked like a rectangular chip of pale mica, as small as a baby's fingernail and not much thicker. Jeff stared woodenly into Lilibit's smiling face, not a trace of gratitude to be seen.

"Thank you," Jeff said without a hint of sincerity.

His sarcasm was lost on Lilibit. With a cheerful grin, she grabbed Jeff's hand and turned it to place the stone in his palm. "His name," she declared with a calm authority, "is Dave."

This was too much for Todd and Marla. The librarian hurried over to shush their crack of laughter, but Marla's eyes were tearing and Todd's face was hot from biting his lip.

"Dave?" asked Jeff.

Lilibit nodded innocently before returning to her book with Devon and Nita, who had been watching with interest.

Jeff turned his stare from Lilibit to Todd and Marla.

"Dave?" he mouthed to them voicelessly. Jeff huffed at their grins and then set the splinter next to the keyboard before going back to work.

Todd watched closely, wondering if Dave was having any effect on Jeff. Evidently not, since it was Lilibit who stood again and, taking Dave from the desktop, placed it on the back of Jeff's hand.

Jeff rolled his eyes and for several moments ignored the chip, continuing his attempts at digital piracy. It took less than a minute, but he stopped still, his eyes lost focus, and his head twitched from one side to the other as if he saw things floating before his face that no one else saw.

"Whoa!" he muttered. Todd and Marla watched in alarm as Jeff's head snapped up and down, left and right, his grin widening as his eyes snatched at the unseen images.

"Whoa!" he said again. The excitement in his voice bordered on ecstasy. "This . . . is . . . so . . . cool!"

"What?" asked Marla.

"It's as if the entire Web is in virtual reality. I can *see* the entire layout of the Internet. I can *see* the firewalls as if they were actual physical barricades."

His fingers rested gently on the keyboard but made no movement. The monitor, however, seemed to flash between screens faster than the light traveled to their eyes. Jeff began making small noises like a human pinball machine as he dived through the Web, leaping over firewalls and plowing through dossiers of data with an unruly joy.

Todd didn't try to hide the sarcasm in his voice. "Jeff, I don't want to interrupt your playtime, but could you squeeze in a little background check on the Institute?"

With an effort, Jeff turned to Todd. It took him a moment to focus on his face, but when he finally saw Todd, he grinned. Turning back toward the monitor, Jeff said, "Well, let's just see what the Nil and Voight Medical Research Institute is hiding."

The screen flashed through several dozen security checkpoints.

"Okay." Jeff's voice grew serious. "We're in."

Todd hushed his voice so the others on the floor could not hear him. "Search for 'Lilibit.' See what you get."

The search revealed several dozen options scrolling down the screen. With an unerring aptitude born from years of hacking, Jeff trained his attention on a likely file. The case file of Research Subject 1717 popped onto the screen.

As one, Marla, Todd, and Jeff absorbed the information on the first page.

```
Research Subject 1717
Birth name: Unknown
AKA Elisabeth Moore; AKA Lilibit
Parents: unknown
```

Todd was surprised to see that her birth date reported that she had turned eleven several weeks earlier. He glanced at Lilibit where she sprawled on the floor with Nita and Devon. She was smaller than the two eight-year-olds and Todd had assumed she was younger.

He returned his attention to the screen, hoping to find the answers to his questions.

DNA analysis showed she was possibly Polynesian, probably Hawaiian in ancestry. No surprise there. It was the next page that made Marla gasp, and Todd felt his blood chill in his spine as Jeff scrolled through the attached documents.

According to the files, starting nearly five years earlier, RS 1717 had been the subject of a series of exploratory research surgeries. These operations appeared to have two objectives. The surgeries conducted by Dr. Nil were concerned with the subject's regenerative abilities, while the surgeries conducted by Dr. Voight dealt more with the "ratio of pain tolerance."

Todd could feel the blood drain from his face as he read the transcripts of the procedures. Amid the reams of technical data, certain phrases dragged his attention.

```
Anesthesia: None
Time: 1 hour 18 minutes, RS 1717 terminates
vocalization...
Time: 1 hour 20 minutes, RS 1717 loses consciousness...
Procedure terminated.
```

An image of Lilibit screaming for over an hour before "terminating vocalization" made Todd nauseous.

The pages flickered past. Jeff was able to absorb them with his inner eye faster than either Todd or Marla could read. "There are hundreds of these transcripts. They must have been operating on her practically once a week for over four years." Jeff's whisper echoed the horror they all felt. Todd glanced at Jeff and saw he was pale, almost green beneath his freckles, and his hands trembled. "Check this out."

Reluctantly Todd looked back at the monitor. The heading on the top was Procedure 187. The date was eight months earlier. He forced himself to read on.

```
Time: 0 hour 42 minutes, RS 1717 enters cardiac arrest.
   Resuscitation instituted.
Time: 0 hour 46 minutes, RS 1717 cardiac activity resumed.
   RS 1717 stabilized.
```

"She *died?*" Marla's voice was barely audible to Todd, even though her face was inches from his.

The pages on the monitor began fluttering past again; Jeff's eyes flickered as he digested the data. "According to these transcripts, she went into full cardiac arrest three different times and was gone from four to nine minutes each time." Jeff muttered. "Check out the last operation transcript."

The date was three months prior.

```
Time: 0 hour 14 minutes, RS 1717 enters cardiac arrest.
    Resuscitation instituted.
Time: 0 hour 28 minutes, unable to resuscitate.
    RS 1717 terminated.
Cadaver sent to Biopsy Research for autopsy.
```

Todd, Marla, and Jeff all turned to look at Lilibit. If they hadn't seen Lilibit in the condition she was in when she arrived at Dalton Point, they would not have believed the girl in front of them was the same child coldly described as RS 1717.

Evidently Lilibit was a very difficult child to kill.

While Todd and Marla mulled over what they read, Jeff turned back to continue his scan.

The files had two more surprises to offer. First, Jeff reported, the case file on RS 1717 had been reopened two weeks ago after eighteen employees were terminated for conspiring to transport "Cadaver 1717" to another research institute. "Reclamation Procedures" were currently underway.

The final revelation made Todd jump. "Pack up; we're moving out," he hissed. Devon, Nita, and Lilibit looked at Todd, surprised by the alarm in his voice.

Jeff quickly darkened the monitor and purged the terminal's history log before the younger kids saw the last entry in the Reclamation Operation file. Where there was now only a black screen, moments before had been the images and history of all six of the others.

And their current location: Little Pine.

The bus accelerated sluggishly as it pulled out of the terminal. The driver announced the towns they were scheduled to pass through over the next six hours, his voice not bothering to reach above a bored monotone. He glanced into his rearview mirror; his interest seemed to be primarily in the two shapely young women who had giggled their way onto his bus. He had little concern for the group of children huddled in the back. They seemed well behaved.

Thirty minutes out of Little Pine, the bus slowed to a stop. The driver was annoyed but not very concerned over the delay. "Four twenty-two to base," he called over his radio.

"Base." His radio cackled.

"We've got a delay here on the interstate. Looks like a state police roadblock. I'll give you an update on our ETA as soon as we clear it . . . Over."

"Confirmed."

A state police officer, followed by six men dressed in dark gray, approached the bus. The driver plastered on his official smile as he opened the door.

"What can I do for you, officer?" he asked, a façade of cheerfulness thinly covering his impatience.

"We're looking for some runaways and we've got a report they might be on your bus. Can we take a look?" It wasn't a request and the bus driver knew it.

"Absolutely!" The veneer of politeness was firmly in place.

The police officer turned to the largest man in gray and gave him a sharp salute. "Go ahead, Director."

The Director brushed rudely past the officer, making a beeline to the back of the bus. A mousy woman with blue hair stood up to block his path.

"Can I help you?" She bristled like an angry French poodle.

Without a word, the Director pushed her aside and continued toward the children. Reaching down, he grabbed the shoulder of the smallest child and spun her toward him with a jerk. The cap on her head fell to the ground and long red-brown hair spilled down her shoulders.

"Did my Dad send you?" The girl tossed her head angrily. "He signed the permission slip! I told him weeks ago about this field trip!"

Furious, the Director's eyes snapped at each of the children before he shoved the girl back into the arms of her blue-haired chaperone. With a growl he pushed a path back to the front of the bus. A frightened hush and the faint stench of oily fumes lingered in the aisle long after he had stormed out the door.

This was a field trip that the Little Pine 4-H Club would never forget.

Chapter Thirty-six

The Demons of Malagua

None of them moved as they rolled slowly to a stop at the police roadblock. They didn't even breathe. The sight of the powerful men in gray suits made Todd pull his head back from the window into the shadows. The hard eyes of the men raked the vehicles as they passed. Todd felt a cold spasm in his gut as the largest of the gray men seemed to lock Todd's eyes with his. Instinctively Todd gripped his staff and his stone tighter.

They were moving again, pulling slowly away from the roadblock, but Todd felt he could never forget the eyes of that man: the eyes of a hunter. Even now, Todd almost felt the eyes following him, almost felt his breath on his neck.

He bit back a startled yelp when a gust of hot, wet air actually brushed his hair. While the brown mare seemed amenable to sharing her trailer stall with the travelers, there was only one small window and she wanted it back. Todd crouched and rejoined the others at the front of the trailer.

"Roadblock," Todd whispered. "We're through it."

The others peered between the slats in the sides of the trailer, watching the flashing lights pull away. They all released their breath at the same time, sounding like one huge sigh. Nita giggled, but Lilibit stayed huddled in the corner, staring.

Clustered together in the rear of the trailer, they watched through the cracks between the floorboards as the highway scrolled beneath them. Donny stood and went to the horse's head, mumbling softly to it, an unusual sparkle of delight gleaming in his eyes. Other than that, there wasn't much talking.

Hours later, when the trailer pulled off the highway, Todd decided not to tempt fate any further. At a traffic light, they bailed out of the back gate, Donny giving the horse a quick goodbye pat. Jeff waved cheekily at the elderly driver of the car behind the trailer who watched them with a cantankerous grimace as they tumbled out the back and piled onto the sidewalk.

The town of Malagua was a large town, almost a city, drenched with a darkness not completely attributable to smog and dusk. The travelers had no difficulty in losing themselves among the busy streets of the downtown area.

Todd saw pine-covered mountains in the northeast. For a moment, his heart beat quickly, but as he looked closer, he realized they weren't at all like the mountains in his dreams.

He knew there would probably be hundreds of mountains they might pass before finding the mountains of Kiva.

Like most cities, there were too many people but too few eyes, and no one noticed them as they walked through the crowds.

Todd watched as a wave of pedestrians veered, dodging one particular section of the sidewalk. Their movements seemed almost subconscious and Todd wondered what they were trying to avoid.

Then he saw him. On the corner, waving his arms and screaming at demons only he could see, stood a shabby man with long black lanky hair and bloodshot eyes. "Leave them alone!" he screamed at a point off to his left. His head snapped to the right and he stabbed his finger in the air. "No! Stop it! I'll kill you! I'll kill you! I swear I'll kill you all if you don't stop!"

Todd led the group away from the man as he ranted and cursed. Jeff snickered. Marla looked disgusted and Nita was frightened to the point of tears. Lilibit was openly curious and would have lagged behind, but Todd grabbed her hand and pulled her away.

Devon stopped to gaze sadly at the man. He looked up and down the street like he was trying to see who it was that the madman was screaming at.

In his left hand was a bottle-shaped paper bag, which he waved as he spun around, screaming in all directions. "I know what you're planning! I know what you're thinking! You'll do it again; I know you will!"

Devon opened his mouth to speak to the man, but Marla grabbed his arm and pulled him away. Marla had no sympathy for the vagrant. For an instant, the burning contempt in her eyes seemed to pierce the man's insanity, but the moment passed and the madness returned. He screamed at a point just beyond her left shoulder and lunged for it.

"Stop it! Don't you dare! Stop it!" he screamed.

Marla's contempt turned quickly to fear and she dragged Devon away. Even from the distance of a city block, the man's eyes followed them until the movement of the crowd cut him off from their sight.

The demons were out in force today. They swarmed up the sides of buildings, pushed their heads through walls, and leaped onto the oblivious pedestrians as they passed. They were vile little demons, hairless and barely human-looking. Their skin was mottled with many colors, mostly a rancid purple with green, festering boils. Sometimes if the madman couldn't get enough alcohol, the festering green boils grew until they covered their skin. If it got really bad, they began to turn black with decay.

Then the carnage would begin.

That the people of the town could not see them was a point of both horror and envy to the madman. The demons would leap onto their heads or cling to their backs. They would reach into their bodies and pull out parts of their souls, eating them like dripping entrails. Sometimes when the pedestrians bothered to look at him, their eyes mirrored the hate and contempt of the demons clinging to their shoulders. Mostly, though, they walked by, ignoring the madman and blind to his tormenters.

Maybe it was the lack of alcohol that caused the demons to be so outrageous today. The alcohol made his head hurt and his stomach wrench, but for a few blessed hours, he was free of their torture.

Yet it could have been the group of strange children that caused today's rampage. The demons certainly seemed interested in the children when they walked down the street, but the demons were unable to attach themselves for more than a moment or two. Part of his mind watched with detached curiosity as the demons leaped onto the group, their teeth bared, their long clawed fingers outstretched to attack. They seemed most attracted to the smallest girl, but whenever they leaped to grab her, they bounced away as if repelled by a mighty blow.

And while there was an aura about the smallest girl that seemed to attract the demons, the madman wondered if it might be the eyes of the smallest boy that repelled them. When the boy looked at him, his large gray eyes seemed to hold some secret knowledge. It was as if he not only could see the demons, but also knew their source: the rotting depths of the madman's soul.

A demon fastened itself to the back of the black girl, and for a moment, the bile of its hatred spewed from her eyes. He tried to swat the demon off her, but frightened, she ran away. As she retreated, the demon jumped off her back and returned to taunt him.

The boy was gone, dragged off by the black girl, but his eyes still haunted him. With a scream of rage, the madman scratched at his own face, trying to claw away the memory. A few frightened pedestrians scuttled away when he smashed his bottle against the nearest wall. As the last precious drops of his alcohol spilled to the ground, he collapsed onto the sidewalk, sobbing. He prayed the escape of death would come soon.

"They are a bit out of control, aren't they?" he heard a small gentle voice say.

The madman pulled his hands from his face to see the boy with the large gray eyes sitting quietly beside him. They sat silent for several long moments. The boy looked up and down the street as if he saw the demons.

"They are your soldiers. You are their chief," he said at last.

"You can see them?" The madman was stunned.

"They're your soldiers," the boy repeated. "They will obey you but not without discipline."

"Discipline?" The madman snorted. "How do you discipline a nightmare?"

"When you discipline yourself, you will discipline your demons," said the boy, his voice serious, "but first you have to purify yourself."

"How?"

The boy gazed into space as if listening to a voice only he could hear. "You know how." He looked as if he was speaking to someone else. "You know what you have to do."

"Devon!"

The madman looked up to see the angry black girl approaching. She grabbed the boy's arm and began to drag him away.

The boy did not protest, but turned back to smile at the madman. "Goodbye, Chief!" he called back.

Chief. Not the derogatory nickname given to him by the local police officers when they regularly locked him up. No, this title was for a man who was the ruler of his demons. A King. A Sachem. A Chief. The Chief looked up and saw all his demons clustered on the street, watching him with apprehension. The Chief gave a small nod. He knew what he must do.

The Chief stood. Leaving behind all his possessions piled into a rickety cart, he walked north into the desert. He was born here in Malagua and never once had he left this blighted town.

He walked through the desert for forty days, eating nothing, drinking only the morning dew or the water from some rocky spring. His demons followed him, taunting him, torturing his body with the lust of alcohol. Some days he could not move at all. He lay curled on the desert floor, surges of pain racking his body, waves of despair pummeling his soul. His demons grew desperate, conjuring him food and drink, offering respite from the pain. And yet the Chief held steadfast.

At the end of the forty days, the Chief looked and saw the vast army of his demons, now brown and golden as the earth, with no will in their eyes but to serve their Chief.

The Chief stood. Somewhere deep within him, he had always known that he must serve. He now had the strength to answer the call. He walked east out of the desert toward the mountains, his soldiers following in his wake.

He knew he was called.

Devon didn't act very sorry as Marla dragged him back to the group. "I needed to talk to him" was all he would say.

Todd cut off Marla's scolding with a shake of his head. It was a waste of breath. Devon was usually the most obedient of kids until he got an idea in his head; then you might as well box up a cloud as try to change his mind.

They used the remains of Jeff's cash to buy food to refill their packs. Todd nixed the idea of Jeff stopping at an

Internet café to use his new powers to replenish their cash or get new bus tickets. Jeff was certain with Dave in his hand, he could mask the transactions so that the enemy couldn't detect them, but Todd had his doubts.

What Todd didn't say was that he had a lot of misgivings about finding Kiva from the inside of a bus. That he had qualms about finding Kiva at all was an understatement. His dreams made him think that Kiva wasn't near any town or road, but as they stood on the outskirts of Malagua, the highway rolling east, the desert stretching out to the foot of the distant mountains, he was overwhelmed. Kiva could be anywhere.

A flutter of movement caught his eye. A large black bird soared high above the desert to the north. The raven hovered almost motionless in the purple sky of dusk for several moments before flying toward the mountains northeast of Malagua.

Todd released his breath with a sigh of relief. He couldn't tell from this distance if the bird was Gray Feather, but at least here was a direction. With a nod, Todd steered the group into the desert, following the raven that floated like a fleck toward the distant mountains.

Chapter Thirty-seven

The Horsemaster

They hiked deep into the desert before resting that night. They huddled together on the rocky ground and stared at a sky with more stars than they'd ever imagined. Was this the same sky they knew from Dalton Point? The carpet of stars was so deep and rich, it looked like a pulsing cloud overhead. Todd smiled when Lilibit reached out her hand as if to touch them. The night sky seemed more vibrant and alive here, as if it were a vital and interested part of their world, not just a meaningless backdrop.

His eyes open barely a crack, his mind dithering on the edge of sleep, Todd sensed rather than saw the shadow of a large black bird pass overhead. A dark patch on a living canvas, seen more for the loss of the stars behind it than by the sight of its wings.

Entrusting his flock into the keeping of the raven, Todd slept.

◆ ◆ ◆ ◆

Into the town of Alamos-Tierra they came. Dozens upon dozens of them. Driven by a need they could not put into words, they arrived by foot, by train, by car, by horse, some even by bicycle. Many were of the People, having received the call during their visionfast, but even more were from far away, answering the call of the Stone.

Most were between the ages of thirteen and fifteen. Some were as old as seventeen or eighteen. A few were as young as eleven or twelve. Some came with their parents, puzzled but supportive of this strange vision driving their children. But most of them were alone, having left what little home or family they had to answer a summons that came from the Stone beneath their feet, an edict they could not deny.

They milled about like geese in the fall, waiting for a sign to move. Then, with one mind, they set out, walking single-file into the desert.

Outside the palisades of Kiva, they camped and waited. And from the topmost ridge of the Sienna Sentries, Gil-Salla watched them arrive.

Ten centuries had passed since the Earth Stone last beckoned the neophytes. This was to be a new generation of stone warriors. It was a good sign.

The neophytes had arrived. The Stone Voice was coming.

Todd woke with the dawn but didn't wake the others. Just because he didn't need more sleep didn't mean he had to push the others. He sat on a nearby stone watching the sky lighten and scanning the horizon in all directions. No creature that did not belong to the desert was seen. Todd waited.

Marla stretched and yawned, then immediately clasped her stone. She spoke with Ulex for a moment before nodding a greeting at Todd. With a twisted smile, Todd accepted the inevitable: Marla's connection with the man from the Nether Rock was as strong as ever.

Lilibit woke next and, not being burdened with any element of consideration for the preferences of the other travelers, climbed over them noisily, calling her good mornings to them all.

Their path that morning took them out of the desert and into the grassy foothills that rolled along the base of the mountains. Cresting a hill, they stopped to scan the meadows below. In the distance, they saw swirls of dust kicked up by something moving quickly across the valley floor. They hunched down and hid amid the scrub. It wasn't until the cloud was within a mile of them that they could make out its features.

"Horses!" Donny grinned happily. He jumped up and ran toward the herd, but the wild horses were too fast and far away. As the herd passed, they saw it was made up of only a dozen or so mustangs along with a few foals and year-lings. At the pinnacle of the stampede was a huge golden brown stallion.

Laughing, Lilibit grabbed Donny's hand and pulled him, following the trail of the retreating herd. When they reached the trodden tracks, they waved and called after the horses. Jumping up and down, Lilibit slipped and fell on her behind, which only made her giggle more.

Lilibit's laugh was contagious, but everyone's smiles faded when Lilibit picked up a stone from the dust. With a now familiar gesture, she brushed the soil from it and held it to her cheek. Her eyes lost focus for a moment, and then she smiled and turned to Donny.

"Here, Donny. His name is Doo-Shi and he wants to stay with you." In her open hand sat a large reddish brown stone. It didn't look that much different from the millions of other stones carpeting the desert floor, and yet they knew it was.

By now, Donny was the only one of them who didn't understand the importance of Lilibit's stones. Todd held his breath as Donny cheerfully plucked it out of Lilibit's palm. He gave a deep gurgle of laughter and pocketed it with a grin. Lilibit turned to Todd and her smile dimmed when she saw how they were all staring at her. She shrugged.

With a wary glance at Donny, Todd resumed their trek toward the mountains. As they climbed the next hill, Donny lagged behind to look at the horses. The herd had stopped a mile or so away, grazing peacefully.

"Come here, horses!" Donny cried loudly. "We want to ride you!"

"Todd!" Marla whispered. "Look!"

The horses stood stock-still, their ears peaked as if they could hear Donny's distant call. Then the gold stallion pawed the ground and reared on his hind legs.

"Come, horses, come!" Donny called again. "We want to ride you!"

The entire herd broke into a full gallop and headed straight toward them.

All too soon, the herd was upon them. From a distance, they had looked noble and handsome. Stampeding directly at them, they were terrifying. Marla screamed and started to run, but Todd grabbed her arm and pulled her behind him. He hefted his staff and motioned for the others to get behind him as well. They all obeyed except Donny, who stood apart, waving his arms and grinning at the approaching herd.

The golden brown stallion galloped directly to Donny while the other horses circled. Even the foals seemed bigger than normal up close, but the stallion was huge. Donny was tall, but the stallion towered over him. It was strange that Donny didn't seem the least bit frightened; he just reached out to pat the muzzle as the horse snorted loudly.

The ring of horses slowed to a gentle walk. Two of the foals dropped out of the circle to graze quietly and one of them wandered over near Todd and Lilibit. Lilibit tentatively reached out to stroke the friendly foal, smiling as it gently nudged its head against her hand.

Todd relaxed and was reaching out to pat the foal too when a powerful jolt hit him from behind. He whirled to find a large black mustang butting against his back. Cautiously Todd stroked the mustang's neck and ran his hand across its back, reveling in the scent and sensation of the animal. Nearby, Donny climbed on top of a large boulder to mount his stallion.

Todd was amazed. He knew Donny had never ridden a horse before, but there he was sitting comfortably atop the trotting stallion. His hands grasped the horse's mane as the animal circled the herd.

"Get on! They're gonna take us to Kiva!" Donny called with a grin. "They say they will serve."

"Serve what? Who?" Todd asked, puzzled.

"I dunno." Donny shrugged. "That's just what he said."

"Hey!" Lilibit cried out indignantly. "Cut it out!"

Todd turned to see Lilibit trying to climb onto the back of a small freckled foal, but a large gray mare kept nosing her away. Todd could see why.

"No, Lilibit." Todd stepped between the girl and the foal. "It's way too small to be ridden yet."

Lilibit looked skeptical, but even though she was reed thin, she was still too heavy for a young foal.

Todd looked around to see what other horse might work for her, but it appeared that this wasn't a decision he was allowed to make. The gray mare nosed Todd gently and presented her flank to be mounted. Todd shook his head.

"No," he said as he patted the mare's neck, "you're too much horse for her."

But the large mare would not be put off so easily. When Todd tried to place Lilibit onto a sober-looking brown nag, he was hit in the back with a much less gentle nudge. The two of them tumbled to the ground, and Todd looked up to find himself nose-to-nose with the determined-looking mare. He shrugged, and with some serious qualms, placed Lilibit onto the back of the gray mare.

Lilibit was delighted. She squirmed around on the mare's back, lay on her stomach, and rubbed her nose into the mane. "She's like an old auntie!" Lilibit sat back up and clutched the mane, as comfortable as if she'd been born on the back of a horse. Old Auntie took a few careful steps and Lilibit hung on, grinning.

After seeing Lilibit trot about, Devon and Nita were ready to try. Todd hoisted Devon onto a palomino colt and Nita on a brown and white pony. They both had worried looks on their faces, but Nita screamed only a little when her pony started a slow walk. Todd walked beside them for a few minutes until they got used to each other.

"SON OF A —" The rest of Jeff's curse was lost as he landed with a painful-sounding thud on the packed turf. He had chosen a feisty rust-colored mustang to ride and his mounting style looked more like wrestling than equestrian. He leaped back to his feet, brushed off his pants, gritted his teeth, and charged the horse again, screaming like a crazed chimpanzee on the attack. The horse waited until Jeff's hands were within inches of its neck then dropped its head sharply. Jeff gripped air, slammed his chest against its flank, and slid to the ground, winded.

The horse snickered.

"Um, Jeff?" Todd wasn't sure what advice to give, but he really thought that Jeff should try a different tactic.

"Shaddup!" Jeff growled, fire in his eyes. He approached the horse like a bear in slow motion. The horse's ears were flat back and its tail flicked the air, but it didn't move. Jeff grabbed the mane and crawled up the flank, flopping all over the mustang's back as he tried to get himself seated.

The horse's ears perked forward, its tail slapped back and forth, but still it did not move.

With a grunt, Jeff righted himself and glowed cockily as he sat astride his steed.

"You see?" He grinned smugly. "All you have to do is show him who's boss!"

With that, Jeff gave the mustang a possessive slap on the butt.

The horse moved.

Jeff clung with both hands to the mane as his mount bucked and kicked. It didn't seem possible, but there were times it looked like all four hooves were off the ground. For three wide-eyed seconds, Jeff clung to its back. With a final buck, Jeff lost his grip and flew through the air, landing flat on his back with a breath-robbing thud.

Walking over to where Jeff lay, Todd winced and looked down, struggling to find something to say.

"Shaddup," Jeff said when he could breathe again.

Todd helped Jeff to his feet and turned to look back at the horses. Donny slid off his horse and walked over to the rusty mustang, patting its nose and whispering to it.

"Try again, Jeff," said Donny. "He says he'll be good."

Jeff walked slowly back to the mustang, shooting a hot glare back at Todd, who fought to keep from laughing. With Donny at its head, the mustang allowed Jeff to get back on. Donny patted its jaw, whispering "good boy" into its ear until Jeff settled. They took a few steps around in a circle and then Donny moved back, letting Jeff ride the horse alone.

"What's your horse's name, Jeff?" asked Nita.

"This trickster?" Jeff watched the horse's ears closely. One was pointing forward, the other was straight back.

"Look at him! He's just waiting for his chance to throw me again!"

Leaving the two of them to make their peace, Todd looked around for a mount for himself.

Afterward, he was never sure if he picked the black horse or if the black horse picked him, but even before he pulled himself onto its back for the first time, he had dubbed his mount Midnight.

He was barely astride when Midnight took off at a trot. Todd grabbed at the mane and squeezed with his legs, trying to get his butt to stop jarring against the horse's back with each step. He had a few seconds of feeling like he might actually have an iota of control when Midnight broke into a canter. Todd's knuckles were white as he clutched the mane. He bent his head next to the horse's neck, wondering if biting the mane might help steady him. He squeezed his legs even tighter, trying to get his body to match the rise and fall of the horse's stride. Midnight took this as a sign to go even faster. They galloped in a huge circle around the herd, only slowing when apparently Midnight got tired. They slowed to a merciful walk. Todd couldn't have released the mane if he wanted to. His fingers shook. He felt as if all his blood were in his feet. He barely saw the others as Midnight walked slowly back to the center of the herd.

"Showoff!" Jeff muttered with a glare.

Todd had no idea what he was talking about. The others stared at him, waiting for him to lead. Unable to trust his voice, he nodded for Donny, who had remounted, to go ahead, and they started off.

"Hey, Donny!" Nita's voice rang out after they had walked for a while. "What's your horse's name?"

Donny looked down at his mount before turning back toward Nita. "Horse," he said simply.

Horse broke into a gentle trot and the others followed, heading steadily northeast.

Todd squinted at the black fleck circling lazily in the distant sky, but it wasn't until they reached the cliffs that he realized that it wasn't a raven, just a vulture. It settled on a bluff and watched them pass.

The bird stared unblinking and unmoving. Todd wondered if this was how vultures normally acted. Maybe it was hoping that one of them would fall off a horse and die. He looked back again. It was still there staring at them. He rubbed his scalp.

When he looked back the third time, it was gone.

Beneath an icy halo of artificial light, Syxx sat inert, his eyes burning venom into the darkened recesses of his office, the dismembered carcass of a vulture at his feet.

The failure of the Director to reclaim the child disturbed

him more than he cared to reveal. The child's escape from the infestation of Nether Rock might have been luck; the interference of the old Stone Warrior in the desert was unfortunate; but for her to have slipped through the noose of his security forces concerned him deeply.

That the child might actually survive long enough to reach Kiva was a possibility that must be considered. Syxx could no longer rely on the corruption of mankind and nature. It might be overkill, but the elimination of the child must be ensured.

Syxx slowed his breathing to a stop. His eyes rolled back so only the whites showed. Anyone foolishly entering his office at this hour of the night might have thought he had died of a stroke sitting upright in his chair.

Yet no one was unfortunate enough to enter his office.

And from the night's blackest bane, the Chee-tola was called.

Chapter Thirty-eight

The Grotto of Chee-tola

The horses had carried them for hours and showed no signs of tiring, but their riders couldn't make the same claim. The sun had set and the foothills cast eerie shadows in the dusk. They passed a grotto nestled between two canyon walls, with a quiet stream running through it.

Todd no sooner said "This might be a good place to camp," when the herd stopped. Since they had no reins to guide them, he wondered if they understood his words.

Lilibit was asleep atop Old Auntie, her arms and legs dangling down the horse's flank. That she hadn't fallen off was more to the credit of the gentle mare than to any aptitude of Lilibit's. Old Auntie waited patiently while the travelers dismounted, their legs stiff and bruised from the unaccustomed riding. Todd helped Devon and Nita off their mounts before hobbling over to unload Lilibit. She mumbled and flopped against his shoulder but didn't wake up.

Todd carried her as he led the group into the narrow

canyon. A wide swath of grass provided grazing for the horses and a soft bed for the travelers. The walls of the canyon were steep and close. Todd felt they could risk a small fire.

They sat in a ring around the fire while they unpacked the rations they had bought in Malagua. Lilibit shot an impish grin at Jeff as she took a peanut butter sandwich from Marla.

"Any brown bread or baked beans left?" Lilibit asked sweetly.

With a roar of mock fury, Jeff leaped, trying to smash her sandwich into her face, but Todd stopped him with a look. With a satisfied chuckle, Lilibit stuck out a peanut butter–covered tongue at Jeff, who retaliated by flicking a pebble at her behind Todd's back. But everyone stopped laughing when Lilibit picked up the pebble and peered at it closely. No one breathed as she held it against her cheek, listening. After a long moment, she placed it back onto the ground and gave it a gentle pat. As one, they heaved a sigh of relief.

Sometimes a stone is just a stone.

A snail twitched.

Alongside a secluded brook, a snail shuddered. Possessed by some malignant force that took control of its meager nervous system, it crawled onto a nearby spit of unmarked sand.

Upon that pristine surface, the snail began to carve a delicate arc. After completing barely half of a perfect circle, its simple network of nerves failed. With a scalding hiss, the snail tipped over, dying with a sizzle of smoke and spume.

The first snail was not quite dead when a second quavering snail inched its way out onto the sand, its trail continuing the arc etched into the silt.

In the colorless light of the waxing moon, one snail after another curled into lethal agony, hissing and fuming into oblivion. Before the night was over, the streambed was littered with smoldering snail corpses. Yet in the end, carved into the sand, was a perfect spiral of thirteen rings. Driven to completion, the last snail sizzled into death at the center of the spiral.

For a long still moment, nothing moved but the gentle current of the brook. Then slowly the spiral began to pulse from beneath as if a fountain of sand were bubbling up from the bowels of the earth.

By the raking light of the moon, a fetid head crested from the center of the spiral.

Chee-tola, Assassin of the Vortex, had been beckoned.

The neighing of nervous horses woke Todd. One hand reached for his staff while the other wiped the sleep from his eyes.

The horses' ears were pointed back, their attention focused on a large boulder a little upstream of their camp. Todd scrambled to his feet, his staff at the ready.

A long shadow grew from behind the boulder and crawled slowly toward the sleeping travelers. From the gloom behind the rock, a figure emerged.

A groggy Lilibit ambled back into the clearing. She was fastening the button on her pants, having gone behind the boulder to add her own contribution to the local ecology.

Todd blew out an exasperated sigh but he knew it wasn't reasonable for him to be annoyed at Lilibit for his own jumpiness.

Lilibit stopped and patted her pants pockets. Frowning, she looked at the ground and then turned to go back behind the boulder.

Todd started to settle back down, but his scalp still prickled. He rubbed at his hair as he glanced around the clearing, but he couldn't see any potential threat. Then the horses began to whinny even louder.

The noise woke the others. They gaped as the stallion reared and pawed at the air as if sparring with some invisible foe. Then, neighing in terror, the horses bolted out of the canyon.

Todd hefted his staff. He scanned the dark shadows that lurked in the recesses of the canyon, but he couldn't see anything that might have caused the horses' panic. Everything was quiet. Very quiet. Unnaturally quiet. The others felt it too; Todd could see it in the way they rose to their feet and looked around.

A screaming caw made them jump. Todd whipped around to see a black blur streak down between the canyon walls. He caught a glimpse of a bird, one gray feather pale against the darkness as it sliced the air overhead. Todd ducked as it passed and turned to watch as it shrieked upstream. It disappeared into the shadows, and the night grew deathly quiet once more.

A movement, black on black, caught Todd's eye and he peered at the spot where he thought he'd seen it: behind a boulder upstream of where Lilibit stood. His voice caught in his throat as something emerged from the gloom.

Twenty feet above the unsuspecting Lilibit rose a huge serpentlike creature. Its snakelike torso glistened scaly black and its body was covered with clawlike barbs that flexed and curled like boneless fingers luring its prey into its reach. Its head looked like a human head, despite its glowing, pupilless green eyes. It was as if this demon might once have been a man but had been so corrupted that his soul had been sucked out and it morphed into this malevolent viper.

Lilibit read the fear in Todd's eyes and turned but didn't have even a second to grasp what she saw, never mind react. With a stabbing lunge, the serpent attacked. Its huge toothless mouth did something no human jaw could ever manage. With a wheezing creak, it opened to a gaping chasm, saliva dripping from its toothless gums. With a stabbing snap, it grabbed Lilibit in its jaws. The creature drew itself up, its head towering above the grotto floor. All that could be seen of Lilibit were her legs kicking from its mouth. It straightened its neck and jerked its head, trying to swallow the struggling girl.

Todd froze for one long second before leaping to grab at Lilibit's legs. He missed and fell to the ground in a heap. He grabbed his staff and slammed it against the monster's body, but it just bounced off harmlessly.

Gray Feather screamed back into the grotto. Todd was confused as it ignored the monster and dived at him instead. Todd swung his staff to sweep it off, but the bird swerved sharply and came back to peck at him again.

Grabbing his thigh as the beak jabbed into it, Todd felt his father's knife where it hid sheathed beneath his pant leg. He pulled it out as Gray Feather flew off. Grasping the haft in both hands, Todd struck deep into the flank of the beast.

The monster thrashed in pain; dark burgundy blood flecked with pale green bile spilled from the wound. It swung its tail at Todd's head, lethal barbs fully extended, but Todd ducked, rolled, and sprang back to his feet. Then he stabbed it again. The serpent lowered its head to see what was attacking it, and Marla leaped, grabbing at Lilibit's twitching legs. It reared again and Marla was pulled off the ground. Hanging on to Lilibit's legs, she was wrenched back and forth in the air as it viciously snapped its head, trying to dislodge her.

Jeff ripped frantically through his backpack. Pulling out the dinner knives he'd snatched from Mesa del Tío's cabin, he clenched one in his teeth and gripped one in each hand. He charged the beast and plunged the first knife into its tail. He pulled back in surprise as the blade sizzled and dissolved into smoke like a chip of dry ice thrown into a flame. The same thing happened to the next two knives, but at least it looked like the beast suffered as well. Todd looked down at his own knife as he stabbed at the beast again, wondering why his blade was not disintegrating. Not that it mattered: though the beast bled, Todd didn't think his little knife was doing much damage.

Gray Feather dove into Todd's face again then flew up to peck at the beast's head at a spot just above its eyes. Gritting his teeth, Todd leaped onto the back of the beast and began shimmying up its back. He ignored the barbs as they ripped into his skin and he stabbed his way up its spine.

Jeff reached back into his pack to grab more knives, but with his attention turned, he didn't see the tail of the beast swinging toward him until it was too late. The tail caught him and he flew across the stream, crashing into the wall of the canyon. Blood streamed from where one of the treacherous barbs had slashed his arm. He pulled off his shirt and was wrapping it around the wound when a crack in the face of the cliff started to crumble.

The crack widened and a huge pair of dark eyes glowed from the abyss. Jeff screamed a warning to Todd.

Meanwhile, Donny stood, his arms fluttering in frustration. Devon and Nita were hurling small stones at the beast, so Donny picked up a boulder the size of a school desk and flung it at the monster like a cannonball. The rock struck its neck and the beast fell.

The earth shook as the snake whipped its tail against the ground in pain and fury. It rebounded to its full height, and Lilibit's ankles and feet were all that could be seen of her. Marla still clung to them, but with a snap, the beast thrashed her against the wall of the canyon. Her hold slipped and the next lash of the serpent's head sent Marla flinging over the stream and across the grotto, landing in the arms of Ulex.

Ulex broke through from the Nether Rock, the cavern wall splitting in front of him. He surfaced next to Jeff just in time to catch Marla as she was whipped through the air. He looked down at the blood dripping from her head and immediately transformed into a rocky pillar of fury. Setting her gently onto the riverbank, he hefted his crystal staff and turned to face the beast.

"Kill!" Jeff ordered, pointing at the snake, as if Ulex were some kind of mutant attack dog.

Ulex could not understand Jeff's words but acted none-theless. With a voiceless roar, he charged the snake. Bearing his staff as he would a spear, he thrust it through its tail, pinning it to the ground.

Lilibit could no longer be seen and the mouth of the beast now bellowed with pain and rage. Its roar caused small rockslides along the canyon walls, and when the beast turned its head toward Ulex, it spat forth a stream of bile that engulfed the young Netherockian in a wave of green acid. The bile sizzled as it dripped, searing the grass and moss at Ulex's feet, but when the flow stopped, Ulex opened all four sets of his eyelids. His crystalline skin was pocked and scored, but the acid dribbled off, leaving him only slightly hurt — and very angry.

All this time while the others were attacking the beast, Todd was slowly crawling up its spine. Pierced and ripped by the barbs, Todd fought to ignore the pain. What was harder to ignore was Lilibit's fate. That she could no longer be seen was a reality he had to deal with. That she might be dead was a reality he refused to face.

Finally, he reached the scaly head. Gripping the back of its neck with his knees, Todd grasped his knife with both hands and plunged it right into the spot that Gray Feather had pecked at: right above the creature's eyes.

The snake roared and snapped its head back and forth. Todd clung to the hilt of his knife and rode the dying serpent to the ground. The beast twitched and frothed, its lidless eyes growing black and dim. Wrenching his blade from the skull, Todd leaped from its back and ran to the point where its torso swelled unnaturally. Frozen with shock, the others watched as Todd ripped open the bowels of the beast, exposing the cold, lifeless form of Lilibit.

He used his knife to cut away a length of intestine wrapped around her neck and then pulled her out. He laid her on the ground. Her skin was blue and cold to the touch. Wiping the bile from her face, he tilted back her head and tried to breathe life back into her mouth. Part of him knew it was futile, but he had to try.

He didn't know how many minutes had passed before Marla, the blood dry on her scalp, placed her hand on his shoulder.

"Todd," she whispered hoarsely, "she's gone."

Devon broke from the circle. He patted Lilibit's pocket then checked her clenched fists. Looking up, he met Todd's eyes.

"Her stone's missing."

The others searched the ground frantically, Jeff even going so far as to rummage gingerly through the serpent's intestines with a long stick.

Todd, however, recalled Lilibit's reaction before the arrival of the beast. With a bound, he leaped over the carcass and ran to the streambed. There behind the boulder, fallen on the sand, was Ewa-Kwan, Lilibit's stone, glittering dimly in the moonlight.

"It's back here!" he called to the others. Without thinking, he reached down to grab it. His fingers were within an inch of it when something that felt like an invisible truck hit him. He landed on his back several yards away.

Devon came around the boulder at a dead run. Before Todd could stop him, he reached down, scooped up Ewa-Kwan, and then ran back to where Lilibit lay. Dumbfounded, Todd followed Devon back into the clearing.

Forcing open Lilibit's fingers, Devon placed the stone in her cold palm. He stepped back and stood with the others, watching her.

Nothing happened.

Todd dropped to his knees, staring blindly at the lifeless girl. Marla leaned against Ulex, sobbing. The others stood staring and confused.

Todd stood and walked away. Where would they go now? For some reason, going to Kiva without Lilibit seemed pointless. The others watched him. He couldn't think of what to do next.

"We need to . . ." His voice trailed off. What did they need to do? Bury her? Go to the police? Tell them what?

A small cough dragged everyone's eyes back to Lilibit. A

gasp, barely a wheeze, seemed to tremble out of her corpse. Todd ran back to her and lifted her into his arms.

In the pale light of the moon, it was hard to see, but it looked like the blue color was slowly fading from her skin. Her cheeks were still ghastly pale.

And then a faint twitch of her left arm quickly spread until her entire body trembled violently. She was still ice cold to the touch yet sweat beaded on her brow. Her back arched, and for several minutes, she flopped and twitched like a beached minnow. When the spasms finally stopped, her eyes opened.

Todd watched helplessly as a wave of hysteria built within Lilibit. He couldn't blame her, and yet there was nothing he could do to stop it. She began to sob uncontrollably.

"Oh, knock it off, Lilibit." Jeff's voice was cold and sarcastic.

Stunned, they all turned to stare at Jeff. Lilibit choked back a whimper and blinked at Jeff, his bloody arm hanging limply, a look of contempt on his face.

"If you're going to cry like a baby every time you get a little snakebite, than you're just too big of a loser to hang out with me."

Todd's first thought was to beat Jeff into a bloody pulp, but a glance at Lilibit changed his mind. Lilibit was biting back her sobs, working to understand Jeff's words.

"Well" — she hiccupped — "stars forbid if I'm not cool enough to hang out with Jeff."

"I know." Jeff nodded graciously. "That's why I thought I'd drop you a hint."

Chapter Thirty-nine
In the Wake of the Viper

Still masked in the gloom of early morning, the offices of the Institute were dark and silent.

Except for one office. High on the top floor, a cold unnatural light filled the domain of Syxx. And seated before his ebony slab desk, the motionless figure of the Deceiver sat as if petrified; his eyes were voids of white, life and intelligence having vacated his body.

Then, faintly at first, a tremble of movement twitched through his fingers. Spreading through his body, the contortions intensified. His head snapped back, and with a thrust from an unseen force, Syxx flew from his chair and slammed against the battery of monitors mounted on the wall behind him. Blood dripped from his nose and ears, and for the first time in centuries, fear dripped from his eyes.

The Assassin had failed. Chee-tola had been destroyed. And still the child lived.

No further efforts could be wasted on subterfuge.

There was always a risk in acting too openly. The humans who were the most obedient were the ones who could be deceived into thinking that they served only themselves. In fact, Syxx had long ago learned that they preferred to deny his existence altogether, even when directly faced with it.

Yet the child was getting too close to the haven of Kiva. He would need to finish the task himself. Any consequences of exposure could be resolved after the child was terminated.

Syxx stood. Crossing to a wall of drapery, he pulled back the curtains to expose a set of doors leading to an exterior balcony. He opened the doors and looked out onto the glittering city below.

In one moment, the silhouette of Syxx was seen illuminated against the night.

The next, it was gone.

Hot and stabbing, the acid burned her skin like a million scalding maggots, tearing and searing as they burrowed deep. Lilibit arched in pain as she dragged her body toward the stream. Maybe the cool water might stop the burning.

The serpent might be dead, but its venom was still doing its job. Todd and Jeff were already unconscious. Lilibit could hear Marla trying to wake them.

"They're burning up!" Marla cried. "Devon! Nita! Wet more rags in the stream! We need to cool them down!"

Lilibit's hands reached the water first. She tried to lower herself gently, but her arms gave out and she plunged in, face first.

"Lilibit! No!" Devon yelled.

Small hands grabbed Lilibit, tugging her out of the water and back to the stream bank.

"*¡Levántesen*, Lilibit!" Nita's voice hiccupped with fear. "Wake up! You can fix this. You got a stone. You can fix anything."

Lilibit was too weak to argue — she could barely think through the pain — but was Nita right? Could she "fix" this with her stone? Her fingers fumbled; her joints were sore as she pulled her stone out of her pocket and placed it against her cheek. Then she closed her eyes and laid her face against the cool silt of the stream bank.

She felt herself drawn softly out of her skin and into the sand. Her body still ached, but it didn't seem important. Deep beneath her, she heard a songlike thrumming as if the earth were a stone with a million separate voices all chiming in a complex harmony. There was some meaning to the song as well, but as hard as she tried, she couldn't understand it. She strained to reach it but couldn't get any closer, and when she tried to call out to it, her voice wouldn't work. She pulled back in frustration, and like a slap, awareness of her aching body returned. The pain whipped her into a senseless frenzy and she pounded the earth with her arms and legs like a spoiled child.

She didn't know how long she'd been lying on the stream bank, but when she looked up from her tantrum, she'd found that the world had changed. She was still in the grotto, but the stream had risen and now the sand she lay on was an island with angry currents raging on both sides of her. The horses were still gone, but so were her friends.

She was alone.

Lilibit punched the sand with a clenched fist. With each strike, a surge of water would rush down the canyon, sweeping through the grotto and coming closer and closer to swamping her little island, but she was half mad with pain and couldn't seem to stop. Her wordless scream was sucked up by the howling wind and she struck the earth one last time.

A wall of water barreled into the grotto, engulfing her. Pebbles and silt pelted her, ripping into the sores on her skin. She choked on the water, but before she could even remember to close her mouth and hold her breath, the wave passed, the wind died, and the water fled downstream.

Exhausted, Lilibit could do little more than raise her head. Soaked to the skin, she coughed out water and then pressed her cheek back down against the mud. From where she lay, she could see that the stream had subsided, and the floor of the grotto had reappeared. But where earlier there had been grass, brush, and a few tenacious trees, now there was only gravel. Nearby something hummed urgently. Her arms trembled as she pushed herself up to look around.

Marla, Devon, and Nita ran out from the cavern, the one that Ulex had made when he'd burst through to the surface.

"Lilibit? Are you all right?" Marla was frantic as she helped Lilibit to her knees. "We couldn't move you! When that storm started, we tried to carry you into the cave, but you wouldn't budge!"

The humming was louder than Marla's voice. Lilibit saw a glint of pale pink on the stream bank. She reached out, and as her fingers wrapped around it, the urgent buzzing faded, replaced by a faint gurgling chime sound. Safe in her pocket, Ewa-Kwan chimed in as well, the two stones speaking to each other. Lilibit would have liked to listen to them as they hummed bits of knowledge to each other but was just too tired to pay attention. It was early afternoon, but everything was getting dark. Not dark like night, but dark like her eyes had given up working.

With her fingers still clutched around the new stone, she felt Donny's arms lift and carry her into the cavern.

Then the world went black.

Splat. Something cool and wet pressed down on Lilibit's cheek. That roused her more than Nita's babbling. She'd been chattering to her in Spanish, but when Lilibit let out a little moan, she switched to English.

"Feel better?" Nita's voice was overly cheerful, almost brittle, as she placed another muddy leaf on Lilibit's burning arm. "*Mi abuela,* my grandmother, always said that my medicine bandages could make her feel better, even more than the doctor's pills. Even on the bad days when she was too tired to get out of bed, I could tell that the bandages helped."

The new stone in Lilibit's hand thrummed anxiously, drowning Nita's chatter into murmurs. She raised it to her cheek.

Boolakya, it hummed. Over and over. And behind the humming, Lilibit could hear it yearning, reaching out, and like the sound of a hungry baby, it was impossible to ignore.

"Here." Lilibit's throat was so dry, the words rasped almost soundlessly, but Nita stopped, midword, her eyes widening. "Her name is Boolakya and she wants to stay with you."

The whispered words echoed through the cavern. Marla and Devon looked up from tending Todd and Jeff and hurried over. All three of them stared at the gleaming pink stone that sat in Lilibit's palm. Nita slowly reached out to take the stone and then stopped, a question in her eyes as she looked once more at Lilibit for permission. But Lilibit was spent and could only watch with hazy eyes.

Slowly Nita's fingertips touched the stone Boolakya. She froze for a moment and then grabbed it, clutching it tightly to her cheek. She stared unblinking at the cavern wall.

"Nita?" Marla sounded concerned as she nudged Nita. Her voice grew panicked as she repeated her name again and again. Finally Marla shook the younger girl, pulling her out of her daze.

Nita blinked and joggled her head to clear it. Lilibit wheezed and coughed dryly.

"Oh, I'm sorry, Lilibit!" whispered Nita, placing another muddy leaf on Lilibit's forehead.

"Forget the leaves!" Marla snapped. "Get her some water! Her lips are cracking!"

Nita scurried away as Marla wiped the mud off Lilibit's arms and face. The wet cloth paused as it passed over her forehead.

"Devon." Marla looked down with awe at Lilibit's face. "Look!" Marla's finger glided over a cool spot on Lilibit's forehead.

"Was that clear spot there before?" asked Devon.

"No," answered Marla. "That's the spot where Nita put the leaf."

Lilibit closed her eyes. There was one spot on her forehead that was pain free, but the rest of her still burned.

"Nita!" Marla called. "Get over here!"

"I'm getting water!" Nita's voice echoed from the stream.

"Never mind that now!" Marla yelled. "Come back here!"

Nita jogged back, grumbling in Spanish as she carried a bottle of water.

Marla snatched the bottle from her hands. "Try the leaf thing again!"

Puzzled, Nita picked up one of the leaves, dragged it through the mud, and then placed it on Lilibit's arm. Quickly Marla wiped off the leaf. Where it had lain was now a leaf-shaped patch of healed skin.

"They work!" Nita's voice rang triumphantly. "My medicine bandages work!"

"Do it again!" Marla whispered.

Quickly Nita began covering Lilibit's face and arms with her muddy bandages while Devon ran out to gather more leaves.

Lilibit wondered if she was finally dying. Her arms and face had stopped hurting. But her torso and legs still burned, so she thought she couldn't be dead yet.

"Do Todd and Jeff," she heard Marla say. "The leaves might work on them too."

Lilibit opened her eyes a crack. She was still in a lot of pain but she could only watch as Nita plastered muddy leaves all over the two boys. They looked like human bushes, but they stopped moaning, and when Marla washed off the mud, their skin was pink and smooth underneath, the burn blisters fading.

Weak and lightheaded, Lilibit lost track of time. It seemed like hours before Nita finally remembered that she hadn't finished bandaging her wounds yet. At last, she scurried back.

When the leaves had washed away the last of the pain, Lilibit rolled over and fell fast asleep.

Gil-Salla sat unmoving, her hands and feet splayed against the smooth red earth floor.

All night she sat, her eyes open yet not seeing the clay walls of the ancient hall or the shifting shades of the flame. Her uneasiness had grown from a faint apprehension into a dread that froze her breath in her lungs. From deep within the earth, she felt the stirrings of the Enemy and heard the echo when he called for the Assassin. Fighting panic, she reached out to Keotak-se's mind, only to find that he too had heard the summons.

Frantically Gil-Salla searched with her fingertips while Keotak-se searched from the skies, seeking some trace of the Infant Stone Voice or the faintest scent of the Assassin. All night they searched fruitlessly.

The Earth trembled when the light of the Infant Stone Voice flickered and dimmed. Tears poured down Gil-Salla's cheeks unheeded as she heard the despair of the Earth Stone.

Yet barely had her grief set in when Gil-Salla quavered

with another revelation. Beneath her palms, the soil trembled with the news. The Assassin was dead. The Chee-tola had been destroyed.

A glimmer of joy quivered from below — tentative and weak but there was no doubt: the light of the Infant Stone Voice was not yet extinguished.

Tears and sweat froze unheeded on Gil-Salla's face. Her mind again leaped the void to speak to Keotak-se, praising him for his triumph. Yet Keotak-se's response left her astonished. Someone had slain the Assassin of the Vortex but it was not Keotak-se.

Who but a seasoned stone warrior armed with the weaponry of Quapan could have defeated a Chee-tola? And what stone warrior besides Keotak-se had not fallen to death or corruption over the past centuries? Could another stone warrior have survived, hiding all these centuries, to return at this time when most needed? Or perhaps another force was rising, one that could defeat one of the Enemy's most potent weapons?

Gil-Salla fought the urge to break from the Earth and rush to the Tower. A search of the Archives of Kiva might give her a clue as to the identity of the conqueror of the Chee-tola, yet she forced herself to remain focused. There would be time to study the ancient manuscripts when the Infant Stone Voice was safely within the sanctuary of Kiva. For now, Gil-Salla must remain vigilant.

While her palms listened to the whisperings of the soil, Gil-Salla sensed the eye of the Enemy sweep the mountains. Ice choked her heart as she felt the Enemy deploy. Reaching out to Keotak-se, she alerted him of the threat.

The Enemy was mobilizing. The Deceiver himself was advancing.

The moonlight flickered against Lilibit's closed lids. Even though the stinging pain was almost gone, she still felt weak and groggy. She opened her eyes slowly. Her eyes adjusted quickly to the starlit glow, but her mind was slow to react.

A towering figure filled the opening, its silhouette blocking the moonlight. It advanced slowly: a long black shadow creeping over the rock floor. Darkness flooded the cavern.

Lilibit rubbed her eyes. "Hey, Ulex," muttered Lilibit drowsily, "when did you get here?"

Ulex glowed dimly in the dark. Two of his four sets of eyelids clicked open as he watched Lilibit squirm to her feet. She was heading for the cave entrance when Ulex put out his arm to stop her.

"It's okay," said Lilibit as she pushed aside a hand larger than her head. "I'm feeling better. I just want to go outside for a few minutes."

Ulex looked as baffled as a granite slab could look, but he let the girl pass. On wobbly legs, Lilibit stepped out of the cave. With a lumbering creak, the man from the Nether Rock followed her.

She stopped to stroke Old Auntie. The horses had returned while she'd been sleeping. She laid her head against Old Auntie's flank, feeling the heat through the silky fur. But then a glimpse of a black serpent tail made her draw back from the horse and she walked over to the stream.

A shiver rippled up Lilibit's back as she stared at the battered carcass of the beast. It lay against the canyon wall where the flash flood had pushed it.

"You know, Ulex," she whispered, safe in knowing that he couldn't understand her words, "I don't remember much about anything, but these kinds of things" — she stared at the carcass — "this can't be normal. Can it?"

She turned away from the serpent and climbed onto a boulder. Her chin in her hands, she stared at the moon and picked at the threads of her splintered memories.

And standing in the shadow of the bluff, Ulex kept watch, a stony sentry of the night.

Chapter Forty

Copper Herald

A stranger's car pulling into the small town of Dry Creek was unusual enough to warrant a second glance from the old men drinking pop on the front porch of Jack Whitedeer's hardware store. This car, however, was so remarkable, it pulled the store clerks out from behind the counter and the women out from the IGA Market. By the time the car rolled to a stop in front of the Morning Star Diner, it seemed half the town was on the sidewalk or looking out their windows.

The old men laughed and buzzed as the long brassy orange limousine jumped the curb as it parked, tilting drunkenly. A short wiry man with a face like a wrinkled shirt tumbled out of the driver's door and scurried to open the rear passenger door. All remarks stopped for several awestruck moments after the passenger stepped out onto the sidewalk. Some events are just too overwhelming for words.

A plump, elderly woman wearing a magnificently flowered dress stood decorating Main Street. The gaudy dress, the abundance of jewelry, and the large round, rhinestone-encrusted sunglasses made the woman look like a huge bug landing on a flower bed. To crown it all, her improbable copper-red hair was sculpted into a beehive tower that added eight inches to her height.

Molly Coppertop had had a very interesting week.

After the Battle of Nether Rock, she woke to find herself in a hospital. Shattered from the loss of her beloved Beryl, she'd lain there listless, waiting for death to catch up with her body.

That's when she learned there'd been two very interesting changes in the Overworld during the past fifty years while she'd exiled herself in the mines of Coppertop.

The first change brought to her attention was that the town of Coppertop, once just a desolate collection of abandoned ruins, was now an oasis of rustic wilderness amid a desert of suburban development. Turned out, the land above the barren minefields was now worth more than whatever minerals once hid beneath it.

And Molly Coppertop was the sole surviving owner of the entire town.

Lying in her hospital bed, Molly endured a series of visits by real estate agents, developers, and opportunists who mistook her lethargy for hardheadedness. When the dust cleared and the papers were signed, Molly was an absurdly wealthy woman.

The second revelation was that the doctors were able to restore most of her vision. She had considered eye surgery a waste of time and effort since she had no intention of ever leaving her hospital bed alive. Yet as she looked out the window, she remembered Keotak-se's parting words.

"Perhaps you are spared because you are called," Keotak-se had told her when he left her at the hospital. "Do not indulge in despair. Listen for the call for you are needed."

Which is how Molly found herself being driven around the deserts and countryside in a garish stretch limousine by a squirrelly little man named Rocky.

Molly smiled at the customary hush that fell over the diner as she entered. The bracelets on her plump arms rattled as she waved at the patrons. She picked up a local paper before toddling over to sit at the counter.

The Enemy must be getting desperate. There was nothing subtle about the headline that screamed of seven missing runaways. Six faces, file photos from the Social Services Department, stared sightlessly up at Molly. Was one of these children the Infant Stone Voice? As she waited for a cup of coffee, she studied the pictures.

The oldest boy, Todd Hawker, had black hair and dark eyes. He gazed from the newspaper with the wary look of a hunted wolf. Molly guessed he wasn't the type to trust others easily. A pretty girl, Marla Fuller, had smiled for the camera, but Molly could see shadows of anger and hurt behind the dimples. Jeffrey Terrance glared like in a mugshot, defiant from the tilt of his chin to the glint in his eyes. Donny Johnson's gaze was unfocused, fear and loneliness seeming to send him hiding deep within himself. Little Nita Rodriguez looked frightened half to death, while the waif-like Devon Brigham looked lost and bewildered. Could one of these sad children be the Infant Stone Voice?

Perhaps it was the seventh child, the nameless one with "no photo available." High on the wall of the diner, the television droned, repeating the same images, echoing the same messages. "If you see these children, please call . . ."

The waitress poured a cup of thick coffee into a mug and glanced up at the television. "Kind of makes you wonder what they're running from, huh?" she said dryly.

Molly smiled as she picked up her coffee cup. She had a job to do.

"Well, Connie," Molly said, reading her nametag. "Let me tell you what *I've* heard."

Chapter Forty-one

The Canyon de la Muerte

A scattering of black feathers froze Todd in his tracks. Stooping, he examined them with shaking fingers. Too many feathers. Some were mutilated and corroded as if they had brushed against acid. He looked around but couldn't see a body. Could a bird have lost this many feathers and survived? Todd poked at the mound and picked up the largest and least damaged ones. His breath caught noisily in his chest when he lifted a solitary gray feather from the bottom. He looked up and down the canyon, hoping for a glimpse of familiar black wings but there was nothing. Carefully he slid a half dozen black feathers along with the one gray feather into the pocket of his backpack, zipping it completely. He continued walking over to Midnight and mounted him heavily, but made no mention of the feathers to anyone.

Todd steered the troop toward the northeast, hoping for

the best. He didn't want to say it out loud, but without Gray Feather to guide them, finding Kiva had just become a lot more doubtful.

The horses picked their way over a trail that wound around gentle foothills in a narrow valley. On either side, mountains speckled with pine trees framed the horizons. Todd was weary and his body ached, but it was a healing pain, and after the roller-coaster ride of fever and near coma of the past day, he was feeling lucky just to be alive.

A glance over at the Trickster showed Jeff was still hurting as well. Lilibit, however, was a point of wonder. Almost completely recovered, she sat atop Old Auntie, clinging to the horse's back with her knees as she rummaged in her knapsack. As she rode, she'd pull out and caress her stones, smiling as she stroked them against her cheek. Feeling Todd's eyes upon her, she turned around so she rode backwards, facing him. She tilted her head like a bird and looked at him.

"Todd, did you have a mother and a father?" she asked. The others looked at her speechlessly. Lilibit had just broached one of the inviolate rules of the inmates of Dalton Point.

Lilibit waited patiently while an unnatural silence settled on the troop.

"Had to have them once," Todd answered shortly. "We all did."

Todd felt everyone's disappointment. They all wanted to

talk about it, but as usual, they waited for him to take the lead. He wished that opening the musty vaults of childhood wouldn't be another one of his responsibilities.

But maybe, perhaps more than food, this was exactly what they needed.

"I don't remember my mother," he offered quietly. "I kind of remember my father once telling me that she was an amazing woman who'd made some bad choices. I guess one of the choices was leaving my Dad and me. Mostly I remember driving around in a pickup truck with my Dad. Then one day he said I had to go to school. He dropped me off one morning and said he'd be back after school to pick me up." Todd's throat tightened. "He never did."

For several minutes, nothing was heard except the muffled clops of the horses' hooves. Todd didn't feel like sharing his vague memories of the last week with his father. Looking back, Todd could see his father had been worried about something and, in those last few days, had tried hard to hide that fear, but Todd had been only six years old and his trust in his father had been unwavering.

It had taken years before Todd stopped expecting his father to come back. At every squeaking door hinge, every sudden footstep, every stranger's shadow, Todd had turned, looking for his Dad. Then after a while, he stopped looking for him. Now even the memories of his face and voice had faded. All he had left was the cherished knife.

"Did he give you that knife?" Lilibit's voice cut through the haze of Todd's memories.

Looking at his hands, Todd hadn't even realized that he'd unsheathed his knife and was gently fingering the haft. He nodded.

The knife was a beautiful instrument. It might even have been expensive. The blade was gently curved at the point and honed on both edges. The haft looked to be sterling silver, though it was probably only silver plate, and was set with a mosaic of tiny turquoise and colored stones. For all of Todd's gypsy childhood, he had kept his knife hidden, a forbidden secret he never shared.

Until today.

"My parents were working in Manila," Devon's voice offered quietly.

Todd was grateful for the interruption, relieved to have the attention diverted from him.

"They left me with some cousins in Naircott." Devon reached down to pat the neck of his horse. "They got killed by some fanatics because they didn't believe in the same things. When my cousins had to move into a smaller apartment, I couldn't go with them."

Left unsaid was the confusion of a small boy who couldn't understand that his parents weren't coming home and the miserable feeling of being discarded. One way or another, they all knew those same feelings.

Except perhaps Lilibit. Her brow furrowed as she tried to absorb all the emotions and experiences the others spoke of. Memory of her life before Dalton Point was so fragmented and incomplete that she barely understood what it was she was missing. Todd saw the confusion in her eyes and wondered if she was to be envied or pitied.

"Don't know who my real Dad is," Marla announced abruptly. "He bugged out before I was born. My stepdad was a piece of work. When my teacher figured out what a number he was doing on me, she called Social Services and they pulled me out of there. The judge told Ma she had to choose between me or my stepdad. I haven't spoken to her since."

Marla clenched her stone tightly and her thoughts went inward. It was obvious the rest of her tale would be heard only by Ulex, who followed them far below, poling along a subterranean river.

"My Mom died when I was a baby." Nita seemed eager to share. "My Dad was a fisherman. I don't really remember what he looked like, but I remember his smell when he came home. The lady downstairs used to complain about that smell, but I loved it." Her grin faded before she spoke again. "He died in a storm at sea when I was four. *Mi abuelita,* my grandmother, she took care of me for a while, but then she got sick. She died about a year ago."

Silence fell.

"Lilibit?"

Lilibit glanced up to find Marla staring at her.

"Do you remember your parents?" Marla asked.

Lilibit shook her head with frustration. "Not a scrap."

"You're lucky," Jeff stated. Lilibit looked surprised at the bitterness in his voice. "My parents have six cars, three houses, five servants, and a dog. They've got everything they want in life, except a son."

"What were you doing at Dalton Point, then?" Marla asked.

"I got sentenced to Juvenile last year. I was at the Hardwell Center, but I got transferred." Jeff's smile aimed for smugness but missed.

"Sentenced? Did you actually commit a crime?" asked Nita, her eyes wide.

"Yup," answered Jeff. "I hacked into the corporate computers of Endrune and 'redirected' about three hundred thousand dollars into my own account."

"You did what?" snapped Todd.

"Why?" asked Devon.

"How?" asked Marla.

"What did you buy?"

The last question came from Lilibit, with complete disregard of the ethics of the situation.

"Lilibit!" Todd glared at her. When Lilibit shrugged innocently, Todd turned back to Jeff, who was still laughing at

Lilibit's question. "Dalton Point was a foster home not a halfway house. Why would they transfer you there?"

Jeff gloated with poorly concealed pride. "My social worker left me alone in her office for ten minutes with her computer. Stupid goat! By the time she got back, I'd hacked into her system and had already processed and approved my own transfer!"

Todd bit back an angry reply. It bothered him that Jeff had no remorse about having pushed some other kid out of Dalton Point and into Juvenile Hall.

It was funny though, Todd thought. Homeless, wandering, burdened with the responsibility of all the others, aching in body, and pursued by an unknown murderous enemy, he still felt luckier than those kids still back there trapped in the system.

The walls of the valley loomed higher and closer and the trail disappeared into a heavily wooded canyon. The midday sun grew hidden and dim as they entered the shadowed forest of the Canyon de la Muerte.

Their escape from Little Pine rankled the Director of Security. That a bunch of untrained brats with no apparent resources had managed to evade him tested his temper further than he could recall being pushed before. This was a personal affront to his expertise and he would not allow it to pass unheeded. The Director had not slept for two days but he was not tired. Adrenaline and determination had overridden biological survival instincts.

It did not concern him that the massive RV parked along a rural highway might attract attention from the locals. Working day and night, his subordinates came, left, and returned again, awed by his stamina, terrified by his temper. They scanned all resources, looking for a sign of the runaways: police reports, bank transactions, even traffic cameras. In the end, a weather satellite provided the key. And it was the Director himself reviewing the data, who picked up the infinitesimal blip that was originally identified as a small herd of wild mustangs, but which, upon closer examination, proved to be traveling in a manner quite unlike the way a pack of feral horses should behave.

Forgoing his usual helicopter reconnaissance teams, the Director hacked into the government's weather satellite's control system and directed its focus on the aberrant herd.

The Director smiled. Not only did he confirm the location of the truants, he quickly ascertained that they were heading into a box canyon. A dead end appropriately named Canyon de la Muerte.

Pausing only to transmit a status update to the absent Syxx, the Director mobilized two hundred operatives into ten ground Reclamation Teams. It might be considered excessive, but the Director would not allow any margin for error.

The children would be reclaimed today or they would be terminated. The Director could not decide which option would gratify him more.

Chapter Forty-two

The Dell of Bocarbolee

A dense canopy of leaves masked the bright morning sun. In the gloom, the air hung heavy with the smell of decaying foliage. The horses' legs waded through drifts of dead leaves as the trees above their heads creaked like old uncles rising to stand after a long dinner. All other sounds were hushed and muffled.

Weary and wary, the travelers plowed through the dusk and the musk of the woods.

They'd been forced to travel due north for the last few hours, unable to find any break in the foothills that might have led them eastward. Todd figured that this canyon might be their best bet to cut across, but as he looked around at the looming trees, he once again wondered if he'd made the right choice.

"Todd!" Marla was jittery. With a jerk of her head, she pointed to the trail behind them.

In front of them, the trail was narrow and clear, but behind them, Todd couldn't see any trace of the path they had just traveled. It was as if the forest had parted to let them enter, but then sealed their route behind them.

They rode silently, the dank murk of the forest stifling any chatter. Even Lilibit seemed spooked. Twice she squeaked when a branch brushed against her face.

Urging Midnight into a canter, Todd maneuvered so he rode directly behind Lilibit. Sure enough, the trees appeared to be moving, bending their branches to touch her as she passed. The contact was more of a caress than an attack, but since this was obviously frightening her, Todd guided Midnight to ride between Old Auntie and the trees. Lilibit shot Todd a grateful smile and he reached over to ruffle her hair.

For more than an hour, they rode silently through the trees.

A brightening ahead on the trail warned them of the clearing before they reached it. A wide grassy vale gleamed in the light and a broad sunbeam lanced through the trees, revealing a solitary figure standing on a small knoll. They gaped, amazed.

A magnificent elk stared back at the travelers; twenty-four points crowned its golden brown antlers. It gleamed bronze in the sunlight.

No one moved. Todd didn't think he even breathed. He lost count of the minutes. Finally, the Elk snorted and tossed his head.

"The Keepers of the Trees wish to speak to the Pilgrims of the Stone. Will you hear?"

Todd whipped his head around, looking to find who spoke, but saw only the others looking around as well. He then realized that, not only was it the Elk speaking, but he hadn't heard the voice with his ears.

"He said, 'The Keepers —'" began Donny.

"We heard," interrupted Todd. He looked at the elk and nodded slowly.

With that, the Elk pawed the ground three times and flicked his head sharply. He then backed down from the knoll to stand quietly at the edge of the trees. Softly at first, then building to a frenzy, the trees began to twitch and rustle. The horses whinnied with alarm when several dozen small figures fell into the grassy clearing, plopping like ripe fruit in a gentle breeze.

Some landed nimbly on their feet. Some landed awkwardly, tipping and wobbling like buoys on the tide. Several toppled over to land on their behinds, while a few dropped directly onto their behinds and then bounced back to their feet like clumsy acrobats.

They were a small and colorful people. The tallest was little more than two feet high; their clothes and their skin were striped and blocked with large bands of bright colors. Their eyes were exceptionally large and black, with pupils so large you could barely see the whites. On top of their heads, their brightly colored hair was pulled into tufts and decorated with colorful beads and painted acorns. They blinked curiously at the travelers and formed a ring along the edge of the clearing.

Todd didn't want to appear menacing so he hadn't pulled out his staff, but he did casually rest his hand on it. With all his attention focused on the Keepers, he wasn't prepared for the thud that hit him from behind.

Lilibit had leaped from the back of Old Auntie and onto Midnight, slamming into Todd's back and wrapping her arms around his waist.

Todd gave a grunt of surprise. Trembling, Lilibit buried her face into his back.

"What is it?" he asked in a whisper.

"I don't know." Her words were muffled into the back of his shirt.

Todd turned and faced the tree people. Wariness quickly replaced his first instinct of trust. He unsheathed his staff and urged Midnight to the lead, gesturing for the others to fall in behind him.

Sensing the change in Todd's attitude, the Keepers tensed. They huddled closer to the Elk and buzzed anxiously among themselves.

A rustling in the woods heralded the arrival of another stranger. The Keepers of the Trees hushed and turned expectantly toward the quivering brush.

The man emerging from the foliage at first looked even smaller than the other Keepers, but Todd quickly realized that was because he was very old and bent with age. His spine was so bowed, he looked like he was wearing a backpack. In his hand, he carried a staff of living wood. While the shaft was worn and seemed to be stained from ages of handling, fresh leaves sprouted from its tip and an exotic-looking flower grew from the very top like an amethyst crown. The patches of color on his face and tunic were faded and grayer than those of the other Keepers, and the tufts on his head sagged like the branches of an overladen Christmas tree. His eyes roamed slowly over each of the travelers, and he paid no more attention to Lilibit, peeking around Todd's back, than any of the others. His gaze fixed on Todd, who returned his stare with what he hoped was confidence. When the little man spoke, his voice was high and raspy, with a singsong cadence.

"Bocarbolee is the name of me. Elder of Keepers of the Trees. Welcome us give to the Children of Stone. Sit with us! Eat with us! Come rest your bones!"

A snort of mirth from Jeff drew a withering glance from Todd, but the others were too amazed by the strangeness of the Keepers to laugh at the Bocarbolee's odd speech. Even

Lilibit peered intently at the little old man. Peeking around from Todd's back, she stopped trembling but did not loosen her grip.

While Todd didn't want to discount Lilibit's instincts, he couldn't sense any threat from the tree people. And the offer of food was tempting: the extra day recuperating after the attack of the monster snake had depleted the food in their packs. He looked over at the others before turning to speak to Bocarbolee.

"The Children of the Stone thank the Keepers of the Trees," Todd said slowly. The formality of his speech seemed somehow appropriate. "And we would like to eat with you. If you please."

His unintentional rhyme made Todd grimace and Jeff rolled his eyes in disgust, but the consequences were as dramatic as they were unexpected. The tree people began to laugh and clap. Some rolled on the ground, holding their sides. Some pulled out flutes or drums or musical pipes and began to play a cacophony of notes that, while there was no definite melody or tune, seemed to harmonize with the laughter and the sounds of the woods. One little female bounded up to land on Midnight's neck and pushed her nose directly into Todd's face.

"Good! Good! You be so clever!" She laughed into his face. "Friends we shall be! Forever and ever!"

With that, she jumped off the horse, tugging at Todd's

arm as she fell, pulling him from Midnight's back to land with a thud on the ground. Looking around, he saw the others were also being pulled off their horses. The tree people danced around them, laughing.

Lilibit alone hung back from all the merrymaking. Walking with the horses as the little people led the travelers down a newly opened path, she scowled at anyone who dared come near her.

The Director did not squint at the desert glare. He tolerated no weakness around him, not even from his own eyes. The convoy of all-terrain vehicles he led ripped a wide scar across the fragile desert landscape. As the mouth of the Canyon de la Muerte came into view, his earpiece buzzed in his ear: his units were moving into place. Strategically located along the rim of the canyon, they encircled the perimeter, tightening the noose around the fugitive children.

The convoy rolled to a halt at the mouth of the canyon. The trees were dense, their branches intertwining only a foot or so from the forest floor. A network of vines wove a web reinforcing the screen of foliage and creating a living wall of timber.

The Director's ATV roared north and south, from one wall of the canyon to the other, but he found no breach. He knew the children must have entered the canyon, but it was as if the woods had closed up behind them, swallowing all traces of their trail.

The Director would not be thwarted by the forest. From the rear of the convoy, a salvo of bulldozers rolled to the vanguard. With a grim smile, the Director gave the order to proceed: the forest would yield to the will of the Director.

The Dell of Bocarbolee was breathtaking, and yet Lilibit had no trouble breathing. She shuffled along in a sullen silence while the others whispered their admiration as the dense woods again yielded to an even larger, sunnier meadow.

A sprightly stream bubbled cheerfully through tall grass. Huge weeping willow trees ringed the clearing, their branches softly brushing the ground. Hanging within the branches of the willows, small yet elaborate nests hung like huge walnuts, their walls woven from the living willow branches, their round windows fashioned from twigs and leaves. Small hatches on the bottoms of the nests served as entries and vine ladders hung from these openings. As they entered the Dell, many little people climbed out of the windows and swung on tree limbs, clamoring to catch a glimpse of the visitors.

In the center of the Dell, an enormous, golden weeping willow towered above the rest; its glistening branches arched gracefully, looking more like a fountain sparkling with sunlight than the living tree it was. Dozens of woven nests filled its limbs, connected by swinging bridges made of vines and branches. Banners of many colors attached to the stems of the nests draped like tresses to intertwine with the branches or to flap gently in the breeze.

Lilibit watched fuming as the little female Keeper who called herself Sillisoso attached herself to Todd and appeared to be amusing him with her rhymes. As they sat under the golden willow, Lilibit was certain they had forgotten all about her. She hung back, standing outside the wall of willow branches while the travelers and the Keepers sat down to eat.

As Lilibit watched, she saw Todd glance around to check on the others. His back straightened when he didn't find Lilibit on his first scan, but then he glimpsed her through the dangling branches and his attitude relaxed into annoyance. With a twitch of his head, he gestured for her to join them and Lilibit saw his irritation grow when she shook her head to answer no.

Todd turned an exasperated shoulder on Lilibit and went back to listening to Nita, who was making up silly songs to the wild melodies Sillisoso played, much to the delight of the tree people.

Lilibit plopped herself among the willows and began to weave herself a bower of branches and self-pity.

"Why do you not join the others in the feast?" she heard a low voice whisper. Lilibit turned to find the Elk standing near her, gazing at her with huge brown eyes. For several moments, Lilibit ignored the question, plaiting the twigs of willows, waiting for the Elk to go away. On her back, Lilibit felt the warmth of his breath and the patience of his gaze.

"I don't know," Lilibit said at last.

"There is naught to fear from the Keepers of the Trees." The words of the Elk appeared in her mind. "They have no malice to any who do not threaten their woods and few powers to wield except their music and their laughter."

Lilibit turned back to peek at the group laughing and singing around the mounds of fruits and nuts and tubers they shared. As she watched, Devon was pulled to his feet by a little laughing Keeper who pulled out his flute and piped a tune while encouraging the boy to dance.

The image of Devon being tugged along triggered a memory within Lilibit. Something about being cold and wet and frightened and wanting so much to trust the colorful little man who pulled at her hand just like the way Devon was being pulled. She felt a surge of terror as she remembered a bolt of excruciating pain. She needed to warn Devon. She scrambled to her feet and was about to run to him when a hand landing on her shoulder recalled an agonizing memory. She screamed.

Todd snapped his hand back from Lilibit's shoulder like

he'd been stung. He had seen the Elk standing with Lilibit, and though he wasn't worried about her, he thought she had sulked alone quite long enough and it was time for her to rejoin the others. But the touch of his hand startled her and she screamed long and loud. When she turned to him, she looked like a hunted animal. On impulse, he put out his arms to her, and when the panic faded, she pounced on him, wrapping her arms around his waist, trembling.

The Dell was hushed. The sound of Lilibit's cry had pierced the hodgepodge of music and laughter and had stunned all the celebrants into a bewildered silence.

The Elk too was stunned. His experience with humans was limited and he was unable to decide which astounded him more: that the small girl projected her memories so vividly or that, in the past, she had crossed paths with a Keeper who walked among the world of men. That she associated this Keeper with a distress and betrayal too intense for her mind to accept triggered a great dismay within the heart of the Elk. With a deafening trumpet, he reared on his hind legs, causing the boy to turn his body to shield the girl. The hooves sliced the air above their heads.

As the Elk's hooves touched the ground, he pivoted on the turf and galloped out of the Dell. If a renegade Keeper was consorting with the Enemy, then he must be found. And found quickly.

The sun was low on the horizon. The shadows of the sa-guaro pointed long accusing fingers at the machinery as-saulting the edge of the Forest. The roar of their engines and the stench of their fumes smothered the peace of the Woods.

And yet the Forest would not yield.

No sooner was a tree felled or an area cleared, than the Forest appeared to rebound, refilling the void, giving no quarter, surrendering not an inch.

And the Forest fought back.

Three bulldozers, two chippers, and a 1070D Harvester had already fallen victims to the trees. Vines, swinging le-thargically in the breeze, haphazardly twined around the ax-les and weaved their way into the gear shafts, using the machines' own momentum to rip the cogs apart. Branches like arboreal kamikazes plunged from the crests of the tree-tops to impale the lumbering invaders.

The Director had long since passed the point of being puzzled. Even frustration was behind him. All that was left was an ice-cold anger that burned and a fiery determination that froze. He buried the excuses of the squad foreman with one glacial glare that left the man stuttering and sweating.

The Director gave the order for the machinery to with-draw. He then grabbed a tank filled with petrol. With a wrench of his wrist, he twisted off the top and tossed the cap away. He strode determinedly to the closest ATV and, with one swift motion, grabbed the operator and heaved him out of the driver's seat.

The foreman watched in confusion as the Director doused the ATV with the fuel, slammed it into gear, and drove it full tilt into the Woods.

The trees seem to part as if to allow the Director's vehicle to enter the sanctum of the Forest, only to seal immediately behind him.

The silence at the canyon mouth lasted only seconds. The blast of the detonation blew engine parts and tree limbs in all directions, scattering flaming wreckage at the feet of the troops. They stood stunned, uncertain what to do next.

Black smoke poured out of the smoldering wound of the Forest. Then the flames parted and the Director stepped from the inferno, flecked with ash yet unscathed. He scowled as he walked to his minions before turning to look back at the Forest.

"Burn it," he ordered. "Burn it to the ground."

Once again seated beneath the willow, Todd avoided the eye of Bocarbolee. He had no answers to the Old One's questions. What made Lilibit cry out? Why was she afraid of the Keepers? And what had driven the Elk from the Dell?

Sillisoso told them the Elk was their last liaison to the world beyond the canyon and Bocarbolee was worried that the Elk might not return.

Creaking like a tree, Bocarbolee stood to speak. A quiet fell over the Dell, and although his voice was soft and scratchy, it carried far in the hush.

"Thank you, new friends, for sharing our food.
Our stomachs are full; we all feel renewed.
Yet pause for a moment to hear our sad tale,
For we pray your assistance will help us prevail,
For the tale of the Keepers is a tale of the ages,
And to tell all of it here would take pages and
  pages.
So here in a nutshell I speak of our plight,
Of betrayal and murder and the onset of night."

By the crackling light of the campfire, Todd could see Lilibit's fears slip away as they all became engrossed in the tale told by Bocarbolee. His voice grew stronger as he continued.

"In an earlier time, countless eons gone past,
The Keepers were many, the Forest was vast,
The Earth Mother listened, the Creator would
  speak,

The Stones they were strong, the Enemy, weak.
The Stone Voice would serve the Earth Stone
*   with trust*
And speak for the People with words wise and
*   just."*

The mention of the Stone Voice caught Todd's attention. Jeff perked with interest too, and Marla leaned over to
whisper into Todd's ear, "Do you think that Lilibit — "

"Later." Todd cut her off. It was not the time for those
questions.

"Yet crept like a viper, the Deceiver did enter,
And counsel the Stone Voice, a most evil mentor.
She turned from the Earth Stone and turned from
*   her calling,*
And blind was the Earth Mother; the balance was
*   falling.*
Now the path to extinction is long but unchecked,
And if nothing is changed, we shall pass from
*   neglect.*
The Woods will fall barren; the land, it will die.
Not even mankind will this fate deny.
Our one hope is seeded, a Stone Voice will rise
For years, we have watched for the signs in the
*   skies.*

*Now the stars are our herald, and our hope once
more springs.
The sky is reopened, the Earth once more sings.
For the rise of a Stone Voice is the last hope for
the trees.
So we beg the young Stone Pilgrims to carry our
pleas,
For the Heart of the Forest, the Stone of the Dell
Still dwells in the canyon, but casts a dim spell."*

With that, Bocarbolee tapped the butt of his staff lightly
on the ground. The pale purple blossom on its apex slowly
unfurled to reveal a small gray crystal. The stone glowed
with a faint violet light shining from its core.

*"Here in the scepter of Bocarbolee
Lies the heartstone, Quaba-ho, the soul of the
trees.
Yet as dark grows the Stone Voice, so too the stone
pales,
And the fear of the Keepers is soon it will fail.
But if a new Stone Voice rises, a new age will
dawn.
The Forests will thrive; the Earth will go on.
So to you, young pilgrims, we wish you great
speed,*

That you may carry to Kiva the news of our need.
Please tell the new Stone Voice, a new stone is
  needed,
And we pray our request will not go unheeded.
Rest now, young pilgrims, for tomorrow comes
  soon,
And your path to the Stone is pain- and thorn-
  strewn.
Sleep deeply and safely in the peace of the Dell.
The Keepers shall guard you, and all shall be well."

Chapter Forty-three

Flight from the Flames

Todd didn't remember falling asleep. He didn't remember being covered with his blanket nor the large foamy mushroom being placed under his head as a pillow.

Some noise was waking him up. At first, his head, still fuzzy with dreams, tried to ignore all the racket, but when he remembered where he was, he rolled to his feet, staff in hand.

A faint smell of smoke hung over the Dell and Todd saw plumes of black striping the starlit sky. The Keepers rushed to and fro in a panic, pulling their nests down from the willows and carrying them into the Woods toward the canyon walls. As Todd woke the others, he heard a high voice squeaking frantically at him.

"Hurry! Hurry! Arise! Awake! The Woods are afire! Haste we must make!"

Todd turned to see Sillisoso bouncing toward them, her arms flapping, her eyes darting frantically. "Close your mouth! No time to gape! The Dell is on fire! This way to escape!"

She grabbed Todd's hand and started to pull him toward the cliff walls on the eastern edge of the Dell. Todd shook her off for a moment to help the others get their gear together. Sillisoso jumped up and down with impatience, bouncing from her feet to fall on her behind and then rebounding back to her feet again. In a very few moments, the travelers were packed and running behind the frantic Sillisoso, placing their feet carefully to avoid tripping over the mob of Keepers bounding among them.

"The caves of the canyon will provide us safe haven; I'll guide you there swiftly, I swear by the Raven!"

The branches of the trees parted to create a tunnel through the dense forest. At first, the smoke seemed to be lessening as they headed east, but when a new path opened in front of them, a cloud of thick ash preceded the appearance of another band of Keepers, Bocarbolee at the lead.

"The flame of the Enemy, it burns on all sides! Between us and the havens, the flame it divides!" Bocarbolee gasped, his face smeared with soot.

The Woods, knowing the fire to be on all sides, would not open another path for the refugees. The trees stood tall against the enemy inferno, but all knew in the end they would fall. As smoke began to roll along the ground between the besieged trees, the Keepers began coughing and stumbling. Since they were shorter, the fumes were overtaking them sooner.

A startled yelp made Todd turn just in time to see the top of Marla's head disappear into the ground. Sprinting to the spot where she'd stood only moments before, he looked into a small gaping hole that had opened on the forest floor. There, glowing faintly in the murk of the pit, stood Ulex with Marla where she had landed in his arms.

"Down the hole! Quick!" exclaimed Todd.

The Keepers hadn't waited for Todd's invitation. They were already bounding into the cavern, bouncing and rolling down the sloping floor of the cave. It was only a drop of about ten or fifteen feet, and most of the travelers landed neatly on their feet, but Devon wavered uncertainly on the rim. Todd reached out his arms and helped him land. A quick head-count made Todd realize they were short one.

"Hey! Where's Donny?" asked Jeff, glancing around the cave and up the opening. "Donny!"

"The horses! The horses!" The faint ring of Donny's voice echoed down into the cavern.

Like a slap, Todd remembered the horses. There was no way they could fit down the small hole and the flames were closing in. Smoke began pouring down the opening, rolling along the cavern floor like a slow flood.

"Leave the horses!" Jeff yelled. "There's nothing you can do for them!"

"No!" There was a ring of strength in Donny's voice the others had never heard before.

Todd glanced around, desperate for inspiration. He saw Marla, her eyes locked with Ulex's.

"Move away from the opening," Marla ordered, her eyes still fixed on Ulex.

Most of the Keepers had already darted down the tunnel, anxious to escape the smoke and flames. Bocarbolee and Sillisoso stood by with a few other Keepers, gawking in terror at Ulex, torn between their fear of this towering horror and their pledge to guard the children. With a gesture, Todd led them all deeper into the tunnel. They turned to see Ulex step to the wall closest to the opening and place his quartz white hand against the stone face. Immediately, a vein of white mineral grew from his fingertips and branched out along the wall like a rapidly growing creeper of crystal. When it reached the opening, the rock wall of the cave began to change. To the eyes of the travelers, it appeared as if the rock itself turned to clay, only to be molded by hundreds of invisible hands. The opening gaped wider and the wall of the cave expanded to form a rude ramp of rock leading steeply but surely to the cavern floor. As the opening grew, the travelers could see Donny trying to calm the terrified horses, smoke draping them, flames rising behind.

"C'mon, Donny!" yelled Marla. "Lead them down here! Now!"

Donny needed no further encouragement. Old Auntie, the dappled gray mare, was the first, trotting gingerly down the ramp, followed by the foals and the others. Last was Donny with the golden stallion, rushing down the slope amid a wave of dense black smoke. The stallion's tail no sooner cleared the opening than the hole began to seal.

For a moment, only the dim glow of Ulex could be seen in the smoky cavern, but then a glimmer of light flickered and grew. Sillisoso's eyes widened in amazement. The light of Ewa-Kwan showed brilliantly in the palm of Lilibit, much brighter than it had in the labyrinth of the Nether Rock. Despite the dense smoke still hanging in the air, Ulex was forced to close his auxiliary eyelids to protect from the glare.

Todd sighed. He had hoped his suspicions that Lilibit might be the Stone Voice would not be apparent to the Keepers. His instincts told him the less others knew about Lilibit's rapport with her stones, the safer it would be for all of them.

By the light of Ewa-Kwan, Lilibit beamed proudly up at Todd. He shook his head and smiled back ruefully. Wiping the soot from his face, he followed Ulex through the tunnel and away from the flames.

From the rim of the canyon wall, the Director of Security watched the inferno surge and envelope the entire forest. He permitted himself a sigh of pleasure. His satisfaction at destroying the children in the blaze was only increased by his delight in watching the flames consume the insolent woodland. He would wait until the fire burned out and then he would locate the charred corpses in the ashes. Only then would he contact Syxx and confirm that the mission had been accomplished. And while it was true Dr. Nil at the Institute would be furious at the loss of her research subject, he knew Syxx would infinitely prefer the termination of all of the troublesome truants.

The flames flickered warm on his face as the Director waited patiently for the blaze to abate.

Todd rubbed at his hair nervously; his scalp crawled with a vague warning. With a wave of his fingers, he hushed the other travelers to silence. Bocarbolee and the Keepers fell silent as well: stone warriors who could beckon the aid of the terrifying Ulex were not to be ignored.

Ulex's maze of caverns had led them to an opening that sat high in the face of one of the cliffs that overlooked the canyon. The travelers could not know that a scarce thirty feet above them stood the predatory Director, but Todd was learning to trust his instincts, and his intuition told him that danger was very close.

They watched in silence as the fire consumed the Woods. Tears poured down Marla's cheeks and Nita muffled her sobs by burying her face into Todd's sleeve. In their own ways, the others grieved as well. Before their eyes, the glories of the Dell and the Golden Willows passed into ashes.

"Grieve not for the trees, for the Woods will return, for the Heart of the Forest the flames cannot burn," whispered Bocarbolee soberly. "So long as Quaba-ho glows in the Vale, the flame of the Enemy will never prevail. The trees will return, the Forests rebound, and once more the willows will spring from the ground."

Todd met Bocarbolee's sad but knowing smile with a nod of his head. He then turned and led the travelers through the tunnels, out of the Canyon de la Muerte.

A solitary condor pierced the plumes of smoke rising above the inferno of the Canyon de la Muerte.

Keotak-se knew the fire raging below had been set by the Enemy. Dread rose in his throat and threatened to choke him. That the Enemy had set a snare of flames to purge the Woods could only mean it thought the children to be in the canyon.

As a bird, Keotak-se landed on a ledge of the canyon wall far above the blaze. As a man, he splayed his fingers on the rock, querying the stone, beseeching the Earth for the answer to the question darkening his soul. The Earth Stone's response brought joy to his heart and the ghost of a smile to his jaw.

The Infant Stone Voice still lived.

"CHEE-ot-say. Toh-GEE-na. Sha-be-KAH." Keotak-se took wing and resumed his quest.

The sun was high in the sky when the travelers reached the mouth of the caverns. With Ulex at the lead, they had passed under the mountains and now they stood overlooking a broad expanse of the grassy plains. Todd decided they should rest underground for the rest of the afternoon. It would be safer to move at night.

Hours ago, the Keepers, who were familiar with the caves, had parted to go their own way. They would find a new valley hidden from men, and there they could replant their willows.

Night was full up when the travelers led the horses out of the caves. Mounted, they waited while Marla parted from Ulex. Trickster tossed his head and gave a snort of disgust.

"I'm with you on this one," muttered Jeff from his back. "C'mon, Marla! It's not like you'll never see him again!"

Marla turned to glare at Jeff. Quickly Todd bent to pat Midnight's neck. He agreed with Jeff but didn't have the heart to cut short her lingering — and maudlin — farewell.

After a moment, Marla emerged from the cave, strutting in a huff, and mounted her horse in a smooth heave powered by her annoyance.

It was a moonless night, but the stars were bright enough to cut the gloom and light a path for the travelers.

"Todd!" whispered Devon urgently, gesturing behind him.

Looking back, Todd saw they left no trail as the horses waded through the tall grass. The land was covering their tracks as quickly as they were laid.

The boots of the Director crushed the slaughtered foliage as he tramped through the vanquished forest.

A weary dog wrangler, blackened by soot from head to toe, approached the Director. An anxious canine pulled at his arm and defeat pulled at his face. The Director did not wait to hear the words of the searcher. The failure of the wrangler's eyes to meet his own told him of the failure of the dogs to find any trace of the children.

A black rage clouded his eyes. A vicious kick sent the dog yelping through the air.

The children had escaped.

The Director felt cold eyes boring into his shoulders. Turning and looking upward, he saw Syxx standing on the rim of the precipice.

Anger fled and with it all vestiges of frustration and brutality.

All that was left within the Director was fear.

Chapter Forty-Four

Passage Through Cow Town

Dawn was just a sliver hinting over the mountains. They'd ridden through the night over broad grassy plains and, despite the darkness, Todd had felt dangerously exposed under the clear, starry sky. Now, with the arrival of morning, his scalp twitched anxiously. They needed to find a place to hide out the daylight hours.

A farmhouse sat alone on a slight hill in the middle of acres of fields. But Todd wasn't ready to risk being seen. They skirted it with a wide margin and saw a ramshackle barn at the far end of a cow pasture.

The cows eyed them warily as they crossed the paddocks. A large bull threatened with a snort and much scraping of his hooves, but Donny let out a rumble that sounded like a deep sneeze and the herd calmed down.

"Jeff? Is this Cow Town?" Nita asked in a very audible whisper.

"What are you talking about?" Jeff snapped, his attention on the temporarily docile bull he was passing.

"You said we all Cow Town to Todd. Is this Cow Town?" Devon hiccupped a giggle.

Jeff looked at Nita coldly. "Nita. Don't think. Don't speak. Just ride."

The barn was smelly, decrepit, but empty. No one complained as they settled in to wait out the sunlight.

Joshua Blackbear stood on his front porch and kicked at the peeling paint rippling free of the railing. Today might just be his last chance to reap the grain from the Cross Creek Field before the frost set in, but to his mind, he already had more than enough grain stowed away to last the winter for himself, his family, and his neighbors. To pull in any more was just greedy. He'd just as soon leave it for the feathered and furry folk to enjoy. Time and plenty to tend to the cattle later as well. A Good Book was calling to him from the kitchen table and he was turning back to answer that call when a speck of movement caught his eye in the distance. He stood still for a long hushed moment while he watched the trespassers trek across the outskirts of his homestead.

Esther stepped out on to the porch, drawn by the silent stillness of her husband. A long quiet descended as they stared unmoving at the specks on the horizon.

"Might be them runaways we saw on the television," said Joshua after a long pause.

Esther grunted faintly. Another lengthy silence ensued.

"Well, I best be making that phone call," commented Joshua, turning to walk back into the house.

Esther watched for another long moment before grunting again and following her husband back into the house. She never minded the fact he was the chatty one. Someone had to be the listener.

Chapter Forty-Five

Sanctuary of the Morning Star

The travelers watched impatiently as the day slowly faded into night. Their stomachs grumbled. There'd been no time when they left the Dell to grab more supplies and no chance since to replenish. They mounted in the dusk.

"Todd!" Devon called, pointing to the sky. "Look!"

A black cloud fluttered on the horizon. Todd smiled. Dozens of ravens flittered in circles before heading off to the northeast.

"A murder of crows," Jeff muttered.

"What?" Todd turned to glare at Jeff.

"That's what you call a flock of crows," he answered. "A murder of crows."

Todd stared at the birds. "And what do you call a bunch of ravens?"

It was Marla who answered. "A beacon," she said, smiling. "A beacon of ravens."

Todd hoped she was right. He nudged Midnight toward the disappearing flock and the others followed.

From where they were hidden under a sparse grove of juniper trees, they could see the lights of a rural village. It was the kind of town that had most people in their own homes as soon as the sun went down. Not one person could be seen walking the darkened streets. Todd was worried. They would have been less noticeable in a crowd, but they needed food.

"Put me in, coach!" Jeff offered. "If you can get me to an Internet terminal, I know I can block them so we can at least get some cash out."

"How can you do that?" asked Todd.

Jeff's eyes lit with a manic delight. He was scary when he was planning complicated mayhem. "I'll jump their security barriers and dump a virus into their database. They'll have to shut down for at least ten minutes to reboot and resecure the system. We'll time it so that you're at the ATM machine when I crash their network. Then —"

"Okay, okay!" Todd had heard enough. "Five more minutes of your plotting and you'll probably have someone scaling buildings or swinging on trapezes!"

Jeff thought for a moment. "Yeah, I could work that in."

They left the horses grazing on the outskirts. Even

though the locals would ride into town as readily on a horse as in a car, Todd worried that the lack of saddles and bridles might be too noticeable. Donny was whispering something to Horse.

"Will they stay?" Todd asked Donny. "Do you think they'll be here when we get back?"

Donny nodded. "Uh-huh," he said, with a final pat to Horse's muzzle. "He says they will serve."

Todd looked closely at Donny as he walked away from the horses. It was as if the horses were giving him a strange new confidence. "What is that all about?" Todd whispered to Horse. Horse just snorted a raspberry at him and bent his head to graze.

The town — if such a small cluster of buildings could be called a town — did not have a real library. The sheriff's office shared a space with the post office and a modest collection of books in the back of the post office was deemed the Town Library. It was just as unlikely there would be a public computer terminal in that building as it was that Todd would lead their band directly into the sheriff's office to find out.

As they peered at it from the shadows across the street, uncertain what to do next, a dour voice called to them.

"You children look hungry," the voice stated.

In the doorway of a quiet diner, a short plump woman

stood, her arms folded strong across her chest, the apron of her uniform soiled from a long day of waiting tables.

"Will you be needing a bite to eat." It wasn't a question.

"Yes, please!" chirped Lilibit, perking up at the thought of food. "I'm starving!" She cast such a look of angelic misery, the face of the waitress lightened into a near smile.

Todd reached out to grab Lilibit and pulled her behind him. "Thanks, but no thanks."

"Todd!" Lilibit rolled her eyes.

"We have no money!" Todd whispered at her between gritted teeth.

"I didn't ask you for your money, proud boy." The woman stared at Todd for a moment before she turned and walked back into the restaurant. The sign would have read "Morning Star Diner" if it didn't have so many lights out. "Come along, then," she called, not looking back.

Lilibit scurried into the door before Todd could stop her. Warily Todd followed with the others.

Lilibit climbed onto the bench of a vinyl booth. A handful of locals were scattered in the diner. Their skin was brown and baked by the sun, much like the land they tilled. If they looked at the newcomers at all, it was with only casual interest. They turned back to their coffee cups and the dregs of their conversations long before the travelers were seated. Todd relaxed. He felt no threat in the diner.

Lilibit's request for four peanut butter and pickle sandwiches drew no apparent surprise from the waitress as she jotted down the orders and turned back to the counter to deliver them to the kitchen.

"Thanks, Connie!" called Jeff with a wink.

The waitress turned a baleful eye on Jeff. Devon and Nita giggled but then quickly fell silent when she looked over at them.

"How did you know her name was Connie?" asked Lilibit, puzzled.

"Because I'm psychic!" intoned Jeff in a mystic whisper.

"Oh," said Lilibit naively.

Again Devon and Nita giggled. Marla stepped in to explain. "He read her nametag, Lilibit."

"Really?" exclaimed Lilibit in awe.

The others laughed, but Todd just shook his head. Lilibit's limited experience made clairvoyance much more plausible than literacy. That the letters Devon had taught her could convey knowledge was far more miraculous to her than talking stones or glowing rocks.

They chatted and joked quietly through their short supper. It would have been pleasant to linger, but Todd itched to get moving.

"Thank you, Connie!" Lilibit exclaimed loudly, drawing the eyes of all the diners. Her voice rang with a seed of pride for learning her name from her written tag. Connie's cheeks ticked with the hint of a smile as she handed a large paper bag to the travelers.

Todd stuttered a thank-you. The bag was full of sandwiches and fruit, enough for several days. He did not know why the woman was helping them and his gratitude was deeper for it.

"Thanks," he said quietly. "We'll pay you back someday."

It was just a sop to his pride, but her response surprised him.

"Yes, you will," she stated quietly.

They had turned to walk out onto the street when a large dark figure filled the doorway. Todd's eyes froze on the silver star on his shirt. He was aware that the big man was looking closely at the travelers, taking more notice than Todd felt comfortable giving. With a mumbled farewell, they hurried past the sheriff, down the street, and back to the horses.

The sheriff stood woodenly, staring out the window of the diner, watching the children scurry into the night. Unlatching his walkie-talkie from his belt, he activated it with a grip and a chirp.

"O'Quette to base," he barked.

"Go ahead, Oak." The response scratched back after a pause.

"Think I got us a twenty on those runaways. Over."

"Copy."

"They're out by Sand Canyon, heading south toward Snake River. Over."

"Ten four. I'll notify State. Out."

The sheriff stood watching out the window for a moment before walking over and taking his regular stool at the counter. A cup of black coffee waited for him, patiently steaming.

"Good eyes there, Oak," Connie said tonelessly as she pulled two cheese Danish from a glass cake bin on the counter.

"Just doing my job, Connie," Oak mumbled, pouring sugar into his cup.

"Real good eyes," said Connie.

A weighty silence descended as she watched the sugar pour like a waterfall into a bottomless lake. Oak finished his pouring before meeting Connie's eyes.

"Just doing my job."

Chapter Forty-six

The Moose Tightens

Secure within the confines of the Central Command RV, the Director gave vent to the anger and frustration he had controlled all night. Turning on the travel stove, he placed his hand over the lit burner. The flame stroked his palm and calmed his rage. He smiled. These setbacks were incidental. In the end, they would succeed. Nothing could eclipse the power of his master, Syxx.

Once more in control of his temper, he studied the map of the surrounding territory. Dozens of flags dotted the chart, each representing a reported sighting of the truants. From the evidence in front of him, the only answer could be that there were two dozen groups of children on horseback wandering about the region. Either that or the fugitives were able to disappear and rematerialize.

This last operation had been a fiasco. The intell they'd received about Sand Canyon had seemed reliable at the time. Called in by a county sheriff. They'd mobilized all the crews and found nothing. The teams had fanned out and canvassed around the canyon in a two-mile radius and couldn't find a sign that the quarry had been anywhere near there.

"They have entered Reservation Territory."

The Director turned and found Syxx standing at the rear of the RV. He had not heard him enter nor could he understand how he'd gotten past him, yet this was not the moment for those questions.

Syxx walked past him to the map. "They are among the People of the Land. They conspire against us. You cannot trust the reports you receive from those sources."

The Director raised an eyebrow. He would not dare to contradict Syxx, but it seemed unlikely to him there could be a movement that well-orchestrated among such a rural area.

If Syxx saw the doubts in the Director's eyes, he did not choose to address it. Instead, he pointed to a portion of the map, the northeast sector, that had the least sightings flagged.

"Concentrate your search in this area. I will be conducting my own search and will be checking in on your progress."

Syxx stepped back from the map as the Director moved

forward to examine the territory indicated. "To what degree should we conceal our presence?" he asked.

When he received no response, he turned to face Syxx, but he was alone.

Chapter Forty-seven

Dry Creek Crossing

In the plains of Dry Creek, one hundred and sixty miles north of Sand Canyon, the riders pulled up from a gallop. Todd smiled as Lilibit laughed and hugged Old Auntie's neck. They all felt the same; as if Kiva might be just over the next ridge. In his pocket, Tai-Kwee buzzed joyfully.

They had ridden through the night and the sky was beginning to lighten. Both the horses and their riders were breathing hard, yet Todd could see they were eager to keep going. But he still didn't feel safe galloping over the sweeping grasslands in the full light of day, so he scanned the landscape looking for a place to shelter.

A small grassy hill had a rocky outcropping on its northern face. The travelers huddled beneath the narrow ledge. Donny sent the horses off to a distant field to rest and graze.

They had just settled in when the first helicopter appeared on the horizon. They did not move, they did not speak, they barely breathed.

Keotak-se waged a small war against his own fears, which threatened to blacken his vision. The need to find the children before the Enemy did drove him to search both night and day without rest. He could feel the Enemy approaching. His presence hung like a gray film over the pine-swathed mountaintops.

Keotak-se circled the Canyon del Muerte in ever increasing circuits yet found no trace of the children. It did not occur to him that the children had passed under the mountains rather than over them, nor did he perceive the earth healing the scars of their trail as quickly as they passed.

He landed on a rocky precipice and looked out over the vast grassy plains that rolled from the edge of the Pine Mountains to the foot of the Stone Mountains. For the children to have gotten even this far was so improbable, Keotak-se assumed some greater force must be guiding their steps. Perhaps he would find some sign of them in the northeast, in those plains that stood between the Pine Mountains and the mountains of Kiva.

From the cusp of the cliff, Keotak-se threw himself off, indulging in the sensation of a freefalling dive before transforming into the condor and sailing off to the northeast.

To search. To find. To prevail.

Failure was not an option.

Crouched against the rock, the travelers watched impatiently as the sun crept slowly toward the mountains. Though they had closed their eyes and rested, they hadn't really slept.

Even though the sun was not quite set, Todd told Donny to call the horses. They hadn't seen another helicopter all afternoon. The only stranger in the sky had been a very large bird they sighted hours ago. It had passed more than a mile away and they had seen nothing unusual since.

Todd knew it might be dangerous to travel while the light was still up, but the roots of his hair were itching to move and they'd got this far by trusting his instincts. He wasn't going to ignore them now.

Todd couldn't tell if the horses ran faster because they sensed a threat in the air or if they were just picking up the riders' fears, but for whatever reason, they almost flew across the hilly plains. Yet as they had reached the top of a tall rise, they all stopped, awed at the view.

The mountains before them were close enough now to make out the details. To the north ruled a towering peak capped with snow. A ribbon of white sparkled along its southern face, marking a waterfall that cascaded into the hidden valley below. The two mountains to the east and west weren't nearly as tall. One was green and lush; the other, rocky and barren. And the fourth mountain, to the south, almost as tall as the northern mountain, looked eerie and dark and was draped with swirling clouds and shadowy mists. Connecting the mountains were palisades of red stone cliffs that had been eroded into hoodoos, statuelike pillars standing shoulder-to-shoulder, glinting purple in the dusk.

Todd slid off his horse and walked forward a few steps, as if the few extra feet would help him see better. These were the mountains he'd seen in his dreams and he was certain that, whatever Kiva was, it would be there in the valley between those mountains.

"Is that Kiva?" he heard Donny ask.

Todd turned to face the others. They too had dismounted and stood staring at the mountains. Todd grinned. "Yes," he said. "That is Kiva."

Todd turned back to study the view, drinking in the details, knowing that these memories wouldn't fade from his mind the way they did in his dreams. He pulled out his map and tried to find the mountains on it, but there was nothing marked. It was as if the outside world had forgotten all about them. Or maybe they were hidden and only those people who knew what they were looking for could find them. He shoved his map back into his pack.

He saw Lilibit's shadow approaching. He looked down at her and her grin made him smile back. He picked her up and placed her on his shoulders. Together their shadow stretched from the grassy hill across the plains toward the feet of the Sienna Sentries. She lifted her arms as if the stone pillars were doting uncles and she was a toddler asking to be picked up. Todd laughed out loud.

So mesmerized by their first sight of Kiva, none of them noticed a large shadow streaking across the plains, heading directly for their grassy hill.

Chapter Forty-eight
The New Wave

Gil-Salla scattered crushed feldspar and dried cactus needles into her hearth, watching the flames leap, pink and gold, the colors of inquiry and welcome. While her eyes gazed into the flickering light, she studied the pledges as they sat nervously in her hall, their backs pressed against the earthen walls.

Oh, by the Stone! They are so young! It had been more than ten centuries since the Earth Stone had called a new generation of stone warriors, but Stars, she did not remember them being so young!

Young or not, she doubted there had ever been such a wave of neophytes that followed the Stone with such blind faith. While some of them were People of the Land and had heard the myths and legends of the Stone since infancy, most of the neophytes knew nothing of Stone Voices or stone warriors and had left their homes to follow the call blindly. The very existence of the Enemy was little more than a scary bedtime story to them. They had much to learn if they were to prove themselves worthy of the Stone.

The dormitory hogans had been prepared and the neophytes had divided themselves between the three halls. Ten centuries had passed, yet youth still fell into the same patterns, reenacted the same rituals. It would be interesting to see how the Infant Stone Voice dealt with their self-inflicted segregation.

The Infant Stone Voice. She was close — Gil-Salla could feel her — but she was not safe yet. Gil-Salla had little time to initiate the neophytes.

Raising her eyes to meet their gaze, she spoke to them briefly, hinting at the skills they must learn, the powers they may earn, and the fealty that they might be called upon to pledge. She then dismissed them and turned her mind to the hearth.

The Enemy was near, closer than she had felt him for centuries. He had grown stronger since their last meeting, feeding upon the corruption and decadence of mankind, thriving in the degradation of creation.

Gil-Salla could not leave Kiva to help search for the lost ones. All she could do was pray Keotak-se would find them before the Enemy did.

Chapter Forty-nIne

Sienna Shadows

A shadow passing before the sun was the first sign to the travelers that they were not alone. The horses snorted frantic whinnies and bolted off the hill in a panic.

With the sun at its back, Todd could see only the outline of a huge winged creature setting down on the crest of the hill. Brandishing his staff, Todd gestured for the others to get behind him. They watched, amazed, as the figure transformed and the silhouette of a man now stood where moments before had landed the winged intruder.

"Lilibit," called the stranger. His words rang like the knell of death in their ears.

Behind him, Todd felt Lilibit trembling. "I don't know you!" Her voice cracked in fear. "Go away."

"Lilibit," repeated the stranger.

There was a note in that voice that made Todd want to obey. He girded himself against that urge.

"I DON'T KNOW YOU!" screamed Lilibit. "GO AWAY! GO AWAY!"

"Lilibit," he called for the third time.

It was at that moment that the sun dropped below the Pine Mountains in the west. Now the travelers could clearly see the stranger. Todd was unsure whether it was the weathered brown of his face or the green mantle he wore over his tan leathers, but while he still looked like a man, he also seemed somewhat like a . . .

"TREE!" squealed Lilibit. Before Todd could stop her, Lilibit darted from behind him and, leaping high at the stranger, wrapped her arms around his neck and clung with her legs to his chest.

"I can't wait to see how she greets people she *does* know," Devon whispered.

The stranger gingerly detached Lilibit from his torso and placed her gently on the ground. His face was expressionless as he looked down at the grinning child, but Todd sensed strong emotions hiding beneath his stoicism.

"I am called Keotak-se. You have done well to have traveled this far. Now I will lead you to Kiva."

Todd felt heat rise in his face. This man's opinion shouldn't be important to him, but he was still flattered by the approval.

"I am . . . Todd." He winced. His name sounded lame in

his own ears. "Marla, Jeff, Donny, Devon, and Nita." He hoped his voice wasn't as sullen as it sounded to him. "Lilibit, evidently, you've met."

Keotak-se nodded to each of the travelers. "We shall now proceed to Kiva."

Keotak-se raised a faint eyebrow when the horses returned at Donny's summons.

Todd hesitated before mounting. "There isn't a horse for you; should we all walk?" Todd asked.

With a hint of a smile, Keotak-se chanted, "Wees Si Key Em" and where a moment before had stood a man, there was now a horse. Its coat was so white, it almost hurt Todd's eyes to look at it. Rearing on its hind legs, it neighed musically, like a cornet, and with a slash of its hooves, set off across the hilly plains. The travelers followed, their mustangs hard pressed to keep up.

The night was so dark, the riders could barely see the horses beneath them. No moon and few stars pierced the muffling blackness of the sky. All they could see was the glowing form of the white steed as it led them across the plains.

Out of the gloom, the pillars of the Sienna Sentries rose black on black in front of the travelers. Still they did not slow their pace. The white steed turned north and the others followed, racing along under the stern glare of the stone sentinels.

They rode for hours without a rest before the white steed finally slowed to a stop. And though they watched him closely, none of the travelers saw how the horse transformed back into a man. And yet there he stood.

Todd's scalp buzzed so urgently it was almost a sharp pain. He searched the open plains, but saw nothing out of the ordinary. The fact that Keotak-se scanned the horizon with a similar intensity did nothing to allay his fears. He felt a looming menace in the air like a dry fog threatening to choke them.

"Dismount," ordered Keotak-se. "The horses can go no farther. We shall travel the rest of the way on foot."

The dismay on Donny's face was painful to see. He opened his mouth to argue, something he rarely did, but Todd cut him off with a shake of his head.

Donny hugged the neck of the golden stallion in farewell. "But they said they would serve!" he muttered sullenly as the horses trotted off into the dark.

"And they have served well. They have earned honor here on Earth for their labors and great will be their rewards thereafter."

Keotak-se's words were curt but Donny seemed to find some comfort from them. He stood gazing toward the herd for several moments after they were swallowed by the night, then shrugging off his grief, he slid his backpack onto his shoulders and turned to follow the others up the path.

The Attack of the B'Ricas

Path was far too civilized a word for the course over which Keotak-se led them. They scrabbled over razor-sharp rocks, hoisted each other up stony barricades, and scaled cliff faces that scraped their skin raw.

Todd realized that, as difficult as it had been getting to the Sienna Sentries, without Keotak-se, they never would have found the path to get over them into Kiva.

Eventually the trail took them between two pillars spaced so closely together only Lilibit could get through without being squeezed by the stones. Beyond that point, the hiking got better. It ran along a narrow gap behind the palisades, switchbacking up the face of the cliff.

Todd should have felt safer sheltered by the cliff walls but instead he felt edgy. He scanned the sky, but couldn't see any threat.

Several times, the path wound around the front of the Sienna Sentries. Marla trembled when they edged their way along the narrow lip. She hated heights and one slip could send them tumbling down fathoms into the teeth of the rock shards below.

As the trail led them around the exposed western face for the fourth time, a vicious wind picked up and blasted the travelers. It was hot and humid and stank like rotting meat. It tore at their clothes and whipped at their skin. Their eyes teared and their breath gagged in their throats.

Keotak-se, leading the march, halted and turned to face the blackening horizon. The sky swirled with thick dark clouds that hung like a canopy of scum over the plains.

"Get back!" he barked.

Todd started to herd everyone back to the cleft they had just passed through, but Jeff's scream made him turn.

"What in the hell are those?" Jeff paled as he stared out over the plains.

Dropping from the greasy clouds were thick funnels of whirling filth. But these weren't tornados like Todd had ever seen or heard of before. There were three separate twisters, each articulated by swirling tendrils that stretched out and retracted like arms as they moved. Near the tops of the columns, the winds spun to form vortexes resembling vacant eyes and a gaping toothless mouth.

"They are the B'Ricas, the Wraiths of Wrath, servants of the Enemy." Keotak-se turned and pointed to a crevice off the trail. "Get back behind the Sienna Sentries. And stay together. You cannot fight the B'Ricas."

They retreated through the cleft and huddled between a large rock and the cliff face. From where they crouched, they could see the figure of the Stone Warrior turn to face the menace, but they couldn't see the valley beyond or the approaching enemy.

With a glance to confirm the children were secure, Keotak-se scaled the face of the palisades, crawling like a spider up the cliff wall.

From where they huddled, Todd and the others could no longer see Keotak-se. They hid their faces from the slashing wind and clutched one another as the tempest tried to pry them apart.

The wind was howling so loud, Todd barely heard Marla's warning scream. Looking back down the trail, he saw that an arm of one of the B'Ricas had breached the Sienna Sentries. One long tentacle of fury was reaching between the columns, slowly advancing toward them.

It moved along the gap, blindly feeling its way down the trail, reaching in to inspect each crevice as it slowly approached their hiding place. Todd screamed a warning to Keotak-se, but even he couldn't hear his own voice over the shrieks of the storm. And then the tendril was upon them.

If Todd felt battered before, it was nothing compared to the touch of the B'Ricas. He felt as if every inch of his body were being shredded. He clung to the others but felt them slipping away. Then, with an almost explosive wrench, he felt one final rip from the storm. The winds abated slightly and he clung to the rocks, gasping.

Through stinging eyes, Todd saw that although the tempest still swirled around them, the worst of the battering had passed. Nita clung to his waist sobbing and Marla clutched at her stone, her eyes tearing and unfocused, her lips moving soundlessly.

A hand pulled at his arm. "Todd!" cried Devon. "Where's Lilibit?"

Todd leaped to his feet as he realized Lilibit was missing. Looking down the trail, he saw the tendril of the B'Rica disappearing as it retracted.

He ran up the trail toward the battle. "Keotak-se!" he yelled. "It's taken Lilibit!"

But the wind still howled and Todd knew Keotak-se could not hear him, nor could Todd reach him.

Todd ran back to the others and screamed over the gale. "Stay together! Marla's in charge! When Keotak-se returns, tell him the B'Ricas have taken Lilibit and I've gone to find her."

Grabbing his staff, Todd ran down the path where he'd last seen the retreating tempest.

Chapter Fifty-one

The Wrath of Syxx

Todd crawled through the gap where the B'Rica had broken through. He crept onto an outcropping and looked out. Off to his left, he saw flashes of light and heard thundering booms from Keotak-se's battle with the monsters. He scanned the cliffs to both sides and the rocks below, but there was no sign of Lilibit. As he edged his way back to the trail, a scrap of movement from above caught his eye. He looked up the rock face.

There, trapped on an isolated ledge high on one of the red stone palisades, lay Lilibit. In the dark, he could barely make out her silhouette, but he couldn't see any path that would bring him close to her. Off to one side, there was a series of cracks and crevices that might serve as hand- and footholds. Maybe if he could climb to the top of the cliff, he could get close enough to reach her.

Sheathing his walking stick onto his back, Todd turned to scale the face of the Sienna Sentries.

◆ ◆ ◆ ◆

The fury of the B'Ricas had whipped at Lilibit as she fought against their pull. She'd felt as if hooks had been sunk in all over her body, dragging her in every direction. She screamed as she lost her grip on Marla and was wrenched from the arms clutching her, but her voice was drowned by the roaring winds.

After that, she couldn't make any sound at all as she was sucked into the foul vortex of the B'Rica. She spun helplessly through the dark until the cyclone flung her against the cliff face of the Sienna Sentries like a cannonball. On the edge of consciousness, she was barely aware of her battered body sliding down the side of the precipice to land with a slam on a narrow ledge.

She tasted blood on her lips and coughed blindly. The world spun like water in a drain when she opened her eyes, so she closed them tightly and pulled herself together. When she was finally able to open her eyes and focus, what she saw made her wish she hadn't worked so hard to regain consciousness.

A figure, like a finger of vapor, rose out of the dark. Lilibit opened and closed her mouth but no sound came out. She backed away, panic rising in her like bile in her throat as she realized she was trapped on the small outcropping. For the first time in her memory, cold rock pressed against her back gave her no comfort.

A manlike creature with black leathery wings towered above her. Twenty feet tall, its wings were nearly twice as wide as its height, dripping with slime and making a fluid, smacking sound as they beat. The bloated, hairless body was covered with dark gray-green scales and the cracks between those scales glittered with red hellfire. Its head too was hairless, mottled gray and black with a ridge of bumps like a ring around its skull. Those bumps grew and retracted into vile horns, cresting and ebbing like a living crown of evil.

It hovered in the air in front of her narrow ledge. Lilibit choked as a blast of its breath hit her; it stank like something that had been dead for a long time.

Then their eyes met and Lilibit, in a flash of memory, recognized the demon's eyes. They were flat and black and bottomless: the same as the bald man who had attacked her so many years before.

Lilibit found her voice. She screamed.

The time for deception had passed. Syxx decided his purpose could best be served by appearing in his true nature to the doomed child. His eyes glittered red and his long green-black tongue flicked the air, tasting her fear, reveling in her terror. *Discipline,* he reminded himself. Now was not the time to indulge in a slow, excruciating execution. He must complete this task quickly, as he should have five years ago.

Not that he regretted the glory of the past five years. At

the time, the prolonged torture of the child had served two purposes. Not only had her torment been delightful, but his enjoyment had increased by knowing that Gil-Salla and the Old Stone Warrior, along with all the other Defiant Ones of Kiva, had felt the echoes of her suffering. A lesson for them all: they had learned the futility of defiance.

But he had been distracted from the true purpose of his calling by indulging himself. While it had been a pleasant diversion to manipulate the fools at the Institute into being his tools of torture, he should not have been surprised that such weaklings were, in the end, so ineffective in destroying the child. Now passed to him the bliss of her final annihilation. With a screech of triumph, Syxx lunged for the cowering child.

Her scream died in her throat as his hands wrapped about her neck. Her fingers raked futilely at his arms as the freezing shards of the Void impaled her body.

Beneath his palms, Syxx felt the strength of the Earth Stone pulsing through the Infant Stone Voice. She had grown stronger since their first encounter, but Syxx channeled the might of the Decreator, and though his veins throbbed and his eyes burned with the exertion, in the end the Power of Destruction was greater than the fledgling power of the Infant Stone Voice. He roared in elation. The end was foreseeable. The child would die.

And she would die now.

◆ ◆ ◆

The Earth Stone trembled as She felt the servant of the Decreator destroying the Infant Stone Voice. The child was still too weak to channel enough power to repel the Enemy. With a shudder of despair, the Earth Stone felt the Infant Stone Voice slip away.

Syxx rejoiced. What could be better than to break the Infant Stone Voice right under the noses of the Defiant Ones? His laughter echoed off the cliff walls and rippled over the plains. The child grew cold and still under his hands.

Suddenly, something unexpected struck his head with enough force to break his grip and rock him backwards. With a roar of fury, he stumbled and slipped off the ledge.

Scaling the face of the Sienna Sentries, Todd had heard Lilibit's scream. Scrambling to the crest of the cliff, he had run along the ridge until he reached the spot above where he thought her trapped on the ledge. He looked down and his blood froze at the vision of horror hovering below him.

A demon from beyond all his nightmares gripped Lilibit's neck in a lethal grasp. Her eyes rolled back in her head showing only the whites, and her fingers, which had been clawing at the death hold, twitched feebly and then grew still.

Todd had no time to think. He leaped from the ridge.

Spears of pain shot through his legs as his bare feet struck the demon's head. The demon roared as it dropped backwards. Todd's panic flared as he felt himself slipping after his fallen foe, plunging toward certain death on the razor-sharp rocks below.

Twisting in midair, Todd reached out and grabbed the ledge with his left hand as he dropped past it. The pain in his fingertips stabbed up his arm as his fingernails bore the full weight of his falling body. The grit on the ledge slid under his fingers and he felt himself slipping again.

Rocking his body, Todd grabbed at the ledge with his right hand and tried to climb back up, but his left hand was numb and his fingers wouldn't close. Swinging his left arm back onto the ledge, he caught his breath. He glanced down and a wave of vertigo gripped him. The base of the cliffs was lost in darkness; all he could see were his own legs dangling. He squeezed his eyes shut and forced himself not to look down. He pulled his torso onto the shelf. His thighs scraped against the stone face as he scrabbled back onto the ledge.

Panting heavily, Todd crawled to where Lilibit lay unmoving. Her face looked deathly pale and her skin was ice cold to the touch. He gathered her into his arms and hugged her against his chest.

"Lilibit!" His whisper cracked. "C'mon! Don't be dead!"

Todd felt no answering movement in the still child. He chafed her icy arms. Tears of frustration stung his eyes. "C'mon, Lilibit! Could you, just for once, do what you're told!"

A faint moan and movement from Lilibit answered Todd's plea. His relief left him as dizzy as the vertigo had, but he had no time to celebrate. A flash of movement emerged from the darkness below. Dropping Lilibit with more speed than care, Todd leaped to his feet and pulled out his staff. Standing above Lilibit's semiconscious form, Todd brandished the only weapon he had and turned to face the returning Enemy.

The beast rose from the inky depths of the valley below. Todd ducked as a torrent of red flame blasted from its mouth and seared the rock face behind his head. Standing before a seemingly invincible enemy, Todd acted on instinct. He struck his staff on the rock ledge of the cliff three times.

Deep within Her core, the despair of the Earth Stone wavered. The destruction of the Infant Stone Voice was close, but it was not complete and now she recognized the summons of an ally. With each progressive strike of his staff, the Earth Stone discovered the new and untried conduit of a nascent stone warrior. Young, it was true, untested perhaps, but not weak. And most important, it had both the will and the opportunity to protect the Infant Stone Voice.

The Earth Stone knew that, in channeling sufficient

power to defeat the servant of the Decreator, She could very well destroy the tool itself.

And yet She had no choice.

Standing on the ledge, Todd fought the urge to drop his staff. On the third strike, he felt it shudder so frantically, he thought his arms would rip from his shoulders. The shaft glowed with a brilliant white light, and at its apex, a blinding orb of energy began to form.

The Demon spewed another volley of flame directly at Todd's head. Todd waved the staff, hoping the flaring globe would deflect it, but instead the globe absorbed the flame. Sweat from his forehead stung his eyes as the white orb of power swirled bright red as it melded with the fire. His hands scalded from the heat as it traveled down the shaft. He smelled searing flesh and knew it was his own fingers that were burning.

A flicker of fear appeared in the eyes of the Demon. Fire continued to pour from its gaping mouth but it appeared to Todd as if the energy orb on the staff was actually drawing the flame out of the Demon. The Demon wrenched its head to the side, as if to break off the link, but the stream continued to flow.

Then there was no mistake: terror flooded the eyes of the Demon. It wrenched its head back and forth like some huge shark caught on a line. The strain on Todd's arms spread like a flash flood through his torso and his eyes clouded with pain. His vision grew dim. His knees buckled beneath him, but his grip on the staff stayed firm.

With a piercing shriek, the Demon dived at Todd, its long black claws extended to shred his face and neck. Todd twisted his staff, the butt catching the Demon in its torso as it lunged toward him. The stream of flame broke off, but the glowing orb of the staff, now white again, shot down the length of the shaft and exploded like a quasar into the chest of the Demon. The force of that explosion sent Todd crashing against the face of the cliff while the Demon blasted backwards off the ledge and fell into the blackness of the gorge.

Todd struggled to his feet, his arms and legs shaking. Leaning heavily against the cliff wall, he brandished his staff and waited for the Enemy to rise again.

Crumbled at the feet of the Sienna Sentries, Syxx emitted a sound that could only be described as a whimper. A clash with such a puerile opponent should have been barely a mild skirmish. True, he had been weakened by his efforts to nullify the Infant Stone Voice, but how had he underestimated his adversary?

That the Infant Stone Voice might live long enough to reach Kiva was now a probability. That the child would survive long enough to reach her full power was by no means assured. This first skirmish may have been lost, yet Syxx still believed in the infallibility of the Decreator. There would be other opportunities in the future. Today, however, there were no options but to retreat and regroup.

Chapter Fifty-two

The Valley of Kiva

Crouched on the ledge of the Sienna Sentries, Todd waited for the Demon to return. His hands ached but it was ages before he dared loosen his grip on his staff. Then he crept to the edge and looked down.

Nothing. Whatever that creature was, it didn't look like it was coming back.

Tonight.

Todd crawled back to Lilibit, who crouched, dazed and trembling, her arms wrapped around a craggy outcropping. Ignoring the bruises and cuts on her face, she pressed her cheek hard against the rasping rock. Todd dropped down to sit beside her and watched the rank black clouds retreat. The returning starlit sky was tinted purple with the coming of dawn. He sagged against the stone but his eyes stayed alert.

Lilibit's color was also returning. He heard a mumbled sob from her, and after a few moments, her eyes blinked groggily. Todd placed his hand on her shoulder and pulled her gently against his chest.

"I think it's gone, whatever it was," said Todd.

A long silence fell as they both watched the sky lighten. Todd heard Lilibit's ragged sobs slowly fade. He could feel her staring at him and he turned to look down at her.

"Thanks," she mumbled.

"S'all right," he mumbled back. She leaned against him and he placed his arm around her shoulder. Her trembling slowly faded.

Raising himself to his feet, Todd glanced up and down the cliff face, mapping out which handholds he could reach from their ledge. The rim of the Sienna Sentries loomed only thirty or so feet above them, but as Todd glanced at his blistered and bleeding hands, he realized it might as well have been a mile away. Yet he saw no other way. He turned to Lilibit as she rose shakily to her feet.

"I'll scale up to the top, then I'll find the others and come back with the rope to pull you up."

"NO!" Lilibit's voice cracked in panic and she gripped Todd's arm with surprising strength. "I won't be left alone."

Todd couldn't see how, weak and shaky as she was, she could manage the climb, yet he couldn't ignore her desperation either. Against his better judgment, he nodded.

Hoisting her onto his shoulders, Todd pointed her to

the first handhold. She bit her lip with determination and clenched her fists to control her shaking hands. She gripped the first crevice and pulled herself up.

Glancing once more at the valley below, Todd anchored his walking stick onto his back and climbed up after Lilibit. Pushing himself to think beyond the pain in his hands, he forced his fingers to grip the stone handholds. He didn't allow himself to notice the blood dripping from the broken blisters and ripped fingernails. And he wouldn't let himself look down to see the chasm looming below him. He focused every conscious thought on the next foothold and handhold. And on Lilibit.

Glancing up, he saw her reach for an outcropping right above her head. In the dim light, Todd could see that a fissure ran along its base. "Not that one, Lilibit; reach for the one higher to your left."

In hindsight, Todd realized it was inevitable that Lilibit would ignore him.

With a crack, the outcropping failed. With a gasp, Lilibit fell. With a lunge, Todd's arm stabbed out to grab her as she plummeted past.

As Lilibit dangled from his right hand, Todd gripped the stone lip with his left. The pain was blinding. Already seared and ripped from his battle with the Demon, his left hand bore the full weight of Lilibit's descent as well as his own weight. For a long moment, the two of them hung from his faltering grasp, swinging high above the chasm floor. His hand was slipping. He couldn't carry them both.

One shall fall . . .

Todd swung his legs, trying to find some foothold, but his bare toes scraped fruitlessly against the stone face.

"Lilibit!" Todd called. "I need to free my arm. You'll have to climb up and hold on to my back."

Lilibit wrenched her eyes from the chasm floor and Todd saw her face pale with fear and vertigo. She nodded and threw up her free hand to grasp Todd's arm. Then she grabbed at his belt and crawled onto his back, clinging to his shoulders.

With both hands now free, Todd regained his grip on the cliff face. The extra weight of Lilibit on his back did not bother him as much as the crippling pain in his hands. Finally finding some sound footholds, he rested for a moment, pressing his cheek against the rock face, allowing the coolness of the stone to relieve the worst of his aches.

Gingerly he flexed his left hand. The fingers were weak and unresponsive but the top of the ridge was close. Clenching his teeth, Todd reached for the next handhold.

Suddenly, something cold and hard gripped his wrist. Without warning, Todd felt himself heaved upward, Lilibit still clinging to his back. They sailed through the air, only to fall in a heap on the crest of the Sienna Sentries.

Todd scrambled to his feet. Pulling out his staff as he rolled, he turned to face this latest attacker.

Keotak-se stood at the rim of the cliff. His body tense, he ignored Todd as he glared down into the darkness at the base of the cliff. Relieved, Todd slumped to the ground, his breath slowing, while Lilibit, crouched like a cat, looked ready to bolt again at any moment. The other travelers ran up the path to the ridge and stood panting.

"Where is it?" Keotak-se barked harshly, peering down into the shadows.

"The monster?" Todd asked. "I think it's gone."

Keotak-se's eyes narrowed as he stared at Todd.

"It was attacking Lilibit." Todd answered Keotak-se's unasked question. "My staff exploded with this blast of white light and blew it off the ledge."

"You repelled the demon Syxx?" There was a note in Keotak-se's voice, but Todd couldn't tell if it was awe or disbelief.

"There was only one," he mumbled, "not six."

Keotak-se turned back to search the horizon, perhaps doubting that the creature was really gone. "It is but one demon, though it has been known by many names. In this age, it calls itself Syxx."

Marla was wiping away the worst of the blood from Lilibit's face, but Lilibit pushed her hand away. "But why is it picking on me?" Lilibit asked between anger and tears.

Todd and Marla exchanged glances, but no one answered.

Keotak-se allowed the children a brief rest. They had earned it.

His eyes rested on Todd. For a boy this young to have met the Deceiver in battle and to have defeated him was a feat that would be documented in the Annals of Kiva. It would become part of their history to be related for centuries to come.

Despite the crushing efforts of the Enemy, the Infant Stone Voice survived. Looking around him at the seven children clustered together, Keotak-se knew that it was due to their bravery and strength that the child still lived. He also perceived something greater: the bond of love that united these children had created a potent force. Their combined might was greater than the strength of the individuals. So long as they remained united, they would always be a power to be reckoned with.

Keotak-se allowed himself a faint smile.

Devon crossed to the edge of the cliff, seemingly oblivious to heights, and looked down. His forehead creased as he stared thoughtfully. Todd walked over and crouched beside him.

"I think I misunderstood it." This seemed to upset Devon a lot. "I didn't get it right."

"Your dream?" Todd asked in a whisper. He didn't want the others to overhear.

"I think it meant that the demon Syxx would reach the palisades."

"Yeah, but it said 'One shall fall.' What was that about?"

"Maybe it meant when Marla fell into the Nether Rock?" Devon offered halfheartedly.

"Or maybe when we lost Lilibit to the snake?" Todd said.

"Or maybe it hasn't happened yet." Devon kicked at the dirt and a shower of gravel fell over the edge, disappearing into shadows below. They were too far up to hear the pebbles land.

It was quiet as they watched the morning sun slowly turn the sky from pink to blue.

"'Yet all shall rise to face the dawning darkness,'" Devon said softly.

"I was kind of hoping that getting to Kiva was going to be the hardest part," said Todd. "At least whatever's coming, we'll be facing it together."

"Yeah." Devon gave a little smile.

Todd gave Devon a little nudge. Keotak-se was watching them. He was far enough away and they'd been talking quietly, but Todd still wasn't sure that the Stone Warrior couldn't hear them.

Todd and Devon walked over to the others as Keotak-se rose to his feet.

"Stand," said Keotak-se. "There will be time to rest when you reach Kiva. Now is the time to walk."

They pulled themselves to their feet and gathered their packs, but Lilibit was still a little unsteady and she stumbled. Todd rolled his eyes at Donny as he handed him his pack. Donny just grinned and hung both packs over his shoulders while Todd hoisted Lilibit onto his back.

The sky was blue and clear as the travelers hiked along a path atop the Sienna Sentries. Rounding a bend in the trail, they looked into the Valley and caught their first glimpse of Kiva. Lilibit pushed herself off Todd's back and stood beside him. Nobody spoke as they absorbed the panorama below.

A waterfall flowed from the tallest mountain in the north. It crashed against a huge stone of white crystal that split the waterfall into the two rivers that ran along the outer perimeters of the Valley. Bridges spanned the rapids: some looked like natural arches formed by the earth and erosion, while others were ornate and intricate as if wrought in silver lace.

A huge domed building stood several hundred yards south of the waterfall; its perfectly rounded terra-cotta roof looked like a massive bubble of frozen red mud. In time, Todd would study and admire the intricate glyphs and paintings that decorated every inch of the Hall of the Flame Voice. The southern entrance to the Hall opened onto a raised pedestal that overlooked a huge semicircular courtyard. Sixteen avenues fanned out from the pedestal, leading to sixteen multitiered adobe buildings that lined the courtyard in a perfect crescent.

But terraced farmlands, lush orchards, dense forests, and the warren of adobe cottages that littered the basin all dimmed into shadows by the majesty of the Tower that loomed several hundred feet over the Valley.

A perfect unbroken, iridescent spiral, like a mother-of-pearl trochus seashell, the Tower glistened pink as it reflected the first light of dawn. Rising seven levels, the first ring appeared to be some forty feet tall, with the rest tapering until the top ring was no more than twelve feet high. At the top of the Tower was a huge white globe like a full moon. Was it a trick of the light or did the Tower pulse and glitter from some unseen source and with some hidden purpose? Although nothing could be seen through the opaque walls, Todd's eyes were riveted, as if he might see something of great importance in the shadows that hinted through that shimmering shell.

Donny nudged Jeff's arm. "*That* is Kiva," he informed him with great authority.

"Thank you, Donny," Jeff replied. "I might have missed it."

Donny grinned proudly.

The path that led to the Valley floor was smooth, sloping gently between pine trees and flowering brush. At the head of the path, a tall wooden pole stood gleaming in the morning sun. At the top, offshoots branched out like wooden wings. As they got closer, they realized that the branches were indeed wooden wings and that the pole was carved with figures.

On the bottom, what looked like a bear stood sleeping, its arms folded over its chest and its eyes closed. On the top was a huge eaglelike bird, its wings spread out and its beak pointing toward the pass through which they had just come. In the middle was a figure that looked like an owl with huge black eyes and wings folded tight against its body.

"Todd!" Devon whispered. "I think that totem pole just moved!"

Todd's first thought was to tell Devon not to be silly, but when he saw Lilibit and Nita walk up to get a closer look, he moved quickly. Stepping in front of them, he looked up, froze, and then pushed them back.

The owl blinked.

Amazed, Todd watched as its head moved slowly, looking them over one by one.

"You're late." The owl sounded like a woman. Actually, she sounded very much like Ms. Gritsavage, his seventh-grade math teacher.

"Sorry," Todd answered instinctively, and pointed behind him toward the crest. "We got held up . . ."

"The other neophytes all arrived a week ago," she snapped. "What kept you?"

"Other neophytes?" Todd didn't know what was more surprising, that he was a neophyte — whatever that was — or that there were more of them.

"Neophytes? More neophytes?" Suddenly the huge bird on top of the totem pole began to whip its head back and forth. "Why didn't you tell me?"

"Oh, hush, Wacky." The owl sounded more annoyed with the bird than she had with Todd.

"The name is Wakinyan." Brimming with self-importance, the bird lifted its beak. When he caught sight of the seven travelers huddled together on the path, he eyed them un-blinkingly, then began to flex his wooden wings. They click-ered like a box of pencils shaking. He stretched his neck and, with a deafening boom, bawled to the Valley below, "NEOPHYTES ARRIVING! PREPARE FOR THE PLEDGES OF THE STONE!"

They all held their ears. The bird's bellow was so loud, the bones seemed to quake inside their heads. The owl rolled her eyes and looked annoyed, while the bear on the bottom grumbled sleepily.

"This way." Keotak-se had ignored the totem as he walked past and was now disappearing around a bend in the path. "The People of the Valley will be waiting."

They hurried to follow Keotak-se, glancing back to see the totem pole return to its statuelike pose. Weathered and still, it once more looked just like a carved shaft of wood.

Except for the owl. Her eye winked once before she again froze unblinking.

As they hiked down from Red Rabbit Ridge, they passed small bungalows and huge templelike structures. Some were made of earth and wood and some looked like they'd been hewn out of a single stone. Some were decorated with intricate silverwork that framed the windows and balconies, but Todd preferred the warm plainness of the adobe homes and buildings. He slowed as they passed a tiny mud-walled cottage huddled under some trees.

In his mind, he could see a little kid happily playing in the sand in front of the home, watched by a pair of loving parents. He stopped and stood staring at the cottage.

"What is it?" asked Marla. The others were ahead of them on the trail, following Keotak-se. Only she and Lilibit hung back and watched him, puzzled.

"I remember this place," Todd whispered. "I've been here before. I think."

"You've been to Kiva before?" Marla sounded skeptical. "Are you sure?"

"I don't know." Todd headed for the doorless archway. "Maybe I just dreamed about a place like this."

Marla and Lilibit followed Todd into the cottage. The main room had an adobe fireplace in the corner, mud walls, and a dirt floor. There was nothing else in the room except dust and cobwebs.

"There'd have been blankets on the walls and covering the door and windows. And a carpet of woven grass on the floor." Todd didn't sound very certain, even to himself.

"Well" — Marla was already heading back out the door — "if I were going to dream about something, I think I'd dream about a less dusty place."

"What's that?" Lilibit's question drew Marla back into the room.

Placed high on the wall, in the corner opposite the fireplace, was a shelf. On the shelf, a heap of sticks was clustered in a huge knot.

"It's a nest." Todd reached up and pulled it down gently so the contents wouldn't spill out. He placed it on the floor.

"Cool!" Lilibit plopped herself down and began pulling out the bits and pieces that filled the nest.

Most of it was trash but very shiny trash. Silver gum wrappers, aluminum pop tops, even a couple of glittering stones, which Lilibit pulled out, held against her cheek, and then pocketed with a giggle.

"Hey!" Todd pulled a wristwatch out from under a scrap of tinfoil. "This looks like Ben's old watch!" Ben's watch had had a gold band set with plastic gems just like this one. He turned it over and looked at the back side, where Ben had scratched his initials. "It is! Look! It *is* Ben's watch!"

"Who's Ben?" asked Lilibit as she fished through the debris, looking for more stones.

"He used to live at Dalton Point. He got pushed out to Hardwell about two years ago."

Marla took the watch from Todd and looked at it closely, her brow furrowed. "I wonder how it got here."

"Maybe Gray Feather brought it," said Lilibit. "Maybe this is his nest."

"I doubt it." Marla shook her head. "We're hundreds of miles from Dalton Point."

"Well, then how did Uncle Mesa's stone get here?" asked Lilibit, picking up a small glittering rock.

Todd wouldn't touch it, but he looked at it as closely as he dared. "Are you sure it's the same stone?"

Lilibit held it against her cheek. "Yup!" she said with a nod. "It's sleeping now, but it's definitely the same one I gave Uncle Mesa when we left his cabin."

"Weird," Marla said as she headed to the door. She looked anxiously down the path to where the others had disappeared. "C'mon. Let's go. The others aren't in sight anymore."

Todd raked his fingers over the bottom of the nest one last time. "You sure you don't want this?"

Peeking out between the woven twigs, a familiar glint of silver caught Todd's eye. He pulled out a small silver, heart-shaped charm, a scrap of chain still threaded through its eye.

"My locket!" Marla squealed, rushing back into the cottage. "My grandmother's locket!"

Todd stared at the nest while Marla examined the locket. Her eyes got all wet and teary.

"It must be Gray Feather's nest," he said almost to himself.

"But if his nest was here," asked Marla, "what was he doing at Dalton Point?"

"I don't know," said Todd as he picked up the nest and dropped Ben's watch back into it. "But I don't think he's your typical bird."

"I suppose." Marla put the charm in her pocket. "I wonder what happened to him. I haven't seen him for days."

Todd reached up to put the nest back on its shelf, hiding his face from the two girls. He didn't want to tell them what he suspected.

"You want to put this back too?" asked Lilibit, holding out a shiny trinket. "It was in the nest."

Todd didn't move for a long minute as he looked down into Lilibit's hand. In her dirty palm was a round silver hoop draped with silver lacing like a spider web. Eight tiny colored stones nested in the webbing and two small feathers hung from one side.

He'd seen this ornament before. Or at least one that

looked like it. A long time ago he'd seen a charm like this on his father, hanging at the end of a gray braid that stood out against his black hair. He took the charm from Lilibit and squeezed it, almost crushing it.

"What is it?" Lilibit asked, her head cocked to one side.

"Nothing," Todd whispered. What he thought, he didn't want to share. At least not just now. Not until he had more time to think about it.

"C'mon!" Marla yelled from outside. "They're way ahead of us."

They left the cottage without a backwards glance. Jogging down the path, Todd tried to outrun the questions in his head. What was Gray Feather?

Or maybe the question should be *who?*

Chapter Fifty-Three

The Hall of the Flame Voice

The others were stopped on the path in front of them. At first, Todd thought they were waiting for them, but then he realized that they'd stopped to greet an old man who stood before them eyeing them up and down.

Like Keotak-se, the old man wore a leather tunic and leggings, but his tunic was covered with silver beads and colored gemstones sewn in intricate patterns. There was no hair on the top of his head, but a long gray braid fell down his back. He shot a glance as the three of them ran into sight but quickly went back to glaring at Keotak-se.

"So, Keotak-se," the old man rasped, "more pledges? And what use are neophytes with no Stone Voice to serve? Eh?"

Todd glanced down at Lilibit, who was far more interested in the old man's tunic than his words. Jeff started to say something, but a bump from Marla cut him off. Nita cupped her mouth to Devon's ear and whispered something. Devon nodded.

Keotak-se faced the old man, but Todd thought that he was very aware of their reactions.

"When the Stone Voice rises, Hihomay," Keotak-se mildly chastised the old man, "the neophytes must be ready. That is our duty. It is not for us to question the stars."

Hihomay harrumped and waddled away, muttering angrily, his back bent under the weight of his bejeweled tunic.

They followed Keotak-se down a path that ended abruptly at the crescent-shaped courtyard.

Since the travelers were not done gaping at the wonders of Kiva, it seemed only fair for the residents of Kiva to stare back. People drifted down from the hillsides, walked out from the woods, and stepped out of houses and buildings. Todd straightened his shoulders, hoping that he didn't look as bedraggled as he felt.

As they stepped onto the red pavestones, Todd saw that the sixteen buildings that lined the courtyard were all adobe and wood with rounded archways for doors. Each had an entry in the center, and on the upper levels, openings led to balconies that looked onto the courtyard. But that's where their similarities ended. Some buildings were two levels high while others were three or four levels. Some had plain adobe façades while the others were inlaid with silver and turquoise. Balcony railings and cornices might be silver filigree with glittering gemstone accents while others were ornately carved wood painted in earth tones and pastels.

Yet several were simple rough-hewn wood weathered into muted hues.

Another totem pole very similar to the one they had passed on the trail stood at the entrance to the earthen dome. While the carvings stood quite still and looked very wooden, Todd could see their eyes move as they watched the travelers' arrival. The owl blinked occasionally, the thunderbird sniffed once or twice, and even the bear opened a sleepy eye, just a crack, to check out the goings-on.

Groups of young people stood around in bunches and eyed them, some warily, some welcoming. Todd was startled to see that, unlike all the people they had seen so far, a lot of the younger people didn't appear to be native. While a lot of them had the dark hair and dark eyes of the People of the Land, more than half were obviously from elsewhere around the world.

Todd saw the grin of a tall black teenage boy directed toward Marla and noticed a small shy smile in return. She'd rarely spoken of it in the past, but Todd knew that being the only black student in their small elementary school always made her feel "a little weird." Todd leaned over to tease her, but stopped when all the chatter suddenly hushed. A figure emerged from the darkened archway of the earthen dome.

She was not the tallest woman that Todd had ever seen, though she had a towering presence. Her jet-black hair twined with silver cords and streaks of gray was braided into two long plaits that fell over her shoulders, down to her knees. Todd couldn't guess her age: she might have been thirty, she might have been eighty. Her face beamed with strength and wisdom. Looking into her eyes, Todd was reminded of his stone Tai-Kwee and the vision of the universe that he glimpsed when he allowed himself to lose himself in its depths.

"I am Gil-Salla. I welcome you to Kiva and I invite you to enter the Hall of the Flame Voice. Come take your place among the other Neophytes of the Stone."

Her voice was low and resonant. Todd shot a quick glance over his shoulder. It sounded like her words were repeated by the crowd, but it was just the echo off the buildings.

She stepped aside to clear the archway. Todd started forward, but he was stopped by a hiss from the totem pole.

"Not yet!" the owl blinked as she whispered.

"THE FLAME VOICE BECKONS THOSE WHO WATCH AND WAIT!"

Wakinyan's bellow made Todd and the others slap their hands over their ears. The bear growled and looked up. Whether he was glaring at Wakinyan or pleading to the heavens for deliverance, Todd couldn't tell. The other neophytes also held their ears but seemed more interested in the shadows that wavered in the alleys between the buildings than the thunderbird's hollering.

Jeff gave a small screech when something large and furry brushed past him. Several dozen huge wolves entered the courtyard, stopping to sniff and inspect the newcomers. Lilibit backed away warily as the largest wolf prodded her face with its snout. She slid to Keotak-se's side and Todd felt a slight feeling of pique. On their long trek to Kiva, Lilibit would have turned to him. Now she turned to Keotak-se.

After the wolves came dogs and squirrels, ferrets and bears, and then the largest rabbit he'd ever seen. A caw from above drew their attention skyward and Todd grinned as hundreds of crows poured into the chimney hole of the hall.

After the parade of animals passed, Todd looked at the owl to see if they could now enter, but she shook her head and covered her ears with her wings. Forewarned, Todd and the others covered their ears as well.

"THE FLAME VOICE BECKONS THE PEOPLE OF THE VALLEY," roared the thunderbird.

The adults moved forward to enter the hall. Some nodded a sleepy greeting as they passed while some grinned widely and others mumbled politely.

Now, only Gil-Salla, Keotak-se, and the neophytes remained in the courtyard. No one moved or spoke.

"Now?" Todd asked the owl in a whisper. The owl just covered her ears again.

"THE FLAME VOICE BECKONS THE NEO-PHYTES OF THE STONE."

Todd didn't think it was possible, but Wakinyan was actually getting more and more pompous with each proclamation.

Then the children and teenagers passed. There was a little less discipline among some of the younger ones, and one boy pushed another into Nita as they passed, giggling. She stuck out her tongue in retaliation. One tall dark boy stared at them coldly as he passed and Todd felt his scalp tingle. Their eyes met and held and neither flinched, but Todd claimed victory since the tall boy was forced to break eye contact first in order to enter the Hall. Todd didn't even try to hide his smirk of triumph. He would have entered behind the rest of the neophytes, but this time, Keotak-se held them back.

At last, the courtyard was empty except for the seven travelers, Keotak-se, and Gil-Salla. A long moment passed as Keotak-se and Gil-Salla silently locked eyes. They didn't speak, but Todd thought that they were talking to each other nonetheless.

Keotak-se turned and silently entered the Hall. Todd looked up at the thunderbird and waited.

"Well?" he asked after a moment. "Aren't you going to announce us?"

Wakinyan looked down his beak disapprovingly. "Why?" he asked. "Who is left to hear?"

Feeling a little let down, Todd turned to Gil-Salla, who nodded for him to enter the Hall, a welcoming smile in her eyes.

Jeff scuttled in front of Todd, shooting a smirk over his shoulder as he entered the Hall first, Donny on his heels. Marla looked at Todd, rolled her eyes, and followed with Nita and Lilibit.

Todd would have gone in, but he stopped in the doorway and looked back. Only Gil-Salla and Devon were left on the pavestones. Devon looked at his sneakers and seemed reluctant to go in.

"Enter young Devontaine. You are welcome at Kiva."

Devon raised his head, startled. Todd had never heard him called Devontaine before, but it seemed as if Devon recognized the name.

Still, Devon didn't move. He just looked down and mumbled something under his breath.

"I did not hear you," Gil-Salla said gently.

"I don't belong at Kiva!" Devon yelled, his voice cracking.

"That is not the choice of the Stone," said Gil-Salla softly. "And it is not the choice of the People of Kiva. If you choose not to enter, it will be your choice alone. If you do not wish to belong, then you will not."

"Everyone else got a stone. Everyone else got powers. I'm just luggage. I don't belong."

Todd hadn't thought of it that way and would have argued with him, but with a flick of her hand, Gil-Salla silenced him. She bent until she was eye-to-eye with Devon.

"When the Stone Voice rises, the Earth Stone will once more share the Song of the Creator with Her children. And the Warriors of the Stone will again hear His Song through their stones. If they are brave and true and strong, it is from the Creator that they will receive their powers." Gil-Salla paused and placed a finger under his chin, gently raising it so that he met her eyes. "Even more rare than a Stone Voice, though, are those who can hear the voice of the Creator without a stone. They are both uncommon and precious."

"Yeah, but . . ." Devon's voice trailed off. The toe of his sneaker scuffed a pattern in the sand.

Gil-Salla stood as still as a windless day. "I cannot answer what you do not ask."

"Yeah, but . . ." Devon stopped again. He struggled with his words before they finally burst from him. "Anyone can hear His voice. All they have to do is shut up and listen."

Staring at his toes, Devon couldn't see the smile that warmed Gil-Salla's face. "There is much wisdom in your words, young Devontaine. And yet it has been over two thousand years since a Voice of the Creator has been heard within the Valley of Kiva."

A long moment passed before Devon raised his eyes from his toes. His cheeks were wet and an unspoken longing haunted the back of his eyes.

"Your stone is here, little one." Gil-Salla's finger gently touched his shirt near his heart. "You are welcome in Kiva. You are needed. Enter."

Devon straightened his shoulders and wiped his eyes with his hands. With a shaky smile and a deep breath, he entered the Hall.

Gil-Salla smiled at Todd as he went to follow Devon. There seemed to be a lot of thoughts behind that smile. Welcome, yes, but also respect and perhaps . . . gratitude? Todd returned the smile with an embarrassed nod and would have turned away, but a flicker of movement on the horizon caught his eye and he froze.

Gil-Salla turned to see what held his attention. A bird, a large black bird, flew toward the courtyard. As it drew nearer, they could see that it was a raven, a tattered raven that flew with an awkward weariness.

Todd held his breath as Gil-Salla extended her staff and the bird landed clumsily on the tip, balancing itself with a flail of battered wings.

It might be Gray Feather, thought Todd, seeing the charred wingtips and the pockmarks on his crown, but he'd always recognized the bird from the gray feather on its right wing. Now that feather was tucked into his knapsack.

The bird looked at Todd, and as if it could read his mind, spread its wings again. While the plumage was sparse and bedraggled, Todd caught a glimpse of a small gray pinion that had probably once been hidden beneath the other feathers. Todd smiled.

"Gray Feather!" he said breathlessly.

"The bird is known to you?" Gil-Salla asked.

"We followed him to Kiva. We found his nest here in the Valley, but he used to live in the canyon near where our foster home was." Todd paused. "Gil-Salla, ma'am, do you know why a raven would keep his nest so many miles from where he lived?"

"Well, young stone warrior" — Gil-Salla looked closely at the bird — "I do not believe that this Gray Feather is a typical raven."

"I didn't think so." Todd's heart beat faster.

"It is not an ordinary bird nor is it one of the Knowing Crows, which are among Those Who Watch and Wait." She reached out with her free hand to stroke Gray Feather's head but did not seem surprised when the bird turned and pecked angrily at her fingers with an annoyed caw. Gil-Salla smiled. "No, this is not a bird at all."

"It's not?" Todd barely got the words out.

"No. Your Gray Feather is a shapeshifter. A very angry shapeshifter at that."

"What's a shapeshifter?"

"Born a man or a woman, a shapeshifter can take on the shape of an animal. Not as powerful as a stone warrior, but they were once crucial allies in the battle against the Darkness. They were not uncommon in the old times, but most have been destroyed by the Enemy. I suspect that your Gray Feather has been locked into this form by Korap, the fallen Stone Voice, and he will be unable to resume his human form until she releases him."

Gray Feather chirped a soft caw as if in agreement.

"Or until a new Stone Voice rises," added Gil-Salla softly.

Todd's hand fished through his pocket and pulled out the feathered charm he'd found in the nest. When he dangled it in front of Gray Feather, the bird cocked his head to look at it, then nudged it back to him with his beak.

"Do you know who he was?" Todd asked.

"No," said Gil-Salla. "Unlike real birds or Knowing Crows, shapeshifters cannot speak to us while in their bird form."

Gray Feather stared back at Todd.

"It's dumb, I know, but do you think . . ." Todd's voice dropped to a whisper. "I was just wondering if he, um, might be my Father."

There was a long silence and the longer it went, the stupider Todd felt, but when he finally looked up, Gil-Salla was staring at Gray Feather with an unusual intensity.

"What does your heart tell you?" she asked.

"I'm not sure." Todd reached out to stroke the bird. It didn't peck at him; instead it rubbed his head against his finger. "I think . . . he is . . . my Dad."

"Then it could very well be so."

With a sudden caw, Gray Feather launched himself into the sky.

"No!" Todd's voice cracked in anguish. He could probably be heard inside the Hall, but he didn't care. He didn't breathe as he watched Gray Feather soar westward, toward Red Rabbit Ridge, over the Sienna Sentries, and out of the Valley of Kiva.

"His job is not yet finished," Gil-Salla said flatly. "We all have much to accomplish before we may claim victory over the Darkness."

They watched as the raven turned into a speck in the sky.

"You too, Todd Hawker, have many tasks, both small and mighty, before you. And perhaps a great destiny. But first, there are many lessons to learn, many skills to acquire. Enter, young stone warrior. For you too are needed."

The sky was clear and blue, with just a faint rim of dawn's pinkness.

Tearing his eyes from the now empty horizon, Todd turned and entered the Hall of the Flame Voice.

Research Lab Scandal

UNITED WORLD WIRE SERVICES

COMMERCE CITY — Warrants were issued for the arrests of Dr. Rebecca Nil, Dr. Stanley Voight, and many key employees of the Nil and Voight Medical Research Institute.

Acting on information published on the underground hackers' website TheDirtyPen.com by an anonymous tipster known only as "Trickster Dave," Law Enforcement Forces raided the NAVMRI facilities in Commerce City and arrested forty-two employees and seized their computer files.

Drs. Nil and Voight are accused of conducting gruesome experiments on humans, mostly homeless itinerants, although there is some evidence that possibly fatal experiments were conducted on abducted children.

While Drs. Nil and Voight remain at large, officials are confident that they will be apprehended soon and they ask for the public's help. If you have any information, please contact your local law enforcement agency.

Progress at What Price?

See related story on page 36

Fugitive Doctor Apprehended

BY L. J. DEKALB

Staff Writer

SHOBROKEN - Suspected Murder Doc Stanley Voight was arrested Tuesday after an observant local resident called in an anonymous tip to the Shobroken Sheriff's office.

Dr. Voight was wanted for questioning regarding 19 murders and 186 felony counts, including kidnapping, assault, and various human rights violations.

Voight was found hiding in a Dumpster at a trailer park on the outskirts of town.

In a statement to the press, Voight's court-appointed attorney, Donna Cayer, was quick to state: "I think what we all need to remember here is that Dr. Voight is innocent until proven guilty and I don't think that the press should be quite so quick to rush to judgment."

Prosecuting Attorney Al Gonahang retaliated that, "when all the evidence is heard, the problem won't be getting a guilty verdict, the problem's going to be keeping the lynch mob away from Voight."

Voight's accused accomplice, Rebecca Nil, remains at large and is assumed to have fled the country.

How reading your horoscope can prevent serial murders.

See related story page 5.

Not Guilty Verdict for Murder Lab Director

BY AMELIA PENNYWAITE,
Contributing Writer to the *Herald*

CAPITOL CITY — Following a brilliant summation by legal maven Serafino Sexton, the Director of Security for the infamous Nil and Voight Medical Research Institute was found not guilty.

Upon the announcement of the verdict, the courtroom burst into applause and would not be quieted until the charismatic Sexton took a bow.

Justice Edward Zane Tafule joined in with the applause and was quoted as saying that it was a rare pleasure to hear such an eloquent speaker in his courtroom.

Jurors leaving the courthouse were heard to attribute the acquittal to Mr. Sexton's persuasive arguments in proving that not only was the Director non-instrumental in any of the crimes, but that he was, in fact, merely following orders.

Accused murderer Stanley Voight still maintains that the legendary attorney Sexton is actually a fugitive ex-employee of the Institute. Voight's insistence that Sexton is the elusive "Syxx" was met with derision from Prosecuting Attorney Al Gonahang.

"This is such a blatant attempt by Voight to cop a psycho plea. None of the others accused have made such a ridiculous allegation. In fact, there is very little evidence that this so-called Syxx ever existed at all. Voight's attempt to manipulate the legal system would be laughable if it weren't so disgusting."

Voight, who has been held without bail since his arrest, is set to go before the jury next month.

Interview with Serafino Sexton tonight 8 p.m. Channel 6

See TV Listings page A-22.

Guilty! Murder Doc Receives 18 Consecutive Life Sentences

BY BETTE FEINGOLD,
Freelance Contributor to the *Times*

CAPITOL CITY—After a record 14 minutes of deliberation, the jury in the murder trial of Stanley "Bloody Hands" Voight returned guilty verdicts on 18 murder convictions as well as guilty verdicts on 112 other felony convictions.

The only not guilty verdict returned was on the alleged murder of the mystery victim identified only as "Research Subject 1717." All records relating to this victim, alleged to have been a six-year-old orphan, were so effectively purged that the state's finest forensic computer experts were unable to restore that data. While eyewitness testimony supports the claims of the torture and murder of the child, no physical evidence nor any corpse was ever located.

Judge Neva Gottfried sentenced Voight to 18 consecutive life sentences plus 412 years. He will be eligible for parole in 1,064 years.

Voight, who had to be restrained numerous times during the trial, broke down sobbing, wet his pants, and had to be carried from the courtroom by two bailiffs.

Accused accomplice Rebecca Nil has been indicted in absentia. Eyewitnesses report sighting her in New Zealand, South America, and Bulgaria. The most recent sighting was reported in Toronto, where it was alleged she was working as a nonunion background actor on a low-budget film.

Runaway Film Production – Who Is the Real Villain?
See related story page A-16.
